RECKLESS

REAGAN KEETER

Summithill Press
Atlanta, Georgia

FIRST EDITION

Printed in the United States of America

ISBN 978-1-7343945-8-0
ISBN 978-1-7343945-7-3 (ebook)

GET AN EXCLUSIVE COPY OF *THE LAYOVER*

Connor Callahan has been through a lot. More than anyone should. It has left him with an overdeveloped sense of justice. Perhaps that is why when he sees a man discreetly tag a stranger's suitcase with a black magic marker, he sets out to discover what is going on. It's a decision that will thrust Connor into a conflict far more dangerous than he could have imagined, and when it's over, he will know one thing for sure: You're not always safer on the ground.

Details can be found at the end of this book.

CHAPTER 1

ALTHOUGH THE SERPENTINE roads of Connor's life had sent him barreling from one mystery into another, he had not officially been a private investigator for long when he found an unsettling note taped to the front door of his apartment. It read:

Hickory, Dickory, Dock.
The mouse ran up the clock.
The clock struck one.
The mouse was Done.
Hickory.
Dickory.
Dock.

His firm, Red Sky Investigators, which he ran with his best friends Dylan and Olin, had received a lot of attention lately thanks to a high-profile case on a UK film set. They had been featured in newspapers from coast to coast. From time to time, they still were, even though their receptionist, Lucy McBeal, did a good job of shooing away the reporters that stopped by the office to interview them.

That sort of attention inevitably brought out a lot of crazies, and apparently, it had brought one of those crazies directly to Connor's door. When exactly that had been, he had no idea. He'd left early and gotten home late. Other than calling it "today," there was no way to pin the time down.

Heart pounding, he slowly turned the knob to see if the door was unlocked. It was not, but there could still be somebody inside waiting for him.

He drew his Glock 22 from the concealed shoulder holster he wore under his leather jacket, then quietly inserted his key into the lock. The repeated clicking of the key as it pushed the pins into place seemed like the loudest sound he had ever heard, only to be outdone a second later by the deadbolt grinding against the strike plate as it slid free.

With the gun held up to his shoulder and his hand back on the knob, he hesitated before stepping inside. *Maybe I should call someone*, he thought. But who? Certainly not the police. He would feel foolish to have them search the apartment only to find it empty.

He could call Olin or Dylan, but he shouldn't need to call them either.

As he did once in a while, he thought back to the time he had been standing in front of another door—this one at the bottom of the attic stairs in his parents' house—listening to an intruder chase his mom around the first floor. He had been frozen by fear then. At moments like this, the shame of that memory kept him from being frozen again.

Connor turned the knob, pushed the door open, and aimed the gun into the darkness on the other side. He could feel the weapon shaking in his hand. He had purchased the Glock after his trip to London because he no longer deemed it wise to do his job unarmed, but he still wasn't comfortable with the gun.

He stepped into the living room and scanned the shadows, now holding the Glock out at arm's length in a two-handed grip. When he determined everything seemed in order, he flipped the light switch and scanned the room again.

When Connor was in college, his bedroom had always been a mess. His desk was regularly littered with fast food wrappers, dishes, and books. His bed was never made. And good luck finding anything underneath all the clothes that seemed to be everywhere but in his closet.

These days, he kept his space neat. His books sat upright on the bookshelf near the door. His clothes, although still not folded, went in the hamper or the dresser. Fast food wrappers were disposed of right away.

All that made it easy to spot the only thing that was out of place. He had not noticed it when the lights were off, but now it stood out like a fly on a wedding cake (to use an expression he had picked up when he was in the UK). But unlike the note on the door, this one item—a mug on the oval walnut coffee table—had not been left by anybody other than him.

Connor moved deeper into the apartment, clearing each room using the same methodical approach. After he determined he was alone, he ripped the note off the door and sat down on the sofa.

Who could this possibly be from? he wondered, reading the modified nursery rhyme a second time.

It was not an answer he was going to be able to discern by studying the author's penmanship. So he placed the note on the coffee table next to the mug and vowed to begin his investigation into this new mystery tomorrow morning.

He would not be a victim again.

To which—it was also obvious that whoever left the note might come back. Although it did not appear the note's author had entered the apartment before, there was no telling what someone like that might do next time. If the note's author was as good a locksmith as Dylan, the deadbolt alone would not be enough to keep the person out.

Connor crossed to the door and slid the chain into place. Looking at the chain dangling between the door and the frame, he realized he would need more. A lock like that could easily be defeated by a good kick or a pair of bolt cutters, so he followed that security measure with one he had implemented in the UK—he grabbed a chair from the dining room and wedged it up under the doorknob. This was also elementary but would not be nearly as easy to defeat as the chain would.

Even if somebody could get past it, they would make an awful lot of noise in the process.

Then Connor checked all the windows to make sure they were locked. His apartment was on the third floor and, unlike the buildings he'd seen in New York, most of the ones here did not have fire escapes. He had little worry about the note's author finding his way in through a window. Still, one could never be too careful.

Once he'd decided he had fortified the apartment the best he could, he put his gun on the bedside table and turned on the TV. When he was stressed like this, the dialogue from one show or another would sometimes drown out his thoughts and help him sleep. A local news broadcast appeared on the screen. Connor decided that would work as well as anything else and let it run.

Nonetheless, sleep did not come easily. Connor tossed and turned. He fought the urge to get out of bed, to start his day as the walking zombie he knew he would be if he did not get even a moment's rest. Because this note was not just a past mystery to be solved. Whoever was behind it had a plan. And Connor needed to be as sharp as he could if he wanted any chance of figuring out what that plan was before the author brought it to some horrific conclusion.

CHAPTER 2

IT WAS NEARLY dawn before Connor fell asleep, and by the time he did, Lucy McBeal was already racing around her home, trying to get her son ready for school. At five years old, Jerry could be a handful. Especially on days like today when he had decided he really *wanted* to go to school.

Jerry was no more or less studious than most kids his age. He prized recess over math and lunch over science, but today his class was taking a field trip to the Georgia Aquarium. That—as far as Jerry was concerned—was the sort of thing that made school worthwhile.

It took Lucy almost fifteen minutes to get him to finish his bowl of Cheerios. He would not stop talking about all the animals he was going to see, even when his mouth was full of food. He was most excited about the shark tank, but the dolphin show and the penguin exhibit both seemed to come in at a close second.

"And then—"

"Come on, honey, one more bite."

"And then—"

"Jerry, seriously."

Jerry shoved a huge spoonful of cereal into his mouth. "And then . . ." This time, the words were almost incomprehensible as he simultaneously chewed. Lucy could only understand them because she had heard him say the same two words seconds earlier. Those that followed might as well have been in a foreign language.

Lucy looked at the clock on her phone for the umpteenth time. When her son finished chewing, she clapped her hands. "Put on your shoes. Let's go."

Today was going to be a big day. She needed to get him to Bower Elementary and get on with things.

As Jerry ran into the foyer, Lucy's own mom entered the kitchen from the hall. Gretchen McBeal was in her mid-sixties. Her hair, once blond and now gray, was trimmed to her shoulders. The lines on her face suggested she was someone who had both laughed often and cried too much. Although that might just have been the way she looked, she had lost her husband to a heart attack six months before moving in with Lucy and Jerry. And that, Lucy figured, meant the latter was almost certainly true, regardless of whether the lines on her face were related.

Today, like most days, Gretchen was dressed in bright colors. Specifically, she was wearing a yellow button-down shirt and a pair of blue ankle-length pants. She was also wearing her wedding ring, and, unlike Lucy, that was something she did every day.

Lucy had stopped wearing hers two months after Gretchen had moved in. She and her husband, Antonio, had separated instead of getting divorced. But, short of a miracle, that was as close as they would ever get to reconciliation.

Their relationship had been strained for years before Jerry was born because of the financial realities that defined their lives—student loan debt, car payments, credit card debt, and so on. Even with two incomes, they couldn't always keep up with all of it.

When that happened, Lucy, who, in those days, had earned her living as a maid at Motel 6, would pick up extra shifts to make up the difference. Or her husband, who was always bouncing from one sales job to another, would log on to Door Dash and start making deliveries.

But add to that the additional stress of a mortgage and a child, and he was no longer able to cope.

Lucy couldn't say for certain whether she or Gretchen had suggested they live together. Since both of their lives changed within a matter of months, they had been talking a lot, and it was no longer possible to sort out who said what. As far as she could recall, it just sort of happened.

Regardless, it meant Jerry was the only man in their lives. For the time being, he was also the only one they wanted.

Lucy got up from the kitchen table and carried her son's bowl to the sink while Gretchen filled her mug with the last of the coffee in the pot.

"You look frazzled," Gretchen said. "If you'd like, I can take Jerry to school this morning."

Lucy knew her mom did not mean for the comment to come across as critical, even though that was how it sounded. The truth was, she probably did look frazzled. She'd forgotten to charge her phone last night, which meant that instead of the gentle melody that usually woke her up at 5 a.m., she was awakened an hour later by her son repeatedly poking her shoulder and calling her name.

There had been no time for her usual morning routine. As it was, she considered herself lucky to have eked out a few minutes to apply makeup and put together an outfit she deemed acceptable for the office.

Now that she thought about it, to say she looked frazzled was probably an understatement.

"No," she said. "I'll see him off." Her blazer was folded over the back of one of the unused chairs. She grabbed it and put it on. "Don't you have your exercise class this morning?"

"I can skip it."

Jerry charged back into the kitchen with one shoe on, albeit untied. "Come on, Mom!" he urged her, then ran back to the foyer.

Lucy smiled at Gretchen. "It's fine." She kissed her mom on the cheek. "I'll see you tonight."

After Lucy dropped her son off at school, she made her way across town to the building that housed Red Sky Investigators and parked in the garage underneath. Despite the morning's chaos, she was pleased to see she was not late. Lucy liked to get to the office before anyone else and did not want to make today the day she failed to do so.

She took the elevator to the third floor, unlocked the door, and stepped inside.

Lucy had learned about Red Sky Investigators the way most people did—through the various articles and TV coverage on actor Chris Miller's death.

As story after story hit the newsfeed on her phone, she began to realize Connor and his team were the kind of people she wanted to work for. They would do whatever was necessary to solve a case, she had decided. She liked that. So she'd sought them out.

She would have taken any job they offered her. But when she stepped into the lobby and saw half a dozen people sitting on plastic chairs and a receptionist desk that was, by all indications, unused, she had known exactly what position she needed to apply for.

Actually, she thought, *I could do better than merely apply.* Red Sky Investigators was staffed by three bold individuals. Likely, they would respond well to someone who was just as bold.

Without waiting to speak to Connor, Olin, or Dylan, she took a seat at the desk and fished around in the drawers in hopes of locating something she could write on. A legal pad would have been ideal. However, upon finding the drawers empty, she remembered she had a small notepad and pen in her purse. That would have to do. She looked around at the people in the waiting room. "Who got here first?"

A man raised his hand.

"Come up here."

She took down his contact information and the basics of his case. Then she sent him back to his chair and repeated the process until she had spoken to everyone in the room. She had barely finished gathering all their information before a door to her left opened.

A distraught woman stepped out. She was hugging a cardigan sweater around her waist. Mascara had run down her cheeks. Connor followed her to the main door, told her they would be in touch soon, and then, once she was gone, turned around to face the waiting room.

That was when he finally noticed Lucy sitting at the desk. She could see the surprise on his face. He opened his mouth to speak, but before he could, she stood up, pointed to the man who was next in line. "Mr. Flores is ready when you are." She ripped the piece of paper containing his information off her notepad and held it out to Connor.

He stepped forward, eyeing her suspiciously. When he was close enough to whisper without being overheard, he said, "And you are?"

"If all goes well, I'll be your new receptionist," she whispered back and winked. Then she directed his attention to the piece of paper again. "Take it. I've gathered the basics from everyone in the room. These are his."

Connor reluctantly accepted the piece of paper. He looked down at it. The paper had the man's name, phone number, and email addresses. It also said he was there because he suspected his wife was having an affair.

When Connor looked back at Lucy, she made a face indicating that it was not a case she would recommend he take. Nonetheless, Connor showed Mr. Flores into the back room. He gave Lucy one last inscrutable look before he closed the door, but he didn't tell her to leave, which Lucy took as tacit confirmation she should continue doing the job she had assigned herself for the time being.

From that point on, Connor spoke to Lucy briefly between visitors, and he did so strictly with the purpose of obtaining the details she had collected. This went on until the waiting room was empty, with only two minor changes to the routine.

The first was when Olin passed through the waiting area, going between the hall and the back room, with hardly a glance in her direction. (Obviously, Connor had told him about her.) The second was when Dylan stepped out to give her an application.

It looked like her boldness might just pay off. She filled out the four sheets of paper between her conversations with Connor. Once the last visitor had left, she handed it to him along with her résumé.

He glanced at the documents. "Wait here," he said, then disappeared into the back room.

Connor was gone for a long time. Much longer than Lucy would have expected. She began to think they might be digging into her background. Although she was not sure about Olin, she suspected Connor and Dylan would have the skill for something like that. Or maybe the three of them were just discussing how they felt about a woman who would throw herself into the role of receptionist without permission.

There obviously wasn't any way for Lucy to know, and as she looked around the windowless room, she decided one was just as likely as the other.

Eventually, Connor opened the door and invited her back.

This room was much larger than the one Lucy had spent the last several hours in, with a round conference table in the center where the four of them sat, floor-to-ceiling windows opposite the waiting room, and a desk for each of the investigators.

Connor offered her a cup of coffee from the pot that sat atop the filing cabinet.

"No, thank you," she said. "I don't drink coffee this late in the day."

"Good choice," Dylan responded, placing Lucy's résumé and application down on the table in front of her. "That coffee's not good any time of day." Then, without any additional preamble, she began to ask Lucy about the merits of her résumé.

Lucy had worked a variety of jobs, most often in one retail capacity or another. She had never been a receptionist before. So why was she interested in being one now?

Lucy smiled. "That's easy. I like what you do. I like how you do it. It might sound kind of corny, but it's something I want to be a part of. I always thought PI work sounded kind of, well, cool."

"You realize you'll just be a receptionist," Dylan said. "I don't want you thinking the job is more than what it is."

"I know, but . . ." Lucy shrugged. "It can't always be as busy as it was today. Maybe in the down time, you can teach me something."

Thirty minutes later, Connor sent Lucy into the waiting room so he could talk privately with Olin and Dylan.

"She's got a good personality," Connor said, once all three of them were back around the table.

"She's a little chirpy, isn't she? Like she stepped right out of a Disney movie," Dylan said.

"Is that a good thing or a bad thing?"

Dylan shrugged.

Olin glanced at the résumé that was still sitting in front of Dylan. "I'm not sure how I feel about her hopping behind the desk and acting like she was our receptionist. It's presumptuous."

"That's the one thing I did like about her," Dylan said.

"She did a good job keeping everybody organized," Connor agreed.

"We can find somebody more qualified."

Connor pointed toward the door that led to the waiting room. "We were going to look for somebody, anyway. As far as I can see, she'd be as good as anybody else we could hire. Do you really want to go through the trouble of interviewing a bunch of candidates when we have somebody perfectly fine out there?"

Olin shook his head. "I don't know."

Dylan picked up the résumé and looked it over once more, as if there was anything on it she hadn't seen already. "Most people would just be here for a paycheck." She slid the résumé to the center of the table. "Lucy really wants the job."

"And that would translate into loyalty," Connor said, "which is worth a lot on the experience scale."

He could tell Olin still was not convinced.

"How about this? We will hire her on a trial basis. If it doesn't work out, we'll do it your way."

"I'm good with that," Dylan said.

Connor looked at Olin. "What about you?"

Olin took a deep breath. "Fine. Yeah, whatever. On a trial basis."

"Good. Then, it's settled," Connor said and called Lucy back in to tell her the news.

CHAPTER 3

CONNOR AWOKE, BLEARY-EYED and exhausted, to his alarm at 8 a.m. He checked the gun to make sure it was still on the nightstand, then the front door to make sure the chair was still wedged underneath the knob.

All indications were nobody had come inside while he was sleeping.

He dressed, read the note one more time, and slipped it into the inside pocket of his leather jacket.

When he had opened Red Sky Investigators with Olin and Dylan, Olin would often show up armed with a Starbucks for him. These days, they regularly met at a coffee shop a block away from the office building so they could drink their coffee in peace before starting their day.

Before leaving his apartment, Connor plucked a strand of hair from his head. It hurt more than he expected it to, and he winced. Then he peered through the peephole to make sure nobody was outside waiting for him and stepped into the hall.

As he closed the door, he wedged the strand of hair between it and the frame. He wanted to make sure he had a heads-up if the stranger who'd left the note broke in while he was away.

Connor was barely aboard the elevator when a door at the opposite end of the hall opened and Rebecca Strauss shouted, "Hold it, please! I'm coming!" He reached one hand out to keep the elevator doors from closing while Rebecca scurried down the hall with a Pomeranian running beside her.

Rebecca was an attractive woman, Connor thought the first time he'd seen her, with curly blonde hair and freckles that, perhaps by their contrast, drew attention to eyes bluer than any he had ever seen.

She boarded the elevator wearing an orange sweatshirt, inside out, black leggings, and a pair of sandals. "Laundry day," she said and flashed Connor a smile as the dog looked up at him, panting.

Normally, he would respond to her quip with something clever of his own. He had, on more than one occasion, tried to work up the nerve to ask Rebecca out. But so far, their brief exchanges in the hall or on the elevator were as far as he'd gotten. Today, it took all of his energy simply to return the smile.

"See ya," she said after they exited into the lobby, and began moving toward a door that would take her to a small yard behind the building.

When Connor arrived at the Starbucks close to his office, Olin was there waiting for him at a table near the back. Ever fastidious in his appearance, he was wearing a blue button-down tucked into a pair of creased black slacks. Connor took a seat opposite him, and Olin slid one of the two coffees he had across the table.

Connor took a sip.

"Didn't sleep, huh?" Olin asked.

Connor pulled the note from his jacket pocket, unfolded it, and placed it on the table. "Found this taped to my door last night."

Olin leaned in to read the modified nursery rhyme. When he was done, he turned his attention back to Connor. "What do you suppose this is about?"

"I don't know."

Then they both sat silently for a moment, staring at the piece of paper. Eventually, Olin said, "It's probably nothing. You know how much attention we've gotten since that case in London. I bet it's just somebody messing with you. Probably someone who's not right in the head. I wouldn't worry about it."

Connor wasn't sure if Olin said that to try to make him feel better, but he suspected there was more to the note than that. This *was* something. However, Connor had been racking his brain for hours trying to figure out what that something might be and had gotten nowhere.

After Olin's comment, it looked like that was where he was going to stay, too, until the guy made another move.

CHAPTER 4

DRAKE HARTFIELD HAD grown accustomed to his life at the Pearlman, an opulent condominium building in Midtown. He was greeted by a doorman whenever he went in or out. There was always somebody at the front desk who could attend to any need he had, no matter how small. Life was good, but it had not always been this way.

Drake had grown up poor. Nobody was surprised when he was arrested at sixteen for boosting a Mercedes. Not even his mother.

That was a long time ago, though. Fifty-seven years, to be exact. And in all that time, the stint he had done in juvie for stealing the Mercedes was as close as he'd ever gotten to going to jail.

Not to say he'd changed his ways. He had just become a better thief.

A variety of carefully plotted cons and capers had netted him over 142 million dollars during his lifetime. Although much of that money was in the bank, he kept a significant portion of it in the form of bearer bonds in a safe in his condo.

Unfortunately, thanks to Alec Garcia, a dirtbag rotting away in the Fulton County Penitentiary, all that money—and worse, his freedom—was at risk right now. The D.A. was bearing down on him with the full weight of his office. The crimes Drake was charged with ranged from various counts of fraud to tax evasion. The D.A., one Matt Riverstone, was determined to make a name for himself and determined to use Drake to do it. He had flat-out told Drake that if he couldn't get him for his more serious crimes, he'd get him for what he could.

"Al Capone was sentenced to jail for eleven years after a conviction for tax evasion," he had said when he arrested Drake. "I'm going to get you twenty-five."

Of course, Drake had made bail, and the case was now playing itself out through a series of motions and countermotions that his lawyer was using to drag the whole thing out for as long as possible.

At seventy-three and with Drake's health declining, twenty-five years was a death sentence. He did not intend to die in jail, and it seemed like his best way to avoid that was to buy himself enough time to get Alec Garcia to shut his mouth for good.

Alec had been Drake's accountant for nearly twenty years. He knew where most of the bodies were buried (none literally—those were well hidden). Matt had busted him on illegal gambling charges and leaned on him for months to make a deal. He would be the D.A.'s star witness. Without Alec, Matt would not be able to make a case.

"Certainly not one that he could win," Drake's lawyer had assured him.

Drake had thought about running more than once. The bearer bonds he kept in his safe certainly provided him the liquidity to do so. In fact, it was half the reason he had installed the safe in the first place.

But that was a long time ago, and Drake no longer wanted to run. He did not want to die in some strange place any more than he wanted to die in prison. So as long as his lawyer believed he had a chance of turning the case around, he was going to stay where he was.

Speaking of his lawyer, Drake had an appointment with him in exactly thirty minutes.

Dressed in an Armani suit, complete with gold cufflinks and a matching tie clip, he took the elevator from the penthouse to the lobby.

The woman behind the front desk was named Maria. Drake smiled at her and she smiled back with no hint of the disgust or disdain that so many people now exhibited toward him.

No matter what the papers said, no matter how many talking heads on one news station or another called him a criminal, the staff at the Pearlman treated him with the same respect they always had. Here, money was king.

She likewise did not bat an eye when, instead of exiting through the lobby, he took the stairs to the basement.

Reporters had been camped outside the main entrance after the story broke, hoping to take a picture of Drake or to catch him off guard with a question he shouldn't answer. Drake had not seen any lately, but that didn't mean they weren't still there—hanging out on the bench across the street, watching—and he did not intend to give them the opportunity to do either.

The stairs took him to a drab, dark hallway. He passed a door on his left with a sign fixed to the wall beside it that read "BOILER ROOM." A similar sign beside a door on the right read "UTILITIES."

Drake continued past them to the loading dock that was straight ahead. He climbed into the backseat of the Lincoln Town Car that was waiting in the alley and smiled smugly from behind the tinted windows as the driver circled the building.

His lawyer, Patrick Erwing, was waiting for him in the main conference room at the Law Offices of Erwing, Cooper, and Harris. Drake had specifically sought the firm out because they often represented clients with deep pockets and, as Drake put it to his driver once, had a more liberal view of the law than some attorneys might.

Just as it was not by chance that he ended up at the firm, nor was it chance that his lawyer was a named partner. After he sought out Erwing, Cooper, and Harris, he had insisted they pair him with the best of the best. Money was no object and, while Patrick was expensive, he also had more experience than anyone else there.

That showed not just in his age—the man was sixty-two—but also in the way he presented himself. With wisps of gray hair brushed back from his face and a suit that was even more expensive than Drake's, he was sitting at one end of the table with a variety of documents spread out before him. But he did not sit like most people. He sat with his back straight, his shoulders squared, as if even when he was alone, he had a command over the space nobody else could match.

That pencil-straight posture remained as he stood to shake Drake's hand.

"Bad news first?" Patrick asked as they both sat down.

"I suppose."

"Our last motion was denied. We're going to court in a month."

"There's nothing else you can do?"

"I'm afraid not."

That was indeed bad news.

"Ready for it to get worse?" Patrick asked.

This time, Drake responded only by crossing his arms over his chest and bracing himself.

"Mr. Garcia isn't willing to talk to me anymore."

"Are you serious?"

"I went by the prison yesterday, and the guards told me he would not see me. He's all in for the prosecution." Patrick took a deep breath, resting his elbows on the table and interlocking his fingers. "I hate to say this. I think we need to try and make a deal."

Those were words Drake never thought he would hear Patrick say, but the change in his posture—the way his spine had reluctantly slumped forward in defeat—made it clear he was not kidding.

Patrick gestured to the papers in front of him. "I've been going over all of your financials. I haven't talked to the D.A. about it, yet, but I think I can get you a reduced sentence."

Drake refused to entertain the idea of any sentence, no matter its length. Still, he asked, "How long?"

"I think . . . fifteen," Patrick said, rocking one hand from side to side to indicate the number was an approximation.

"*Fifteen*?" Even if Drake was willing to consider a plea deal, that would still be a death sentence and, compared with Al Capone's eleven, still way too much.

"We've got a lot working against us."

Drake got to his feet. "Fifteen years is a long time."

"It's a lot less than twenty-five. If you calm down, I can show you what I've worked out."

The meeting was scheduled to last for an hour, but Drake did not intend to spend the next fifty-seven minutes discussing a plea deal he had no interest in taking. Patrick should have delivered this news on the phone and saved them both some time.

He circled around the conference table. "I have to think about it."

"Where are you going?"

"I said I have to think about it."

"It's the best deal you're going to get."

Don't count on it, Drake thought, as he yanked open the door and charged out of the office.

From behind, he heard Patrick say, "Don't take too long! The clock's ticking on this!"

That was no doubt true, but Drake had a plan. It was one he had been reluctant to put into motion until now. Before he packed up his life and left town, though, he owed it to himself to pull out all the stops.

CHAPTER 5

SITTING AT THE conference table in their office, Connor and Olin were once again reviewing the notes they had on prospective clients. Driven predominantly by suspicious spouses or child-custody battles, none of the cases seemed particularly appealing. Nonetheless, they weighed the pros and cons of those they had not already ruled out and eliminated the losers.

"How's it going?" Dylan asked when she arrived. She was wearing a red plaid shirt, blue jeans, and a pair of Dr. Martens boots. She also had her hair pulled back from her face with a pair of bobby pins, but that had a practical purpose beyond simply keeping her hair out of her eyes. Dylan was a hell of a lock picker. She had a set of professional tools in her desk drawer. However, when she was in a bind, she could still do the job as long as she had a pair of bobby pins on her. Were it not for that, she probably would have let her hair fall any which way.

Connor looked up from the mess of papers spread across the table. "Fine, I guess."

"Show her the note," Olin said.

Dylan hung the small purse she was carrying over her desk chair and joined her partners at the table. "What note?"

Connor pulled the note out of his jacket pocket and passed it over.

"This is interesting," she said after she read it. She placed the note on the table.

"Any thoughts?" Olin said.

"Poor penmanship. Probably a guy."

Olin looked offended. "That's presumptuous."

"Call it what you want. You can tell." Dylan went over to her desk and grabbed a pen. Then she grabbed one of the many pieces of paper scattered across the table and wrote *Hickory. Dickory. Dock.* on it. She slid it and the note over so Olin and Connor could see them side by side. Unlike the sharp, jagged letters the note's author had used, hers seemed to flow from one into the other with smooth curves that almost bordered on cursive. "See the difference?"

"That doesn't mean anything."

Dylan offered Olin the pen. "You try it."

He did. The difference was unmistakable. Although his handwriting was obviously not identical to that of the note's author, the neat, straight lines of his letters certainly had more in common with the author's than they did Dylan's.

"See?"

Connor did not bother to test the theory with his own handwriting. He knew his would also be closer to the note's author than hers.

This morning, Connor assumed the author was a man. At the time, he couldn't say why. Perhaps he had picked up on that same subtle indicator.

"That doesn't mean it's not a woman," Olin insisted.

"Okay," Dylan reluctantly said. "But it's more likely a man than a woman. Can we agree on that?"

Olin shrugged.

Connor folded the note and put it back in his pocket. "If you're right, that rules out fifty percent of the population, but that's still a long way from identifying the person who left the note."

"I think it's just some crackpot who's seen us in the news," Olin said.

"Possibly," Dylan said.

"You don't think so?"

Dylan sighed. "It wouldn't be the first time one of us has been targeted, would it?"

Connor again thought about the man who had come into his house and abducted his parents. This time, he also thought about how that same man had killed Olin's. It certainly would not be the first time one of them had been targeted, which might be the reason he was reluctant to accept Olin's theory the first time he'd proposed it.

"Maybe we could take the note to the police," Olin said. "They might be able to pull a print off it."

Dylan frowned. "That seems like a long shot. If there's anything at all to this note, the guy would have worn gloves. It's pretty much 'Crime 101.' Besides, I don't think they're going to put resources into something like that. Right now, the best it amounts to is probably harassment, and it's barely even that."

Lucy opened the waiting room door. "There's someone here to see you." She gave the trio a wink and a thumbs-up to indicate this was a case that might be worth their time.

"Show him in," Connor said, happy to put the discussion about the note and what it might mean out of his mind for now.

A man entered. In his blue polo shirt and tan slacks, he was GQ from head to toe. But unlike the models who graced the magazine, he was visibly uneasy. His thinning blond hair was brushed away from his face, drawing attention to the worry lines on his oversized forehead. The bags under his eyes suggested he hadn't slept in days. He placed the briefcase he was carrying by his feet and fiddled with the wedding ring on his left hand, suggesting a problem with his marriage. At this point, the only thing Connor could say for sure was that he doubted the man was worried his wife was having an affair. Those were not the sorts of cases Lucy gave a thumbs-up to.

"Reid Wilburn," Lucy said to the guest, "meet the team."

Connor gestured to an open chair at the table. "Come in. Have a seat."

Reid did, ferrying the briefcase with him across the room.

Olin stacked up the client files that were spread out in front of them and carried them over to his desk.

After a brief round of introductions, Connor said, "What can we do for you?"

"It's about my sister."

So, Connor thought, even though the man continued to fiddle with his wedding ring, *it's not about his wife at all.* The gesture was nothing more than nervous energy.

"Go on," Dylan said.

Reid's gaze passed over each of them. Connor could tell he was about to say something heavy and was perhaps sizing them up before proceeding. Although he must have given Lucy some information when he arrived, his reluctance to speak now suggested he hadn't told her everything.

"Alissa works in real estate—has something to do with buying properties and then reselling them. It's made her a lot of money, which is all fine and good, except that . . ."

"Except what?" Dylan asked.

"She's done some deals recently that don't seem to add up to me. Several of her properties in the last six months have sold for significantly more than their market value. It seems strange."

Connor leaned forward in his chair, the note he had received a distant memory for now. "So you think—what? She's involved in some sort of fraud? Or money laundering?"

Reid shook his head. "I don't know. It sounds crazy to me. She would never do anything like that, but . . ." He trailed off again.

"So she told you about these deals?" Olin asked. "If she was involved in something illegal, wouldn't she want to keep that to herself?"

"She mentioned one, but it was almost like she told me by accident. We went out to dinner, and she offered to pay. She said she had made this great deal on a condo she had sold, so it was her treat. There wasn't anything to it. Not really, and I probably should have brushed it off. However, something about the way she said it made me curious. I asked how much she had sold it for, and she just said, 'A lot.' Then she changed the subject. So I looked up the sale online. It wasn't hard to track down. She had told me the name of the building, and I was able to get the rest of the information I was after from Zillow. 'A lot' was an understatement."

"You said there were several," Connor reminded him. "How did you find out about the others?"

"I went to her company's website. And, yes, I mean *her* company. She owns a small firm called Platinum Plus Real Estate. It highlights the most luxurious properties they have available as well as those that have recently closed under a section they call 'Too Late.'"

Dylan made a face.

Reid frowned to suggest he didn't like it either. "Anyway, most of the deals fell in line with the market value for the property. Some were a little high, but not enough to raise an eyebrow. But there were two that were way out of whack. The first was the one she had told me about at dinner, and the second was a house in Midtown. That was six months ago. I've been monitoring that section of her website ever since and have seen another four deals like it."

He fidgeted with his wedding ring some more. "Like I said, I don't know if there's anything here. Maybe she just made some exceptional deals. It bothers me, though, and, well, I want to know for sure."

"You said it's a small firm. Is she the only one there closing deals?" Connor asked.

"No, but the six deals I noted were all hers."

Connor looked from Dylan to Olin. They all seemed to be thinking the same thing. This was the kind of case they had been looking for. "We'll take it."

Reid sighed. "Thank you. Thank you so much. It's my sister, you know? I couldn't go to the police with this. Especially since there might not be anything there. I just have to know."

"So what are you going to do if you find out she is laundering money?" Dylan asked.

"I don't know," Reid said. "Hopefully it won't come that. You won't tell the police, will you?"

Connor, Olin, and Dylan had already discussed how they would handle such a situation. It was one of the many gray areas Connor and Dylan were more comfortable with than Olin was. Nonetheless, they had all agreed that if nobody had been hurt or was in danger, they would keep the information between themselves and the client. It was similar to the commitment psychiatrists made to their patients and seemed equally applicable. After all, Reid had come to them because he felt like he could trust them, and if he hadn't, they wouldn't know about the issue to begin with.

"No," Connor assured Reid. "We will not."

CHAPTER 6

JERRY SAT AT his desk with his head in his hands, listening to his teacher drone on about the migration patterns of birds. His gaze shifted to the clock. It was 10:01 a.m. Shouldn't they be on their way to the aquarium by now? This was torture. How could Ms. Grindon expect anybody to pay attention when the whole class had a field trip like that waiting for them?

10:02 a.m.

Ughhhh. Will this ever end?

Then the classroom door opened, and the principal stuck his head in to tell Ms. Grindon that the bus had arrived. The class cheered and, without waiting for instruction, began swarming toward the door en masse.

Ms. Grindon was shouting for the students to stay with their assigned partners and listen to their chaperones.

When Jerry got into the hall, Marcus Redding caught up to him. Marcus was a slight kid who was small even when compared with the smallest in his class. He had an oversized nose and a bowl haircut that made him look a little like a member of the Beatles, Jerry's mother had said, in the kindest way possible.

"This is going to be awesome," Marcus said, fishing his inhaler out of his pocket. He lifted it to his lips and took a breath.

"It sure is," Jerry agreed.

The two had been friends since the first day of school. They had bonded over their love of the Transformers—a conversation that had been started when Marcus pulled out a lunchbox featuring Optimus Prime—and believed they would be friends for life.

"I want to see the sharks," Jerry said.

Marcus nodded. "Yeah."

They had not originally been paired up together for the trip. Jerry had been assigned a girl named Sarah and Marcus a boy named Nick. But since the four children had approached Ms. Grindon as a group, requesting to switch partners, she did not object.

From behind them, they heard a boy cackle. It was a sharp, sinister sound that cut through the enthusiastic conversations happening around them. Jerry immediately knew who it was.

Eddie.

As far as Jerry knew, every class had a bully. Eddie was theirs.

What Marcus lacked in size, Eddie made up for two times over, in both height and girth. But Eddie was not just a bully. He was a first-rate a-hole. (Even when Jerry's mother wasn't around, that was as close as Jerry would get to cursing.) Just as Jerry and Marcus had become friends on Day One, so Marcus had found himself in Eddie's crosshairs.

Eddie made fun of his haircut and his nose, his size and his inhaler. Basically, everything that made Marcus who he was became fodder for Eddie's taunts. Even the Transformers lunchbox.

And since Jerry was friends with Marcus, he was a target, too.

Jerry looked around to make sure Eddie wasn't close. As he did, Marcus squeaked out a "Whoa!" as he stumbled forward and had barely regained his balance before he stumbled forward again. This was not some accident caused by a loose shoelace or an innate clumsiness. This was all Eddie's doing.

Eddie must have been right behind them when Jerry had heard him cackling before, perhaps gloating over his newest plan to torture Marcus. Now, with Marcus struggling to stay on his feet, he cackled even louder.

The third time Eddie pushed Marcus, he seemed to use all the force he could muster, nearly knocking Marcus off his feet.

"Stop it!" Jerry said to Eddie as he grabbed Marcus's arm to keep him from falling.

"Or what?" Eddie taunted. "What are *you* going to do about it, *Mary*?"

Jerry knew Eddie had not used the wrong name by accident. He was trying to imply that Jerry was weak and girly. Jerry's mom would have called the insult immature and sexist. If Jerry were a few years older, he might have done the same thing. Instead, when Eddie pushed Marcus again, Jerry pushed Eddie back. He'd had enough of the bully's abuse and knew Marcus had, too.

The response was unplanned and emotional and—Jerry would later think—couldn't have been better timed.

Eddie stumbled backward. He slammed into the children behind him, lost his balance, and fell to the ground the way he had hoped Marcus would fall. Surprised, the children closest to him stopped first. As they started to point and laugh, the other kids swarmed in to see what had happened.

Eddie's face turned red as he slung threats at Jerry and tried to scramble back up to his feet. Only the world continued to work against Eddie. Halfway between standing and sitting, he slipped on the linoleum floor and fell again. This time, the crowd laughed even louder.

Jerry and Marcus, who had front-row seats to this embarrassing display, laughed right along with them.

Ms. Grindon scurried over, pushing her way through the crowd like a bulldozer. "What's going on here?" Eddie had gotten back up by the time the teacher arrived. She looked at him. "Are you causing trouble?"

"No, I—"

"He slipped," Jerry interrupted, with a grin on his face. "It was pretty funny."

Ms. Grindon cast a doubtful eye at Jerry, then turned her attention to Marcus. "Is that what happened?"

Marcus nodded.

"Is it?" she asked Eddie.

He stared at Jerry and, through gritted teeth, said, "Yes, I slipped."

"All right. All of you, head toward the bus," Ms. Grindon said, addressing the onlookers. As the crowd dispersed, she pointed at the three boys involved in the incident. "There had better not be any *slipping* at the museum. You hear me?"

Jerry nodded. "Yes, ma'am." Then all three boys melted into the crowd.

Once they were coming up the stairs that would take them to the school's entrance (and a good long way from where they had encountered Ms. Grindon), Marcus whispered to Jerry, "Maybe when we're there, Eddie will get eaten by a shark."

Like Ms. Grindon, Eddie was no longer within sight. He had presumably gone in search of his own partner, or perhaps some other kid to harass. Nonetheless, when Jerry responded, he whispered, too. "One can only hope."

CHAPTER 7

REID PRODUCED A list of deals he was suspicious of from his briefcase before he left. All six transactions he had mentioned were on it. The cheapest property listed had sold for $1.7 million.

"All right," Connor said, sitting down at his desk with the list beside him. "Let's check this out."

He started by pulling up the company's website. Platinum Plus Real Estate had more than forty featured properties for sale. They ranged from luxurious Buckhead houses near the governor's mansion to swanky condos in buildings like the Brookwood and the Majestic. Every single one of them was priced well beyond anything Connor could afford.

Reid had said Alissa bought properties and resold them. Connor got the impression from the website that they also represented properties they didn't own. Many of the listings were noted as Platinum Plus Exclusives. If he was right, that was likely Alissa's way of distinguishing the properties the firm owned from the ones they merely represented.

He then clicked over to the site's TEAM page and found information on six agents. Each agent blurb included a photo and a brief bio. Alissa Wilburn was at the top of that list. She was wearing a fitted gray suit over a white blouse. Her auburn hair had been brushed to one side and spilled down over her shoulders. Her arms were crossed over her chest in a way that suggested she meant business, but an easy smile assured potential clients she was also friendly.

Dylan and Olin were standing behind Connor and leaning in so they could see the laptop's screen.

"So, that's our target," Dylan said in one ear.

"You think she did it?" Olin asked in the other.

"If she did, she has to have a reason why. And if that's true, I want to figure out what it is before we go back to Reid." Connor spun around in his seat to look at Dylan. "You think you could get a list of all the deals she's made in the last year? If there's something here, the six Reid gave us certainly aren't everything."

"On it," Dylan said and walked over to her computer.

Connor directed his next question to Olin. "How would something like that work, anyway?"

"You mean money laundering?"

Connor nodded. He had a vague idea of what the term meant. It seemed to come up in the news once in a while. However, the specifics of it remained fuzzy. As private investigators looking into such a crime, he needed a more concrete understanding.

Olin had been on track to become an accountant when their lives intersected. If there was anyone who could provide the clarity Connor was after, it would likely be him.

Olin pulled a chair over from the conference table and sat down. "Well, let's say you own a bar. That's got to be one of the easiest ways to launder money because so much cash passes through a place like that. Since the purpose of laundering money is to make any ill-gotten gains appear legitimate—"

"*Ill-gotten gains*?" Dylan interrupted. "Really? That's the term you're going to use?"

Olin looked over his shoulder. "You like 'illegal proceeds' better?"

She shrugged.

"Anyway, if you start spending a lot of money you can't account for, the government is eventually going to come knocking, right? So let's say you've got some money you need to launder and, lucky you, you have a friend who owns a bar. What do you do next? You make a deal. You agree to provide this or that at such a price, and, on paper, that is exactly what happens. In reality, the owner of the bar inflates his receipts to cover the money you want laundered. You then give him enough money to make it worth his trouble and he *pays your invoice.*" Olin used air quotes around the last three words. "And just like that, every dollar is accounted for. You're happy. The bar owner's happy. The government is happy. It's a win-win."

"How would that work for Alissa?" Connor asked. "Real estate isn't a cash business."

"No, but the same principle would apply. If she's laundering money, maybe she's claiming she had extensive renovations done before she sold the properties. In that case, there would need to be at least two people involved in the scheme besides Alissa. You would have the person who provided the renovations and the person who bought the property for an inflated price. Of course, they would be working together, and no actual renovations—or only minimal ones—would be performed. The money would pass from the buyer to Alissa to the renovator, and at some point in the future, the buyer would sell the property back to Alissa's company, which would then sell it on the up-and-up. Since she buys and sells property regularly, nobody would think too much about that."

"All right, so if that's what she's doing, it should be easy enough to find out. All we have to do is find out who bought the properties. We might not even need to dig any deeper than the six Reid gave us."

"There might be more than one buyer," Olin said. "But, yes, we should see the same name pop up several times."

Connor rolled his chair back from his desk. There was no longer a need to be close to his keyboard. If they were going to get anything else right now, it was going to come from Dylan. After all, she was the queen of internet research—both public and on the dark web. "I think you might need to switch gears. See if you can find out who bought the properties."

"I heard," Dylan said, typing furiously on her keyboard. "I should have something for you soon."

While they waited, Olin returned to his desk, where he turned his attention to his phone, and Connor's mind drifted back to the note that had been taped to his front door.

Hickory. Dickory. Dock.

"Got it!" Dylan exclaimed. "All six properties were bought by a man named Franz Ludwig."

Olin tossed his phone onto his desk and frowned thoughtfully.

"We have a common buyer," Connor said.

"I suppose we can check the first item off our money laundering list," Dylan said.

Olin shot her a look. "Sounds like you're rooting for Alissa to be guilty."

"I just want the case to be interesting."

Connor had not heard this last exchange. Since he had observed they had a common buyer, he had been thinking about the way the scheme would work. Laundering money through a bar made perfect sense, but there seemed to be a missing piece when it came to real estate. "If the purpose is to clean the money, wouldn't the buyer eventually have to get the money back? After all, if he has this outgoing expense, he has to have money coming in to cover it."

"He could be independently wealthy," Dylan said.

"But the money still wouldn't line up. Right, Olin?"

"Well, the third party—the renovator, we are assuming—would contract the buyer for another service, and out the money would go, thus completing the circle."

There was a knock on the door that led to the waiting room and Lucy poked her head in. "What did you think?"

"We're taking the case," Connor said.

She smiled. "I thought you would. I had a feeling that was right up your alley." Then she hesitated, one hand on the doorknob, neither in nor out of the room. She looked to Connor like there was something else she wanted to say.

"Yes?"

"I know I haven't been here long, but my son is taking a field trip today to the aquarium. I was hoping to knock off around two o'clock so I could meet him when he gets home. I know he's going to want to tell me all about it."

"By all means," Connor said. "You should be with your son whenever you need to."

Lucy smiled again, offered up a quick, "Thank you," and closed the door.

Connor turned back to Olin and Dylan. "All right, if Olin is correct and this is our buyer, then we need to figure out who the third person involved is if we are going to complete the loop."

"We can probably get that by taking a closer look at Franz," Dylan said. "He and Alissa must have some history together."

Connor nodded. "Let's do it. It would probably be a good idea to know a little more about him than just a name, anyway."

CHAPTER 8

THE SCHOOL BUS dropped the children off in front of the Georgia Aquarium. Jerry had seen pictures of it online. Because of that, he thought he knew what to expect. He was wrong. The massive facade, shaped to resemble the bow of a ship at the entrance, was even more impressive than he was prepared for it to be. And impressive as it was, it still paled when compared with the inside.

Jerry and Marcus were about as close as they could be to the middle of the pack without taking out a tape measure and counting the inches from one end to the other.

With chaperones both leading and following the students, they made their way through a glass tunnel where fish swam all around them. Well, not quite *all* around, Marcus observed. There were none swimming underneath their feet.

"Not unless they're swimming under the carpet," he added with a wheezy laugh.

"Close enough," Jerry responded.

Then a whale shark swam past overhead and, along with most of their classmates, they both let out small gasps. It was awe and surprise all rolled up in one.

"Looks like you got to see your shark," Marcus said.

When Jerry said he was looking forward to seeing the sharks, he was thinking about the shark tank they had not yet reached. This, though, was pretty cool, too.

Neither of the boys noticed the man in the Braves baseball cap who was meandering along with the crowd of students. Sometimes he pulled ahead of the group and sometimes he fell behind, but he was always lingering somewhere nearby. If they had, they might have realized he was alone, which was unusual for a place like this, or that whenever he was within Jerry's line of sight, he turned his head away as if he did not want the boy to see his face.

After the children finished touring the exhibits, Ms. Grindon announced they would take lunch in the aquarium's cafeteria before seeing the dolphin show. Jerry selected a personal-sized pepperoni pizza from underneath a heat lamp and a carton of milk from the refrigerator near the register. Then he met Marcus at a table, where the two of them excitedly discussed the exhibits they had seen.

Eddie was, for the moment, a distant memory.

Or at least he was until Jerry took his tray over to the trash can, where his nemesis seemed to be waiting for him. Jerry did his best to pretend Eddie wasn't there.

But Eddie, carrying a pudding cup with a plastic spoon sticking out of the top, wasn't having it. "Hey, you think what you did this morning was funny?"

Jerry glanced at him, dumped the remnants of his meal in the trashcan, and placed the tray on the receptacle above it.

"Did you hear me?"

Jerry could tell he was not going to be able to put an end to this discussion by simply ignoring Eddie. The bully would no doubt follow Jerry back to his seat, getting increasingly agitated with every step, where he would then train his ire not just on Jerry, but on Marcus as well. Best to deal with this now.

Jerry turned toward Eddie. "Can't you find somebody else to pick on?"

Eddie smiled. "Why should I find somebody else when I already have you?"

Of course, Eddie had other students he picked on. That was hardly the point either of them was trying to make, though.

Jerry rolled his eyes. He decided he wasn't going to let this kid ruin a perfectly good field trip. He was going back to his seat, and if Eddie did try to follow him, he would just tell the closest chaperone. Although a second confrontation with a teacher would annoy Eddie, it probably wouldn't make any vengeance he dealt out later worse.

But he didn't even manage to turn ninety degrees before Eddie scooped a glob of pudding out of his cup with his fingers and smeared it across Jerry's shirt.

Jerry was mortified. He did not know how to respond. And Eddie, who was already laughing, seemed even more amused by the expression on Jerry's face.

"Think twice before embarrassing me again," Eddie said, and then walked away.

Jerry hurried to the bathroom. He needed to get this pudding off his shirt before anyone saw him.

When he did, the man who had been discreetly accompanying the children around the aquarium stood up from a nearby table and followed him.

Marcus pulled his cell phone out of his pocket when Jerry got up to take his tray to the trash. He wasn't searching for anything in particular. Looking at his phone—pulling up one social media account or another—was something he reflexively did when he was alone.

He lost all interest in it, though, when he saw Eddie smear pudding across Jerry's shirt and Jerry slip away to the bathroom. If Jerry had a cell phone, too, Marcus would have called to check on him. However, Jerry had said his mother insisted he was too young for such a device, so calling him was not an option.

That left him in the predicament of deciding whether he should follow his friend into the bathroom or stay where he was. As someone prone to overanalyzing every decision he made, that was not an easy choice for Marcus, and he remained where he was, weighing his options, long enough for Jerry not only to enter the bathroom but to exit it, also. Only, Marcus noticed, he did not exit it alone. He was with a man—the same one, Marcus now realized, he had seen go into the bathroom after Jerry.

The two of them headed toward the stairs. Although the man was holding Jerry's hand, he was not forcibly taking the boy with him. Nonetheless, the whole thing struck Marcus as strange. Even after getting pudding on his shirt, why would Jerry suddenly leave the aquarium? And if he was going to leave the aquarium, wouldn't he tell somebody first?

Marcus decided Ms. Grindon must know what was going on and decided to go ask. At the very least, he probably needed to be partnered up with someone else.

Ms. Grindon, however, began to panic. She did not know why Jerry was leaving. She did not even know he *was* leaving. "What did you say?" she asked Marcus, hoping against all reason she had misunderstood him.

"Jerry left. I was just wondering if you knew why."

"He left by himself?"

"He was with a man."

Ms. Grindon stood up. "Which way did he go?"

Marcus pointed toward the stairs.

"Stay here," she told him and hurried away.

Once she reached the bottom of the stairs, she looked left then right, scanning the crowd of visitors for any sign of Jerry. There were a lot of families, which meant kids were everywhere—many of them boys about Jerry's height. Since she didn't remember what he was wearing, it would be impossible for her to tell if any of them were Jerry unless she sought out each child so she could look at him straight on.

She gave up on that idea and turned toward the exit. If somebody had decided to kidnap him—because that was the only reason she could see for what had happened—they would not continue touring the aquarium together. The kidnapper would want to get out of there as fast as possible.

Jerry was not among the children she encountered between the stairs and the exit, and the security guard by the door could not say for certain whether he had seen the boy.

"Maybe if you have a picture," he said.

But she didn't. Why would she? So she spent no more time on that conversation.

She rushed out the doors, heart pounding. Since she had entered the aquarium that morning, the clouds had burned off and the temperature had warmed to a perfect seventy-two degrees. It was as nice a day as any she could ask for. Not that she noticed.

She spun around, overwhelmed and looking at each of the children she could see. Unlike inside the aquarium, where potential Jerrys were everywhere, here there were none.

Ms. Grindon pulled out her cell phone and placed two calls. The first was to the police. The second was to Jerry's mom.

CHAPTER 9

CONNOR, OLIN, AND Dylan had spent the better part of the morning digging into Franz Ludwig's life. When they were done, they knew almost as much about him as they did about each other.

Franz had been born in Berlin to Karl Ludwig and his wife, Christa. He had no major health issues, had never been married, and—at nearly fifty—posted pictures on social media with the frequency of a teenager.

He had plenty to post about, too. Karl had made a fortune as a shipping magnate and, as such, Franz, being their only child, was independently wealthy.

He spent his fortune on lavish vacations, a private jet, a yacht that was big enough to sleep twenty, and more property than any one person could ever use. All indications were he didn't care how much things cost. He wanted what he wanted, and he paid whatever it took to get it.

Which, of course, lent credence to the possibility that the property sales were legitimate.

Add to that the fact that his list of friends on Facebook and Twitter showed no connection to anyone in the real estate industry, let alone someone shady enough to write out fake invoices to Alissa for work that hadn't been done, and Connor was just about ready to tell Reid everything was on the up-and-up.

"You know," Olin said at lunch, "there is another possibility."

The three of them were sitting in a booth at Sue's Diner. The restaurant featured a lot of chrome and neon, and this booth, like most, offered an uninspired view of the road. Still, they ate there often. At four blocks from the office, it was close enough to walk to and had enough variety on the menu to appeal to all of them.

Olin put his burger down. His gaze shifted between Connor and Dylan, who were on the bench opposite him. "We assumed Alissa was laundering money for somebody else. However, if *she* was the one who needed to launder money, there wouldn't have to be a third party involved. She would just need someone to buy the property at an inflated value. And if they didn't want to keep it, then they could just sell it back to her for less money."

"It would still have to be cash," Dylan clarified.

"Absolutely. They couldn't get wrapped up in the complications of a loan for that to work."

"So, in that scenario, Franz could still fit the bill," Connor said, realizing the outcome of the case was not a foregone conclusion.

Olin nodded.

There was no need for any of them to suggest they check the buy and sell history of the properties he was involved in when they got back to the office. Since the exchange of property from seller to buyer and back had been an integral part of the scheme as Olin had first proposed it, that had already been their plan. Sure, in this scenario, Franz might not have sold all the properties back to Alissa—for *this* version of the scheme to work, he only had to pay an inflated price on paper—but it was likely he would have sold some of them back, no matter how many homes he wanted to own.

They paid the bill and stood to leave. They were barely two steps from the booth when Connor's phone rang. He pulled his cell out of the pocket of his jeans and checked the Caller ID. It was Lucy McBeal.

"What's up?" he said when he answered, as the trio continued heading for the door.

"It's my son," she replied. Lucy sounded like she was on the move, maybe even running. She also sounded alarmed.

Connor could feel his own heart rate picking up in response. He had a terrible feeling he knew what she was about to say next, and he was right.

"He's missing. He left with somebody from the aquarium. Nobody knows who. I'm on my way there now. Can you guys meet me there?"

Connor heard a car door open and close in the background and figured Lucy must have been heading to the parking lot when she called. Then he passed through the front door of the diner and reflexively came to a stop. He grabbed Olin's arm to get his attention, who in turn got Dylan's, and he gestured for them to wait.

"We're at Sue's Diner," he told Lucy. "Why don't you come by and pick us up on your way? We'll all go together."

Lucy stumbled through a series of incomprehensible thoughts. "I . . . I need to. . . Well . . ." She was running on fear, that much was clear, and not thinking straight because of it. Connor was reluctant to tell her she shouldn't be driving like that. He hoped he wouldn't need to. But if she refused to pick them up, he would say whatever was necessary to convince her. Since the diner was on her way, it not only made sense from a logistical perspective, but he also did not want Jerry's mom, high on emotion, causing an accident that left Jerry without a mother no matter how the situation turned out.

"Okay," she finally said, perhaps reaching the same conclusion.

"We'll be on the street in front. Pull up to the curb and we'll hop in." Connor slid the phone back into his pocket, then filled Dylan and Olin in on what had happened.

Dylan jerked open the driver's-side door when Lucy pulled up to the curb. "Move over."

Between the three of them, she was the right choice to take the wheel. Olin did not handle pressure well, so he probably wouldn't have driven much better than Lucy, and Connor, even as good as he was, was not as good at it as Dylan. She could handle a car with the grace of a race car driver, speeding fearlessly through lights and able to leverage the way one car was moving relative to another to swerve between them with even the narrowest of wiggle room.

Which was exactly what she did now.

Sitting in the backseat with Connor, Olin held tight to the grab handle. Although by now he certainly knew she could control the car no matter how dangerous her driving might appear to be, he still couldn't help telling her to "Stop!" and "Be careful!"

The reason Connor knew this was that she and Olin had been in a similar situation once before, rushing across town in hopes of beating a pair of detectives to a hotel. According to the story he'd been told, Olin had shouted similar commands at her then. This time, though, instead of keeping quiet, she said, "Shut it, all right? I've got this." Then she sped between two cars seconds before one of them merged into her lane, closing off the opening she had just leveraged.

Lucy, who seemed largely oblivious to Dylan's driving, worked through the numbers in her phone, hoping one contact or another might know something about the man Jerry had left with. Her voice trembled and cracked, but so far, she had not started crying.

"Could it have been his father?" Dylan asked between calls.

Lucy shook her head. "No, it wasn't him. I already checked."

When she finished her calls, she continued to hold tightly to the phone, now with both hands in her lap. "Nobody knows anything," she said, turning to face the window.

Connor glanced at Lucy but did not respond. Neither did Dylan or Olin. They all seemed to understand the best thing they could do for Lucy was to give her a moment to process the situation.

By the time they reached the aquarium, Lucy had managed to pull herself together. Crying, she said, was not going to help her get her son back. She had to be strong.

Connor could tell from the way her hands shook that she was still a mess of emotion inside. He knew from experience that sooner or later, it would all come flooding out. But she was also right. Crying was not going to help her get her son back, and he was impressed by the strength and resolve she seemed to have harnessed at this moment.

Ms. Grindon was waiting for them by the entrance. Lucy made a quick round of introductions, and Ms. Grindon clarified that they should call her Ellie. Then Ellie said a detective from the Atlanta Police Department was inside reviewing the security footage. "There are cameras everywhere here. Detective . . ." She paused to look at the card she was holding. "Detective Stewart Pierce said there's a good chance we'll be able to get a look at the guy. He seems pretty confident we'll get Jerry back soon."

"Let's hope you're right," Connor said. He turned to the same security guard Ellie had questioned earlier. "You didn't see anything, did you?"

The security guard shook his head. "Nothing unusual. Like I was telling her,"—he nodded at Ellie—"maybe if I could see a picture—"

"A picture?" Lucy said as she began fishing around in her purse. "I've got a picture." She withdrew her phone, tapped and swiped, then turned the screen around so the security guard could see it. On the screen was the image of a young boy smiling for the camera.

The security guard looked at it for several seconds, then said, "I'm sorry. I thought it might help, but there are too many kids coming in and out of this place. They all start to look the same, you know?"

That was probably true, Connor thought. If the security guard was paying close attention to anything, it wouldn't be the faces of the children who passed through these doors from open to close. He turned back to Ellie. "How many chaperones came on the trip?"

"Four."

"While we're waiting for Detective Pierce to come back, do you mind if we talk to them? Maybe one of them saw something."

Ellie cast a doubtful glance in Lucy's direction. "I don't know. Maybe it would be best to let the detective handle this."

When Lucy introduced Connor and his team, she had done so only by name. "They're PIs," she now told Ellie. "They're good, too. Remember that case with the actor that was all over the news not too long ago? Chris Miller? They're the ones who solved it."

"You brought PIs with you?"

"I work for them."

Ellie mulled this over, then shrugged in Connor's direction. "I guess if Lucy thinks it's okay for you to talk to the chaperones, it's all right with me."

"Maybe the kids, too," Dylan suggested.

This time, Ellie looked even more reluctant.

"They might have seen something the chaperones didn't," Connor added.

"Are you sure you don't want to let the detective handle all this?" Ellie asked Lucy.

"I want my son back. As far as I'm concerned, the more people who are looking for him, the better."

Ellie sighed. "Well, there was one kid. Marcus Redding. He's the one who told me he saw Jerry leaving with the man. He's Jerry's best friend."

Olin shrugged, then looked from Connor to Dylan. "I guess that's a good place to start."

Ellie gestured for the group to follow her. "They're still in the cafeteria. Come on. I'll introduce you."

CHAPTER 10

ELLIE LED MARCUS away from the other students so they could talk to him privately. Surrounded by so many adults, he looked uneasy. "I'm not in trouble, am I?"

"No," Ellie assured him.

"We just want to hear what you saw in your own words," Connor said, pulling over a nearby chair and sitting down. He hoped it would help put Marcus at ease if he had at least one fewer adult towering over him. "What did you see?"

"I mean . . . I don't know," Marcus responded, then looked up at his teacher. "Ms. Grindon, I told you about this already. Jerry left with a man. They came out of the bathroom together and just left. That's all I saw. Really."

"Could you describe him for us?"

Marcus shook his head. "He was wearing a baseball cap. I couldn't see his face. Not really."

"How tall was he?" Dylan asked.

Marcus looked back at Connor. "Like you, I guess."

"What about his weight? Was he a big guy?"

"Average."

"What was he wearing?" Connor asked.

"Just, like, *clothes*, you know? Nothing special."

Connor leaned forward, clasped his hands together, and looked

Marcus in the eye. "This is very important. Do you remember anything at all that stood out? Anything that might make the guy different from me or"—he pointed to Olin—"him."

Marcus nervously shoved his hands into his pockets and looked down at his feet. "He had a beard."

"Okay, that's good. That's something, right?" Connor said, looking up at the other adults, who nodded in response. "Do you remember what color it was?"

"It was dark. Like, brown . . . or black, maybe."

"Does that sound like anyone you know?" he asked Lucy. "A man who's about my height and weight with a beard?"

She shook her head. "Not that I can think of."

"I have a question," Ellie said. "You were supposed to stay with Jerry. Why weren't you in the bathroom with him?"

"It just kind of happened."

"What do you mean?"

Marcus looked toward some kids in the distance. "I've had enough trouble with Eddie for today, Ms. Grindon. If I tell you, you gotta promise you won't say anything."

Ellie did not look happy, but she crossed her heart and said, "I promise. Now, what is it?"

"Jerry just got up to take his tray to the trash when Eddie smeared pudding all over his shirt. That's why he went to the bathroom. So I stayed where I was, you know, to save our seats."

Ellie's face reddened with annoyance and she, too, turned to look at the same kids Marcus had. One of them, Connor figured, must be Eddie.

They wrapped up their conversation with Marcus quickly. There was not much else he seemed to know, and Connor was anxious to see if Eddie might be able to fill in any details Marcus had not.

After all, there was a good chance Eddie had been watching the bathroom after Jerry went inside, if only so he could make fun of Jerry when he came back out. Maybe he'd had a better view of the kidnapper.

Although Connor thought he might have to tell Eddie he knew the boy had been picking on Jerry to elicit the truth, he assured Marcus they would not mention his name before they told him to return to his seat. It turned out, though, he did not even have to tell Eddie that much.

Eddie burst into tears as soon as Ellie called him over. "It was all a mistake, really. I thought it was just supposed to be for fun. If I had known how this was going to end up, I wouldn't have taken his money, I promise."

When Eddie had started talking, Connor was certain he was referring to the pudding incident. Now that he had mentioned money, he wasn't so sure. "What money? What are you talking about?"

"A man gave me five dollars to go up to Jerry and smear pudding on his shirt," he said through his festival of snot and tears.

The adults looked at each other. All of them seemed to understand who that man had to be.

"Can you tell us what he looked like?" Connor asked. He could feel a glimmer of hope beginning to take root. No matter what Detective Pierce found on the CCTV footage, it sounded like they had a witness. Somebody who had seen the man up close. That could be worth a lot in a case like this.

Eddie took several short breaths as he tried to get control of himself. He wiped away the tears on his cheeks, even though new ones continued to fall. "He was wearing a baseball cap. One of those with, like, a Braves logo on it. And a sweatshirt."

"What about his face? Was there anything distinctive about it?"

"I don't know. I couldn't see."

"What do you mean you couldn't see?" Lucy asked. "How could you not see? You were standing right there in front of him." She sounded like she was starting to panic again.

Eddie began to sob more loudly.

Connor shot her a look. Talking to Eddie like that was counterproductive, he wanted to tell her. But she didn't see his expression—all of her attention was on the boy—and Connor decided that, no matter what Lucy had said, he should keep his eyes on Eddie, too.

"It's all right," he told Eddie. "Just tell us what you can. Why couldn't you see what he looked like?"

"Well, there was the baseball cap, and he had a beard, and he had these *huge* sunglasses on." Eddie stopped wiping his cheeks long enough to hold both hands up to his eyes to illustrate how big the sunglasses were.

"Ms. Grindon."

Ellie, along with everyone else, turned toward the man's voice. Connor could tell from the gray suit he was wearing that this must be Detective Stewart Pierce. After all, who else would come dressed like that to an aquarium?

"So, it's the famous Connor Callahan," Stewart said after Ellie made the introductions and sent Eddie away. He pointed a finger at Connor. "Listen, I don't know what you're doing here, but this is not your case, got it?"

Connor barely even nodded before the detective ran a hand through his disheveled hair and asked to speak to Lucy alone.

Lucy accompanied the detective down the stairs. They were gone for a long time. After a while, Ellie said she should get back to the students, leaving Connor and his friends alone to wait for Lucy's return.

They silently watched Ellie confer with the other chaperones and then lead the students away. Whether the plan was to continue with the field trip or take the students back to the school, Connor couldn't guess. Either way, he thought, it seemed like a good idea to get them out of the cafeteria. He wasn't sure they knew what happened, but with Eddie and Marcus to spread the story, it wouldn't be long until all the children would be talking about the man who had taken Jerry away. And the more time the students spent confined in the cafeteria, the more serious it would seem.

At least if the news spread while they were on the move, it would be couched in some semblance of normalcy and thus perhaps shared with more curiosity than alarm.

The last thing kids that age needed was to be afraid of every stranger they met, scarred by their proximity to an abduction.

"I guess the kidnapper used the pudding trick to get Jerry away from the rest of the students," Olin said.

Connor nodded in agreement. "Seems like it."

"Are we really going to sit this one out?" Dylan asked.

Connor looked at her. His face told her everything that needed to be said. Still, he replied, "Not if Lucy doesn't want us to."

CHAPTER 11

THE DETECTIVE SPOKE to Connor and his friends only briefly when he returned, and only to find out where Marcus had gone.

"Pierce wants to see if he can get prints off the money," Lucy explained.

"They went that way," Dylan said, pointing. "We're not sure if they left or . . ." She did not bother to finish her thought since the detective was already walking away.

Lucy watched him go. Once he was out of sight, she turned back to Connor. "There's nothing useful on the CCTV."

That did not surprise him. From the moment he heard the kidnapper was wearing a baseball cap and sunglasses, he assumed it was in an effort to thwart the security cameras. He doubted the detective would do any better with the money. A man that careful would have applied liquid latex to his fingertips or found another way to obscure the prints.

"Detective Pierce had a technician install some software on my phone, though," Lucy continued. "It will let the police listen in when the kidnapper calls. So no matter what, it's not like we're at a dead end."

Connor remembered the police in New York had installed something similar on his phone when his parents were abducted. It had been pointless, since no kidnapper ever called, and Connor worried it might prove pointless for her, too.

Of course, the statistics were on Lucy's side. Most kidnappings were about money. He shouldn't let his own unusual experience color his expectations of hers, he told himself. They would just have to wait.

There wasn't anything else they could do, anyway.

Lucy drove the group back to the office where Connor, Olin, and Dylan had left their cars. When she came to a stop in the parking lot, she looked over at Dylan and asked, "Would you mind coming back to the house with me?" She then turned her gaze to Connor and Olin, who were in the backseat. "All of you? I'm going to have to tell my mom about this, and I'd rather not do it alone. Besides, I'd feel better if you all were around."

"What's wrong?" Gretchen asked Lucy when her daughter entered the house. "What are you doing home so early?" Then, before Lucy could answer, she looked at Connor, Olin, and Dylan, and followed up her first two questions with another: "Who are all these people?"

Lucy directed Gretchen to the living room and told her to sit down. Gretchen selected a spot on the sofa and Lucy sat beside her. Then she relayed the story of the abduction as succinctly as possible. Every so often, Connor or Dylan, who had perched themselves on floral-print chairs on the opposite side of the coffee table, would add an additional detail where they felt it was important. Olin, who was standing behind them and seemed uncomfortable to be part of this intimate moment between mother and daughter, did not speak at all.

By the time they were done, the blood had drained from Gretchen's face. She collapsed back into the sofa as if she no longer had the strength to sit upright.

"We're going to get him back," Dylan assured her.

Lucy took hold of her mom's hand. "I know how you feel. I'm scared, too. But between them"—she was referring to Connor and his friends—"and the police, we've got the best people we could have on this. Right now, we just have to try to be strong."

Suddenly, Connor's phone rang. He didn't recognize the number, so he silenced the ringer and let the call roll over to voicemail. No matter who it was, he thought, it couldn't be more important than what he was already dealing with.

Then, seconds later, the phone rang again, and he decided that if he wanted to get rid of the caller, he was going to have to answer after all. He excused himself from the conversation, walked into the foyer, and clicked on the display to answer.

"Hello," he said, trying to keep his voice down so that it didn't carry into the living room. He suspected it might be Reid, looking for an update on the case. Of course, it was too early to expect an update of any substance. They had spoken only hours ago. Nonetheless, Connor had learned some clients expected to hear from him every few hours, even if there was nothing to say, and Reid struck him as the kind of person who might expect just that.

But it wasn't Reid, and the first three words out of the caller's mouth chilled Connor in a way few things had. "Hickory. Dickory. Dock."

The voice that delivered those words was deep and raspy. It sounded like the caller had stepped right out of a horror movie, and the silence that followed was all-consuming. Connor could no longer hear the conversation in the living room or the floorboards squeaking ever so slightly when he shifted his weight. For several seconds, he even forgot to breathe. When he did, he inhaled sharply and let the air out with a sudden, "Who is this?"

The question came out louder than he meant for it to. Everyone in the living room turned to look at him. He met their eyes for a moment, and then looked away. Softer now, he added, "What do you want?"

"I have the boy."

"*What do you want?*" Connor repeated, with more intensity but without raising his voice.

"I want you to try to find him."

"Excuse me?"

"Good luck. I'll be in touch soon."

The caller hung up before Connor could speak again.

Connor felt trapped in a whirlwind of emotion as he slowly let the phone fall away from his ear. He looked from the device to Lucy and back, trying to make sense of the call he had just received.

Was this a game? A contest of wits? A madman out to prove he was smarter than Connor and his friends?

He pulled the note that had been left on the door out of his pocket and read it again.

Hickory, Dickory, Dock.
The mouse ran up the clock.
The clock struck one.
The mouse was Done.
Hickory.
Dickory.
Dock.

He now saw similarities between it and the abduction he had not noticed before. The first was obvious—*The clock struck one.* Connor had received the call from Lucy at roughly 1:15 p.m. That meant the kidnapper had been planning a lunchtime abduction from the beginning.

The second—*Hickory. Dickory. Dock.*—was clearly intended to be a calling card of sorts. Any generic claim of responsibility for the kidnapping would have been met with skepticism. Especially since the call had come into Connor's phone instead of Lucy's.

Although there were not yet any news stories about the abduction (and there might never be), word about it had no doubt spread through the aquarium staff. On top of that, teachers had probably told teachers, children had probably told their parents, parents may have told their friends. It was quite possible there were already hundreds of people talking about what had happened.

As hard as it was for Connor to get his head around the idea, he knew there were always people out there trying to take credit for crimes they hadn't committed. Perhaps they were looking for fame or attention however they could get it. Or perhaps, in this case, it was just another student playing a prank, unaware of the consequences. Whatever the reason, Connor knew a call like this should not be taken at face value.

The nursery rhyme was proof positive that the man who had called him was the one who had left the note.

If he was right, the kidnapper had practically laid out his plan for Connor. Although he told himself there was no way he could have realized that at the time, he knew he would still beat himself up for missing the clues until the boy was safely returned.

If he was safely returned.

After the other clues Connor had found in that note, he could no longer assume "Done" had been capitalized by accident. That was intended to deliver a message, just like the rest of the nursery rhyme had been.

The word suddenly seemed foreboding in this context, and Connor's first thought was that "Done" meant "Dead."

Would the kidnapper really have abducted Jerry with the sole intention of killing him?

Connor hoped he was wrong.

Then he looked down at the phone in his hand and realized there was one more clue he had at his disposal. Unlike those in the note, which could only tell him what he already knew, this one might help him find Jerry.

He put the note back in his pocket, navigated to his call log, and committed the kidnapper's phone number to memory. After all of the precautions the man had taken at the museum, Connor could hardly believe he would place such a call without hiding the number, which meant it was likely a burner.

But even if the kidnapper thought he was safe because he was calling from a burner, he might have paid for it with a credit card or been caught on camera buying the phone without a disguise.

He turned back toward the living room. "Olin. Dylan. Can you come here?"

Olin and Dylan had been engaged in quiet conversation with Lucy and Gretchen, no doubt trying to comfort the two women. All four of them looked in Connor's direction.

"It will just take a second," Connor assured the group.

Dylan frowned. She said something to Lucy that was too soft for Connor to hear, and then, accompanied by Olin, she joined Connor in the foyer.

"If this is about anything other than Jerry," she began, "it can wait—"

"It's not," Connor interrupted. "I wish it was." Then he filled her and Olin in on the call he had just received and how it related to the note that had been left on his door.

Olin's eyes grew wide. "You think this is personal?"

"Kind of seems like it," Dylan said.

"We should let Detective Pierce know. He can track the number."

Dylan shot Olin a sideways glance. "*We* can track the number."

"Olin's right," Connor said. "We need to let the detective know. But let's keep the part about the note to ourselves for now. He doesn't seem to like us very much."

"He didn't say anything about me or Olin," Dylan pointed out.

"Fine. He doesn't like *me* very much. Better?"

Dylan shrugged.

"Anyway," Connor said, "if we tell him about the note, he's going to want to start looking through our past cases for a possible suspect, and I'd rather we do that ourselves." He did not have to tell Olin and Dylan that they owed it to their clients to maintain their privacy. Olin and Dylan already understood that. He also did not have to mention that if there was anything to find in their past cases, they would be best suited to find it since they knew the ins and outs of each case in more detail than any of them would have put on paper. "Let Detective Pierce track down the number. If it goes to a burner, he has a better chance than we do at figuring out who bought it."

"You think this could relate to a past case?" Dylan asked.

Connor nodded. "I mean, it makes sense, doesn't it? At least as much as anything else."

"Okay, but I still think there could be fingerprints on the note," Olin said.

"And I still doubt it," Dylan countered.

"If he's going to find any prints, he'll find them on the money," Connor agreed.

"Fine. But we have to tell him, eventually," Olin said.

"We will. Once we've been through our case notes."

"What are you talking about?" Lucy asked from the living room.

Connor and his friends simultaneously looked in her direction. "Follow my lead," he said quietly, then returned to the wingback he had been sitting in with Olin and Dylan in tow.

"The call I got," he said, now addressing Lucy. "It was the kidnapper."

Lucy rocked forward, perching herself on the edge of the sofa and staring straight at Connor. "What did he say?"

"Not much. He said he would call later with more information."

"Why did he call your phone instead of mine?"

"Maybe he suspected yours would be tapped." Connor was still holding his phone in his left hand. He reflexively looked down at the screen, where he could see the call log. "What matters is that we've got his number. Let's get this to Detective Pierce so he can trace it."

Lucy was already fishing his card out of her pocket.

CHAPTER 12

DRAKE HARTFIELD PARKED in the visitor lot outside the Fulton County Penitentiary. He could feel his heart pounding and pressed a hand to his chest. So far, today had been bad news all around. After he had been to see his lawyer, he stopped by his doctor's office, only to find out his cardiomyopathy was advancing more quickly than expected, despite the ACE inhibitor he was on.

He wasn't sure if it was the illness or the stress of being so close to a prison that was making his heart act up right now, but it hardly mattered. He still had to do what he'd come here to do.

Drake took several deep breaths. That helped sometimes, although it didn't seem to make much difference now. He headed toward the entrance.

Drake had left his gun at home, so he did not have to worry about the metal detectors just inside the door. Since he was not on the run from the law (not yet, anyway), he did not have to worry about the guards manning it, either.

He dumped his keys and wallet into a little yellow basket and stepped through. The machine nonetheless beeped. Then he removed the gold tie clip and cufflinks.

Throughout the entire process, the two guards on duty watched him with something that might have been annoyance. He didn't blame them. An honest living was often tedious, which was part of the reason Drake had chosen—as he put it—the road less traveled.

"Just because I'm a thief does not mean I'm uneducated," he had told his associates over the years when they raised an eyebrow at that description. Then, he would add, "And that has made all the difference."

Some of them realized his answer was a reference to the Robert Frost poem "The Road Not Taken." Many did not. Regardless, he had never mentioned the poem or the poet by name. He simply used each individual's reaction as one of many gauges he employed to judge their education and intelligence.

The way he saw it, the more he knew about the people he was working with, and in particular about the way they thought, the better he would be at successfully planning any crime or con in which they were involved.

He stepped back through the metal detector. This time, there was no annoying beep from the machine.

The guard on Drake's left passed the basket from one side of the machine to the other.

With an easy smile, Drake said, "See? Just the cufflinks."

"I see, sir," the offer replied, dryly.

Drake's smile fell away. He grabbed the items from the basket, returned his keys and wallet to his pocket, slid his gold tie clip back into place, and reattached his cufflinks. When he was done, he tugged gently on the sleeves of his jacket to make sure the cuffs of his shirt did not stick out too far and stepped deeper into the prison.

As he headed away from the metal detector, he heard one of the guards say, "Enjoy your freedom while you can. You'll be in here soon enough."

Drake was certain it was no accident the guard had said that loud enough for him to hear, but he did not bother to turn back and confront the man over it. Such a confrontation would not do him any good. With his heart the way it was, it might even do him some harm.

There was only one person within these walls who was worth that sort of risk, and that was his accountant, Alec Garcia.

Drake approached a desk, asked to speak with the inmate, and a different officer directed him to a row of booths. Thick plexiglass divided the visitor's side from the inmate's. Phones were mounted to the walls on both sides.

This officer did not seem to have the same chip on his shoulder the first two did. Perhaps he didn't know who Drake was, or perhaps he was one of the few people who truly believed you were innocent until proven guilty, Drake thought.

"He'll be right out," the officer said before he walked away.

Drake had no doubt that was true. Alec might be unwilling to speak to Drake's lawyer, but Drake knew damn well the man would speak to him. He would be a fool not to. While Alec might be a lot of things—a turncoat, a liar, a snake—he was not a fool.

When Drake had explained his attitude toward his career to the accountant all those years ago, not only had Alec recognized the poem, but he responded with a line from the poet's lesser-known work "A Time to Talk."

When Drake thought back on that conversation now, he remembered he had been impressed not just by Alec's knowledge of Frost's work, but by the wealth of knowledge he seemed to hold on so many subjects.

In the years since, there had been many "times to talk." Some had been good; some had been bad. But none were as important as this.

Alec shuffled through a door on the other side of the plexiglass wearing an orange jumpsuit. He looked tired, weak. His hair, which had been a thick mane of brunette locks the last time Drake had seen him, was now thinning, greasy, and gray. His five o'clock shadow looked like it was closing in on eight. His lip was split and his right eye was swollen, both likely the aftermath of a fight with another inmate.

Once Drake had processed everything he saw, he realized he was staring at a man who had been taken down to his final peg. A man who knew his life, in all the ways that mattered, was over. A man who lived on only because he did not have the will or resources to end it.

Alec lifted the phone on his side of the glass, and Drake did the same.

"What do you want?" Alec asked.

Drake smiled. "I want to talk."

"There's nothing you can say that's going to change my mind. All I did was what you asked me to do. You're the mastermind behind this whole thing. I'm not going to rot in here for you."

Drake looked like he was hurt. "I don't want you rotting in here. Nobody wants that. Not me. Not your wife. Not your baby boy—what's his name?"

Now it was Alec's turn to smile, only his was followed by a soft chuckle.

"What's so funny?" Drake asked.

"So that's why you're here. You came to threaten my family."

"I'm not here to threaten your family. I'm just saying it would be a shame if the grief your wife is going through right now caused her to . . . *do* something."

"Like what?"

"How should I know? What do women usually do? Overdose on

pills? Drive off a cliff? These things happen. And then who would be left to take care of your son? The state? That wouldn't do, would it?"

Alec ran a hand through his hair. "You think they're just sitting around at home? You'll never find them. I know you, Drake. Frankly, I'm surprised it's taken you this long to make such a threat. I've been expecting it for weeks now."

Drake could feel himself getting worked up. If he could have reached over and grabbed Alec by the throat, he would have. Instead, he balled his right hand into a fist and squeezed. "Don't testify against me, Alec."

"It's over, Drake. Go home. Get your affairs in order. You're going away for a long time." Then Alec hung up the phone and stepped away from the booth.

Drake called for him to come back several times, even though he knew he could not be heard through the plexiglass. He slammed the phone down in its cradle.

Alec was mistaken if he thought he was going to win this battle.

CHAPTER 13

LUCY PHONED DETECTIVE Stewart Pierce to tell him about the call Connor had received. She put it on speaker so everyone could listen. The detective wrote down the phone number, said he would get a trace on it, and asked if Connor was with her. She said he was. Then, he told her he would be at her house in fifteen minutes and asked her to make sure Connor stuck around until he arrived.

Connor had expected that. The detective would want to install the same software on his phone he had installed on Lucy's. That was okay with him. He was, however, taken by surprise when the detective wanted to install the software on Dylan's and Olin's phones, too.

"The guy's playing games," Stewart said, directing his comment at Connor. "He obviously knows about Lucy's relationship to you. We don't know who he'll call next. We need to be ready for anything."

Olin readily handed over his phone. "Anything to help get Lucy's son back."

Dylan, who probably liked the idea of such an application on her phone as much as she liked Connor hacking into her computer a few years back, did so as well, but not as fast.

Then the detective passed all three phones to a man in a blue windbreaker with the letters "APD" stitched into it. Without so much as a nod at anyone, the man carried the phones outside. Through the window, Connor watched him follow the front path to a police van parked along the curb, where he climbed into the back and shut the door.

Connor assumed the man was a technician of some sort, but that was just a guess, since Stewart had not introduced him when they arrived. If his behavior now was any indication, he likely never would.

While the man was gone, Stewart asked Connor to repeat the words the kidnapper had used to the best of his ability. That was, quite obviously, not something he intended on doing, since it would also mean revealing the existence of the note. Besides, the exact words the kidnapper had used were not what mattered here. What mattered here was the kidnapper had called, had told Connor he had Lucy's son, and would call again later with more information.

So that was the story Connor told the detective.

"That's it? That's all he said?" Stewart asked.

"He said, 'I have the boy. I'll be in touch soon.'" Strictly speaking, that was all true. Never mind that there had been other words before and between the ones he repeated now.

Stewart jotted the words down on a notepad and slid the notepad into his coat pocket. "All right. Hopefully, the phone number will get us somewhere."

When the detective left, Connor told Lucy he was going to go back to the office with Olin and Dylan. "Like Detective Pierce said, the guy knows you work for us," Connor told her when she asked why. "If he didn't, he wouldn't have called my phone. We are going to review all the information we have on past cases, plus any notes we have on those we turned down."

"You think you'll find anything?"

Connor shrugged. "It's worth a look, isn't it? Maybe somebody will stand out."

"Thank you," Lucy said, hugging Connor. "Thank you for helping me find my boy." When she let go, she wiped her eyes and stepped back.

"We'll let you know if we come across anything," Dylan said.

Back at the office, Connor, Olin, and Dylan reviewed their notes on every person they had spoken to, whether they had taken the case or not. All three investigators had known from the beginning their best suspects would be those they had put away, and it was the same conclusion they reached when they were done. Connor could imagine any one of them kidnapping Lucy's son as some sort of revenge. But finding out if any of them had been released—or escaped—was not something Connor was going to be able to dig up using his computer.

No matter how good a hacker he was, he'd need an IP address to start with. Probably multiple, since an IP address inside one prison system would not give him access to the others. Of course, he had no way of getting those.

Dylan tried her luck with the dark web but came up empty. She had once said you could find anything in the sketchiest corners of the internet if you knew where to look. It seemed that was not entirely true. Apparently, even the dark web had its limits.

She closed her laptop and returned to the conference table, where Connor and Olin were waiting for her. The documents they'd been reviewing were spread out across the table, making the top of it nearly impossible to see. Some were bound together in folders that included copious notes about the cases they had worked on. Others were loose sheets of various sizes that included handwritten comments about potential clients.

"That's okay," Connor said. "I think I know somebody who can help us answer those questions."

"Who?" Dylan asked.

"You remember Detective Shaw?"

Olin, who was in the process of scooping up the closest papers and stacking them into a pile, stopped what he was doing to look at Connor. "You mean the detective we ran into when we were looking for the Thompson sisters?"

"The very one," Connor said.

Dylan leaned forward, resting her elbows on a pair of folders and looking doubtfully at Connor. "Why would he help us?"

"Well, first, we solved the case. Second, he falsely arrested me. And third, he nearly got me killed when he refused to follow me into that motel room." Connor raised one finger after another as he ticked off his reasons. "I'd say he owes us. Besides that, why wouldn't he help us? He knows what we can do."

Olin reached across the table and pulled the two folders Dylan was leaning on out from underneath her.

"Hey!"

"We don't want these getting damaged," he said, looking the folders over. Then he placed them on the growing stack in front of him and turned his attention back to Connor. "I guess we can ask him."

Dylan huffed. "Fine. Whatever."

CHAPTER 14

CONNOR CALLED THE downtown police precinct and asked to speak to Detective Shaw. The officer who answered told him Alex was out, and Connor left a message for the detective to call him when he returned.

Hours passed. Together with Olin and Dylan, Connor went through all the potential suspects one more time. Even though the ringer on his phone was turned all the way up, he compulsively checked the device every ten minutes or so to make sure he had not missed a call from the detective or the kidnapper.

Finally, the three of them admitted to each other there was nothing else they could do for now and headed home.

"There's always tomorrow," Dylan said, locking the door to their suite. "We'll figure this out."

Connor wanted to believe that was true. They had solved a lot of cases, but rarely had they been in a situation like this—where all they could do was wait. Over the last couple of days, though, it seemed to be happening a lot. When Connor found the note taped to his door, they had been stuck until the kidnapper called. Now they were stuck until the detective or the kidnapper called back.

However, as it turned out, they would not have to wait until tomorrow to move the case one step closer toward a resolution.

Connor was halfway between the office and his apartment when his phone rang. The Caller ID revealed only a phone number. Connor braced himself for the possibility that it was as likely the kidnapper as it was Alex (and, he had to admit, just as likely to be a telemarketer).

He pressed the button to answer, and the call was routed through his car's speakers.

"What can I do for you, Connor?"

Connor recognized Alex's voice right away and breathed a small sigh of relief. He wasn't ready to speak to the kidnapper again yet. If possible, he needed to level the playing field first. And that meant finding out who he was up against.

"Can we meet? I have something I need to talk to you about."

"What's going on?"

There was an edge to Alex's voice, Connor realized. He shouldn't have been surprised. Connor had not spoken to him since the Thompson case had been solved, so Alex had every reason to be concerned. After all, people don't call cops out of the blue simply to ask how they're doing.

"It would be better if we spoke in person," Connor said.

"All right. When?"

"Are you free now?"

"Yes, I am. I'm down at the station. I'll wait."

Connor pulled up to a traffic light, looked around, and quickly considered his options. He wasn't going to the police station if he could help it. There wasn't a lot of privacy there, and he didn't need other cops listening in on their conversation. "Actually, there's a bar in Midtown called Smith's."

"I know it."

"Can we meet there?"

Alex seemed to hesitate for a moment, then said, "Sure, I guess that's fine, too. I can be there in twenty minutes."

When Connor arrived at Smith's Bar, he could hear a rockabilly hit he vaguely remembered coming from inside before he even opened the door. It was exactly why he didn't like the place. The music was too loud for his taste. But, tonight, that was also what made it a good spot to meet. After all, Connor didn't want some stranger eavesdropping on their conversation any more than he wanted a police officer doing it, and there was no way somebody would be able to overhear their conversation in there. Connor was pretty sure he and the detective would barely be able to hear each other.

Connor stepped inside. The bar was dimly lit and looked exactly like it had the last time he was here. Neon beer signs littered the windows and walls. A pair of unused pool tables occupied an outsized percentage of the floor space near the back. Aging and chipped tables occupied the rest.

He found a booth that gave him a view of the door and watched it until Alex stepped inside. The detective was wearing a blue suit, a wrinkled dress shirt, and a tie that hung loose around his neck. He needed a shave and, even from here, Connor could see bags under his eyes. All of which was to say, Alex looked exactly like he had the last time Connor had seen him.

Connor waved to get his attention. Alex came over and took a seat on the opposite side of the booth. There were no drinks on the table and no server to bring them. If they wanted a beverage, alcoholic or not, they would have to go to the bar. Connor chalked that up as another benefit to this place since it meant not only was there no way for them to be overheard but there was also no one to interrupt them.

"What did you want to see me about?" Alex asked over the music.

"A friend's son was kidnapped from the aquarium today."

"Oh, hell. How long ago?"

"It happened at lunch."

"And you waited until now to report it?"

"The boy's teacher called the police as soon as she realized what had happened."

"Then you must have a detective assigned to the case."

"Yes."

A heavyset man with a long, matted beard in a Rolling Stones tee-shirt walked past their booth and headed to the restroom. Alex watched him until he was out of sight, then said, "Not to be rude, but why am I here, then?"

"I don't think the detective likes me very much," Connor said.

"Color me shocked."

"I'm serious."

"I am, too. You should have let us handle the missing Thompson woman. The way you go around sticking your nose in other people's business, I'm surprised more people don't dislike you."

Connor pulled his PI license out of his wallet and flashed it at the detective. "I'm not just a concerned friend. The woman is my receptionist."

Alex's eyes widened ever so slightly with surprise. Although many people knew about Connor's involvement in the Chris Miller case, apparently he did not. In a subtle display of respect, the detective nodded at Connor. "Glad to see you've made it official. Still, why am I here?"

"I need some information."

"Ask the detective working your case."

"Like I told you—"

"He doesn't like you," Alex interrupted.

"Right. So he's not very forthcoming."

Alex shrugged.

"You can't sit by and expect me to do nothing."

"What's his name? The detective?"

"Stewart Pierce."

Alex frowned. "If it makes you feel any better, he's that way with everyone. Likes to keep his cards close to his chest."

"Yeah, well, the case isn't as cut and dried as he thinks it is." Connor removed the note from his jacket pocket. He unfolded it, read it once more, and, after a brief pause, slid it across the table.

Alex picked up the note and read it.

Connor waited until he was done before he said, "That was taped to my door last night when I got home."

"You think it's related?"

Connor told Alex about the kidnapper's call and the direct reference the man had made to the note. "So, yeah, I think it's related."

"Are you saying this has something to do with you?" Alex asked.

"I don't know. Maybe it has something to do with one of the cases we worked on. That's why I wanted to meet."

"Have you told Detective Pierce about this yet?"

Connor shook his head. "I wanted to talk to you first."

"You're going to have to tell him about this. If you don't, I will. This is his case, and the longer you wait, the worse it's going to be." Alex paused, then looked at the note once more. "You know, this is exactly the kind of thing that got you in trouble before."

Connor thought back to the Thompson case and the cell phone he had not handed over.

Alex watched the guy with the long beard walk past their table in the opposite direction before he spoke again. "It's withholding evidence. You must know that. And PI or not, if you keep this from him for much longer, he's going to charge you."

"I promise I'll tell him."

"When?"

"As soon as you tell me what I want to know."

"This isn't a negotiation."

Connor looked around to make sure no one was nearby. Then he leaned in and gestured for Alex to do the same. "I know about the room key."

"What are you talking about?"

"You took it out of my wallet after you arrested me. I know, because it was gone once I got my things back. You weren't supposed to do that, were you?" The question was rhetorical. He already knew the answer.

Alex leaned back, crossed his arms over his chest, and stared at Connor for a long time. "What do you want?"

"I want to know if anybody we put away has escaped or is out on bail."

Alex frowned.

"I promise, once you get back to me, I'll tell Pierce everything. I just want to make sure I don't get left in the dark."

Alex still did not seem satisfied.

"You have to admit, we have a pretty good track record."

"Who is this 'we' you keep talking about, anyway?"

"Olin and Dylan. We're in business together. Do you remember them?"

"The jock and the thief. Yeah, I remember them."

"Dylan's not a thief. She's just damn good at picking locks."

Alex shrugged as if to suggest one implied the other. Then he folded the note up—"I'm keeping this"—and placed it in his own jacket pocket. "I'll find out what you want to know. But I'm giving this note to Pierce."

"Do what you have to do." Connor passed another piece of paper to Alex. This one contained the list of names he wanted Alex to research. "Just get me what I want to know."

Alex sighed, stood up, and turned toward the exit. "Don't pull this shit again!"

CHAPTER 15

CONNOR PARKED IN the lot attached to his apartment building and followed the path into the lobby. At the same time he stepped through one door, Rebecca Strauss stepped through another. Once again, she had the Pomeranian at her side. Now, though, instead of the inside-out sweatshirt and black leggings she had been wearing earlier, she was dressed in a tight pair of jeans and a white sweater that clearly weren't meant for, as she had put it, "laundry day."

They both stopped. The look on her face suggested she was as surprised to see Connor as he was to see her.

"How about that?" she finally said. "Twice in one day." She smiled. "It must be a sign."

After the day he'd had, Connor would not have thought he was in any mood to smile. Yet, he did. Although it must not have been as bright as hers, since the next thing she said was, "Hard day?"

"That's an understatement."

Rebecca bit her lip, looked down at her dog, then back at Connor. "You know, I just finished making some spaghetti. It's too much for me. If you're looking for someone to talk to, you can join me."

Connor hesitated. The only thing he wanted to do was go to bed, to put this day behind him. He hated the idea of Lucy sitting at home with her mom, both of them worried about Jerry and unable to do anything about it. He hated that he had kept the note and the truth of the kidnapper's phone call from her. He hated that all he could do was wait for Alex or the kidnapper to call back.

But that was where he was, and whether he went straight to bed or joined Rebecca for dinner, none of it was going to change.

Maybe the company would do me some good, he thought. A small slice of normalcy certainly couldn't hurt. Besides, if he turned down this invitation, would he ever get another one? If he rejected her offer, would she even consider one from him?

Connor had been working up the nerve to ask Rebecca out for a long time. Tonight might not be the perfect evening for an impromptu date, but you don't always get the opportunities you want at the times you want them. Sometimes, you just have to grab hold of them when they come your way and hope for the best.

He would not, however, go into the details of the abduction. That wasn't something Rebecca needed to hear about. He would keep it light, he told himself. Bad day at the office. That sort of thing happened to everyone.

And he managed to follow through on that plan, avoiding the specific nature of the work he did in the process . . . at least until she caught a glimpse of the gun he was carrying underneath his jacket.

CHAPTER 16

BEFORE REBECCA SAW the gun, the evening was going exactly as Connor might have imagined. She told him she liked to be outdoors, and that she enjoyed hiking in particular. Almost every weekend, she said, she was up in the North Georgia mountains with her dog, Chloe, on one trail or another.

If Connor had been a little smoother (and wasn't distracted by the horrible things going on in his life), he might have told her it showed. Instead, he asked, "That little thing can keep up with you on a hike?"

"Sometimes," Rebecca said, smiling again. (Or perhaps, Connor thought, "still smiling," since she hadn't really stopped since he had agreed to dinner.) "I bring a backpack with me. When she gets tired, I carry her. It works out for both of us."

Connor dutifully smiled at Chloe, who had taken a spot underneath the table where she could keep an eye out for crumbs.

Although their apartments had an identical layout, Rebecca had decorated hers with the eye of a designer.

They were sitting at a small table in the dining room with a white tablecloth draped across it and a mismatched assortment of dishes that somehow looked like they were part of the same set.

As interesting as all that was, none of it came as a surprise to Connor. It might have even been the life he would have scripted for her if he had been the one in charge of writing it.

What did come as a surprise was that she was also an inventor of sorts. In college, she told him, she had participated in various robotics competitions and still tinkered with one idea or another. Her apartment was outfitted with half a dozen of her creations. She had made a motion-activated sensor that would turn on the lamps when she entered the living room, a similar device that would open or close the blinds, and an automatic dog food dispenser that would refill Chloe's food bowl whenever it was empty.

"But my favorite thing I ever made had to be in high school."

"What was that?"

"I shouldn't tell you," she said, laughing.

"Oh, come on."

"All right, all right." She pulled herself together. "So I had this test coming up. Something about the American Revolution, if I remember right. I hadn't studied. I knew I was going to fail. So I made this little gadget. It was kind of like a remote-activated smoke bomb. I hid it behind a plant in the cafeteria. Anyway, the teacher passed out the test, and once I got a look at the questions, I triggered the device, which set off the smoke detectors. Everyone was ushered outside for probably fifteen or twenty minutes while they cleared the building. By the time we got back into class, it was too late to take the test, so the teacher postponed it to the next day. And, because I got a look at the questions, I knew exactly what I needed to study to make sure I passed."

"That's pretty sneaky," Connor said, also amused. "You got an A, I take it?"

"I got a C, but I passed."

"Why didn't you try to do more with any of your ideas?"

"Like what?"

"I don't know. Get a patent. Start a business."

Rebecca shrugged. "It's just a hobby. Doing something like that would take all the joy out of it. I'm happy with my job at Georgia Tech."

"What do you do?"

"I work in the mechanical engineering department. Research, mostly."

Then Connor shifted in his seat, and her smile fell away. She slowly finished chewing, placed the fork on her plate, and slid her chair back from the table.

Connor wasn't sure what was going on until she pointed at his chest and said, "What's that?"

Rebecca must have caught a glimpse of the Glock underneath his jacket, Connor realized. At the same time, he also figured out she had slid the chair back from the table so she could make a run for the door if she needed to.

"All right, look," Connor said. "I may have fudged a little bit when I said I worked with computers."

Rebecca slid her chair back another inch as she started to stand.

Connor held out his hands. "Hold on. I do work with computers. I'm a private investigator." He reached a hand around toward his back pocket.

"What are you doing?"

He froze. "I'm just getting my wallet. I'm going to show you my PI license."

After a moment, Rebecca nodded for him to continue.

Slower now, he pulled out his wallet, opened it. The license was in a pocket with a clear plastic window so that it was easy to show when he needed to. He held the wallet up so that it was directly in Rebecca's line of sight.

She slowly sat back down. "Why didn't you tell me the truth?"

Connor put his wallet away. He shrugged. "It seemed like a lot for a first date." Then he cursed himself for referring to this meal as a date. He had no idea if that was in fact what Rebecca's intention had been when she'd invited him up.

But he couldn't have been entirely wrong because her smile was back. She sat back down and pulled her chair back in to the table. "How did you become a PI?"

"That's not first date material, either."

"I think it probably is. If there's something I should know about you, wouldn't it be better if I find out now?"

Connor rolled more spaghetti onto his fork while he considered the question. After he had finished chewing, he launched into the story about his parents' abduction.

When he was done, Rebecca said, "I guess I might have become a PI, too, if I'd lived through something like that." Then, she paused, and added, "This work problem you're dealing with—I guess it's more serious than a crashed computer, huh?"

"A lot."

"You want to tell me about it?"

"Not yet. If it's all right with you, I'd rather not think about that right now."

CHAPTER 17

REBECCA ACCEPTED THE answer without protest and changed the subject. She was not going to make Connor talk about his "work problem" if he wasn't ready. That didn't stop him from thinking about it, though.

It bounced around in his head for the rest of their meal. It was front-and-center when he said he should probably go back to his apartment and get some sleep. It distracted him when Rebecca walked him to the door and asked if she could see him again.

Of course, he said "yes," but the answer did not come as readily or smoothly as it should have. He could see the disappointment on Rebecca's face, the concern that his response was not genuine.

"I'm sorry," he said. "It's just . . ."

"The work thing. I know."

Connor left Rebecca's unsure whether he should have tried to kiss her goodnight. With so many thoughts running around in his head, he couldn't tell whether she wanted him to, especially after his conversational fumble seconds earlier.

When he reached his apartment, he kneeled down in front of the door to look for the hair he had wedged between it and the frame that morning. The single blond strand was still there. He plucked it out, went inside, and made his way to bed as quickly as possible.

He thought about the abduction all through the night. He worried about whether Jerry had enough food or a place to sleep. He remembered the nursery rhyme—*the mouse was Done*—and hoped, even if Jerry didn't have enough food or a place to sleep, that he was, at least, still alive.

Tonight, not even the TV could drown out his thoughts.

At Starbucks the next morning, Connor could tell Olin hadn't slept well, either. His carefully parted hair was not quite as carefully parted as it normally was. His button-down blue shirt, which would normally be pressed to the point that it could stand up on its own, was wrinkled. The bags under his eyes were big enough to carry Connor's laptop.

Connor sat down at the table, and Olin slid a coffee over to him.

"How did it go?" Olin asked. He was talking about the conversation with Alex.

"As well as I could have hoped."

"He's going to look into the list of names for you?"

Connor nodded. "But we're going to have to tell Detective Pierce everything."

"We were going to do that, anyway."

"Yeah, well, now we *have* to. He has the note."

"You gave him the note?"

"I showed it to him. I wanted to make sure he understood the urgency. He kept it, said he's going to give it to Detective Pierce."

Olin shook his head but did not seem as alarmed by this news as Connor would have expected. Perhaps because Olin had wanted to give the note to Pierce from the beginning.

"Did he say when he would get back to you?"

"No, but he knows what's at stake. I'd be surprised if we don't hear from him today."

Connor felt his phone vibrate in his pocket. He pulled it out and checked the Caller ID. He recognized the number as the same one from last night. "Speak of the devil." He clicked to answer and pressed the phone to his ear. "Alex?"

"I've got the information you're after."

"That was fast."

"The boy is still missing, isn't he?"

The question was rhetorical. Connor did not bother to answer.

"All right," Alex continued. "Listen up. I looked into the names you gave me. Most of them are behind bars."

"*Most*? Someone escaped?"

"No, nothing like that, but Leon was paroled."

"Paroled? Really?" Connor said.

"You shouldn't be surprised. He didn't kill anyone. He didn't even do most of the dirty work."

"Still . . ."

"Don't forget he also flipped on his accomplice for a reduced sentence."

Olin waved to get Connor's attention. He mouthed the word *Who*?

Leon, Connor mouth back.

"However, he's down in Savannah now. That puts him too far away to be a good suspect."

"You're sure?"

"Yeah, I'm sure. He works for Surplus Storage, checks in with his parole officer and everything. Never missed a day of work."

"All right," Connor said, disappointed. "Thanks."

"Also, as far as the note goes—it's with the lab. I've asked them to run it for prints. They're supposed to get back to me later today. You've got until then to tell Pierce about it."

"I understand." Connor ended the call, slumped back into his chair.

"Well?" Olin asked.

"It's not him. He lives in Savannah now."

"So that's it, huh? We're stuck."

Suddenly a third chair appeared, and Dylan collapsed into it, grinning enthusiastically. Connor and Olin looked at each other and then at her.

"What are you doing here?" Olin asked.

"You're never up this early," Connor added.

"I heard you say we're stuck," she replied.

"Alex called. No good suspects."

Olin took a sip of his coffee and placed his cup back on the table. "Don't forget to tell her about the note."

"What about the note?"

Connor told Dylan the same thing he had told Olin. She did not take the news as well.

"It's fine," Connor said. "We got the information we were after, and I made a photocopy of the note before I met with Alex, just in case something like this happened."

"You expected this?"

"No, not this exactly. But the note's important. We were going to give it to Pierce eventually, anyway. I just wanted to make sure we had a copy of it in case *anything* happened to it."

Dylan stared at Connor for a long time, then exhaled through her nose and said, "Fine. I guess it could have been worse."

"Why did you say we're in luck?" Olin asked.

"I've got a name."

"What do you mean you have a name?"

"I know you said not to bother with the phone number, that it probably went to a burner, blah, blah, blah."

"Could you get to the point?" Connor asked.

"Well, I got home last night, and I decided I might as well look, anyway. You know, just to see." She grinned again. Apparently, she was too excited about her own news to stay upset with Connor for long. "I got a name."

"He wasn't using a burner," Olin said once the implications sank in.

Connor, who had already reached the same conclusion, could hardly believe it. "Are you sure?"

Dylan made a face. "Really?"

"All right. I'm just surprised."

"His name is Blake Graham. He's an investment broker. Works for a firm called Powell and Striker. Forty-seven. Married once, no children. No hobbies either, as far as I could tell. He basically works all the time."

"Sounds like you got more than a name," Olin said.

"I wanted to be thorough."

Connor racked his brain for the name Blake Graham. He hadn't been a prospective client, and certainly not anyone they had done work for. So why target Connor? There was only one way they were going to get the answer to that question, and Dylan beat him to it:

"You want to go talk to him?"

CHAPTER 18

WITH OLIN AND Dylan at his side, Connor stepped off the elevator into the Powell and Striker lobby. Along the wall to their left, floor-to-ceiling windows offered an amazing view of the city. At fifty-two floors up, that shouldn't have been a surprise. There were so many buildings blocking your view at ground level, you couldn't see much farther than the street you were on, but few rose to the staggering heights that this one did.

On the ride up, Olin had observed that Blake might not be in. "If he's our kidnapper, do you really think he'd go about his normal routine like nothing at all was going on? Wouldn't he want to keep an eye on the kid?"

"Maybe," Dylan had responded. "Then again, skipping out on work might cause his colleagues to worry. He probably wouldn't want that sort of attention. If he's locked Jerry in a basement or chained him to a radiator or—who knows?— Blake may not feel like he needs to keep an eye on the boy."

"I guess we'll have to wait and see," Connor said, who considered both scenarios as reasonable possibilities. At this point, the only thing he knew for sure was that Blake was not at home. That had been stop number one when they left the office. And thanks to Dylan's skill with a lock pick, they also knew Jerry wasn't there.

The house, which might have been better called a mansion, was slow to search, but nothing struck them as suspicious. There was no radiator to chain Jerry to. The basement was home to a pool table and a private theater instead of a dungeon. None of the doors was locked, and there was no shed or storm shelter on the property that they had been able to find.

If this had been Connor's first case, he might have assumed they were zeroing in on the wrong person. However, he had long since learned not to jump to conclusions. People were not always who they appeared to be. There were monsters everywhere. They did not show up with two heads or scales. They did not breathe fire or bare fangs. They could not be killed by sunlight or holy water. They were rarely even disfigured.

The worst, in fact, were quite the opposite. They were attractive and charming. They knew what to say, how to make you laugh, how to make you feel like you were the most important person in the world.

Worse still, they knew how to use all of that to destroy you.

Take Charles Manson, for example.

Blake Graham might be no better.

"Can I help you?" the receptionist asked when they reached her desk.

Connor asked if Blake was available and, without any further questions, she called Blake to the lobby.

"What did I tell you," Dylan mumbled to Olin.

Blake stepped out of a hallway on the other side of the desk. Connor knew from Dylan the man was in his late forties, but he had the skin and hair of someone much younger, which Dylan would later chalk up to Botox and hair plugs. He smiled at his visitors and invited them back to his office.

The space was barely big enough for a desk and the chairs that surrounded it.

As Blake circled his desk, he used the windows behind it as a mirror to straighten his tie. Once he sat down, he gestured to a pair of chairs on the opposite side. "I was only expecting two of you, but I can have a third chair brought in." He looked at Dylan. "You must be Mrs. Everwood." Then, after a quick glance at Connor, he said to Olin: "And I take it you must be Mr. Everwood."

Connor, who, along with Olin and Dylan, remained standing, could not decide whether he was offended. Then again, clearly Blake had mistaken them for other people. Likely potential clients. If he was judging them by the way they were dressed, the assumption was not entirely out of line. Connor, in his black tee-shirt and jeans, did not look like he had the sort of money Olin did (which also happened to be true).

"We're not the Everwoods," he said, intending to clear up that mistake quickly so they could get down to business.

"Oh, no?" Blake glanced at his computer screen, perhaps checking a digital calendar. "Well, I'm afraid I don't have long, then. They should be here any minute. What can I do for you?"

Connor had paid close attention to Blake's expression when they first made eye contact. He'd expected to see some sign of alarm. Short of that, he certainly thought that in one small way or another he would be able to tell the man recognized him. If he did, he was playing it as cool as anyone could.

Psycho cool, he could imagine Dylan saying.

Well, if that's what he was doing, it wasn't going to fly. "Where's Jerry?" Connor blurted out, hoping the direct nature of his question would throw Blake off his game.

At first, it seemed to work. Blake's smile faltered. "Who?"

"We know who you are," Dylan said, following Connor's lead.

Blake held out his hands. "Whoa, hold on there."

"Next time you kidnap someone's child," Dylan continued, "block your number before you call anyone about it."

Then blood rushed to Blake's face. He pointed at Dylan. "Listen, I don't need this crap. I don't want you coming in here with these bullshit games."

"Games?"

"I already told the other detective everything I know."

He pulled open a drawer, grabbed a business card, and flicked it across the desk. The card landed at Connor's feet, but nobody moved to pick it up because Blake was already laying into them again.

"That's his card. Talk to him if you want to know what I had to say. Or, better yet, why don't you all go have a look at the CCTV footage from downstairs, like I already told you guys to? Maybe you'll be able to find the guy who stole my phone and come up with a *real* lead, huh? Whatever you do, don't send any more cops down here with these same bullshit questions. What did you think was going to happen? Did you think you were going to get different answers this time? I already told you guys—I'm not who you're looking for."

He stood and, instead of pointing at Dylan, he now pointed at the door. "Get out of my office. If you send anyone else back here, you're going to talk to my lawyer, you got it? I'm pretty sure this right here amounts to harassment."

But none of them moved. After a couple of seconds, Connor picked up the card by his feet. The name on it, no surprise, was Detective Stewart Pierce. He slid the card into his pocket.

Even though Connor knew the detective was going to look into the phone number, he had assumed they would beat him to Blake's office. Apparently, that was not the case.

"We're not cops," he said, hoping to clear the air and reset.

"Excuse me?"

Connor flashed his PI license. "I'm sorry for the way I came at you. The boy who was kidnapped—he's the son of a friend. I thought . . ."

"You thought you could surprise me into making a confession."

Connor shrugged.

Blake eyed the three of them in turn and waited another beat. "Well, I guess you don't look like cops."

Connor took that as a sign that the conversation was moving in the right direction. "Listen," he said, "I'm glad that you talked to the police, but I would appreciate it if you would take a few minutes to talk to us, too. We need to do everything we can to find that boy."

"You know," Dylan added, "so we can work on coming up with *real* leads."

Connor put a hand on her shoulder, gently encouraging her to take it easy on him.

Blake took several deep breaths. He looked from Connor to his friends. "I'm sorry. It's just the way you guys started this conversation . . . I was certain for a minute there this was some sort of good cop, bad cop routine, you know?"

"It's fine," Olin said.

Blake collapsed back into his chair. "All right. What do you want to know?"

Connor considered that. Clearly, Blake had not been the man who had called him yesterday, which explained why he saw no hint of recognition when they arrived. That honor almost certainly belonged to the person who had stolen Blake's phone, or somebody the thief had sold it to. Either way, getting a little more information about that theft seemed like the place to start.

"Tell us about the robbery."

CHAPTER 19

DETECTIVE STEWART PIERCE had gone straight from Blake's office to the lobby, where a pair of security guards manned a large desk made of black marble. He flashed his badge, explained what he was doing there, and was immediately led to a room deep in the building with a dozen or so monitors affixed to the wall and a lone computer that sat on a desk beneath them. On each of those monitors, Stewart could see one part of the building or another, thanks to the security cameras mounted throughout. Every few seconds, the screens would refresh, providing a new set of views until they cycled back to the first ones Stewart had seen.

Nobody was monitoring those screens, he noticed. That did not come as a surprise. Buildings like this rarely fell victim to the sort of incidents that would make such a job necessary.

The security guard moved toward the only chair. "Let me show you how this thing works."

Stewart held up a hand. "No need." He had reviewed a lot of security footage during his career. It was his go-to move at the start of any investigation when such footage was available. Even if the equipment wasn't intuitive, he could tell by looking at the digital controls on the computer monitor that he had used this exact software before.

"You sure?"

Stewart nodded.

"All right," the security guard said, heading back into the hall. "If you run into any trouble, you can use the phone right there to give us a call. Just dial pound-one-one, and it will go straight to the front desk."

Stewart took a seat. "Thanks," he said, without turning around.

The door closed a second later.

The detective was finally alone. That was a rare thing these days. His brother, Allen, had come to stay with him a month ago, even though he had promised it would be no more than a week when he did. He was between apartments, he said. Just needed a few days to find something.

Stewart should have known better than to buy into that story. Allen was a mess. He had never had a steady job, had not finished college, and yet always claimed to be on the edge of one great success or another. His latest venture had had something to do with cryptocurrency.

Stewart had stayed away from that sort of thing. He saw it as a fad, a get-rich-quick scheme that rarely paid off. From his point of view, the best way to succeed financially was to choose a proven career path and work hard to get as close to the top as you could.

Take him, for example—he planned to be the chief of police by the time he was forty. It was an ambitious goal, for sure, but not one that was beyond the realm of possibility. Especially if he kept closing cases like he had been over the last few years.

All that aside, he *had* bought into Allen's story. He wanted to believe his younger brother would follow through on his word. He wanted to believe, despite this recent cryptocurrency scheme, that Allen was finally starting to grow up.

Stewart's wife was not thrilled with the arrangement, but she'd put up with it for a while without complaint.

However, Allen had not grown up. He slept until noon, stayed up until 4 a.m., and spent most of the hours in between on the computer or watching TV. As far as Stewart could tell, Allen had not been to look at one apartment.

That meant, these days, when Stewart wasn't stuck listening to his brother rave about the merits of some new cryptocurrency, he was stuck listening to his wife complain about their living situation.

He rarely had a chance to sit and think anymore, to ruminate on his cases with the peace and quiet his home normally provided.

Not that he would be doing that here, but at least he could enjoy a little silence while he worked.

Blake had told him his phone had been stolen while he was eating lunch in "the quad."

The quad, he then explained, was a greenspace that existed between Blake's building and two others, all designed by the same architect intending to provide a campus-like feel.

He had been sitting at one of the many picnic tables reading a Harlan Coben book on his iPhone when a man came up behind him, grabbed the phone out of his hand, and took off. Blake said it happened so fast it took him a couple of seconds to realize what was going on. Once he did, he hopped up, looking around for the thief, but the man was gone. The quad was accessible directly by all three buildings as well as the sidewalks between them, so there was no telling where the thief had gone.

"Did you put in a police report?" Stewart had asked.

"What would be the point?" Blake had replied. "They weren't ever going to find the guy, and I was just going to have to buy a new phone, anyway."

Blake had said the incident occurred the day before at about 2 p.m., which put it at an hour or so before the kidnapper had called Connor. It didn't take Stewart long to find the footage that verified Blake's story.

The footage was also able to fill in some additional details, like where the man had come from and where he had gone. The answer to both was a sidewalk that led directly toward the picnic table where Blake had been seated.

Unfortunately, the one question neither Blake nor the footage could answer was what the thief looked like. He had moved too fast for Blake to see him and, like at the aquarium, all the security cameras could tell Stewart was that the thief was wearing a large pair of sunglasses and a baseball cap.

Stewart suspected this was a crime of opportunity. Blake had in no way been targeted. The kidnapper must have known employees ate lunch out there and that they would be an easy mark.

That was not worth much, Stewart figured. There had to be thousands of people who knew that quad was there—maybe more—and since it was accessible to anybody, the best Stewart could do with that information was narrow down the pool of suspects to people who lived or worked in Midtown.

Actually, now that he thought about it, even that might be too narrow. The quad was partially visible from the street, so quite literally anybody who had driven past it might know about it.

Stewart rolled the chair back from the computer and sighed. *I should try to get a look at the security footage from the surrounding buildings,* he told himself. The location of the theft might not have helped him reduce his pool of suspects any, but maybe he would be able to find out where the kidnapper had gone, and that could be worth a whole lot more.

In the meantime, he had other business to address.

Halfway between the security room and the lobby, he pulled out his phone to call Connor. Stewart intended to ask whether he had heard from the kidnapper. Although that was not the entire reason for his call. It wasn't even the most important part. Since the tech guys had already installed their software onto his phone, he had little doubt he would already know about such a call if one had come in.

No, right now he was after something else.

CHAPTER 20

THE ELEVATOR DOORS opened just as Connor's phone started to ring. Leading Olin and Dylan into the lobby of Blake's building, he pulled the phone out of his pocket. "It's Detective Pierce."

Before he could answer, the phone stopped ringing, and instead he heard a man calling his name. Along with Connor and his friends, a dozen or so people making their way through the lobby glanced toward the voice.

Olin tapped Connor's shoulder and pointed at a man coming out of a door on the other side of the lobby and repeated the same thing Connor had said only seconds earlier. "It's Detective Pierce."

"How about that?" Dylan said. "He's still in the building."

"I bet that's where they keep the security footage."

"Maybe he'll be able to verify Blake's story for us," Olin said.

On their way down, they had agreed they would ask the security guards in the lobby if they could see the footage, but Connor wasn't sure the odds were even fifty-fifty that they would get their way. Their history with that sort of thing was hit and miss. With good reason. Whether they were licensed PIs or not, they weren't police, and there were all sorts of reasons the security guards might not be willing to let anyone other than the police see the footage.

"I wouldn't count on it," Connor said as they made their way across the lobby.

They met the detective in the middle of the room.

"What are you doing here?" Stewart asked.

"Our job," Dylan said before Connor could answer.

"You tracked down the phone number, didn't you?"

Dylan shrugged.

Stewart took a deep breath, perhaps to calm down, then directed his next question at Connor. "Have you heard from the kidnapper again?"

Connor shook his head. "Not yet." He hesitated. He had told Alex he would bring Pierce up to speed. Now, with the detective standing right in front of him, he didn't see how he could put it off any longer. If he let this conversation go without telling Stewart everything, he could pretty much guarantee himself the obstruction charge he very much wanted to avoid. His first stay in jail had not been pleasant. He couldn't imagine another would be any better.

He also decided he needed to clear the air before he asked about the security footage, since to do it the other way around might appear less than forthcoming.

Connor glanced at Olin and Dylan, who seemed to know what he was thinking. Not only did neither object, but Dylan actually nodded at him, indicating he should get on with it. Apparently, they wanted to put this behind them, as well.

Connor steeled himself for the uncomfortable conversation ahead. "There is something I needed to tell you about," he said to the detective. The words came fast, if only so Connor could get them out before he changed his mind.

"What is it?" Stewart asked.

Connor gestured at the nearest corner with a nod of his head. "Can we talk over there?" If he was going to have this conversation, the last thing he wanted to do was have it with so many people milling around them.

"Sure."

Once the four of them were out of the way, Stewart repeated his question.

Connor glanced once again at Olin and Dylan. They still seemed to be on board. Then, to Stewart, he said, "All right, look. I didn't tell you everything yesterday."

Stewart's eyebrows went up. "Really?"

Although the expression was clearly intended to convey surprise, something about it looked disingenuous.

"The kidnapper—he knows who I am."

"Obviously. He called your phone."

"It's more than that. This seems like it's personal. He challenged me to find the boy."

Stewart's eyebrows went up again. This time, he didn't say anything.

"He left me a note."

Olin took a step forward. "We should have—"

"Stop," Stewart said. "I already know all this. There are no usable prints on the note, by the way, in case you were wondering. Just like the money we got from Marcus. We got the results back first thing this morning."

Now Connor looked surprised. Only, unlike Stewart's, his expression was sincere.

"Alex told me about your conversation last night," Stewart continued. "You didn't really think he'd keep this to himself, did you?" He looked at Dylan. "We have a job to do, too."

He turned back to Connor. "I wanted to see if you would really come to me with this information like you told Alex you would." Stewart crossed his arms over his chest. "Maybe I was wrong to shut you out of the investigation. Alex has nothing but good things to say about you. If you weren't so hard-headed, he said he might never have solved his case. You obviously know a thing or two about what you're doing."

"Thanks, I guess."

"But, if I'm going to share with you what I know, you can't hold out on me again, you got it?"

"I guess that seems fair," Connor said.

Stewart stared at him for several seconds, perhaps deciding whether he believed Connor. Then he said, "I take it you talked to Blake."

"Yeah," Dylan said. "That's why we came here."

Stewart's gaze cut to her briefly before returning to Connor. "I've been through the security footage. His story checks out. Unfortunately, I couldn't see the man who stole Blake's phone any better here than I could at the aquarium. I'm going to see if I can pull any useful footage from the buildings in the area."

"That sounds good," Connor said.

"Can't you trace the phone?" Dylan asked.

"We already tried that," Stewart said. "The phone's off. You got anything for me? Remember, this is a two-way street now."

Connor shook his head. "No, nothing you don't know already."

"All right," Stewart said, "stay in touch. I'm going to try to trust you. Don't make me regret it."

"I won't."

"If you find out anything useful, I want to know about it right away, okay?"

"I promise."

Stewart held out his hand and, as soon as Connor shook it, the detective took off, heading toward the exit that would take him into the quad.

CHAPTER 21

DYLAN DROVE CONNOR and Olin from Blake's office to Lucy's house. They had no more leads to follow at the moment, and they wanted to stop in to see how she was doing. On the way to the car, Dylan had suggested they could have accomplished the same thing with a phone call, but Olin had insisted a phone call would not be personal enough.

"Her son's missing. The least we can do is stop by in person."

Lucy answered the door wearing the same clothes she had been wearing yesterday. The wrinkles in them, however, were new. "Have you found anything?" she asked as soon as she saw who it was.

"Not yet," Connor said. "Mind if we come in?"

Lucy stepped aside to let them into the foyer. Then she closed the door and brushed her hands through her frazzled hair, trying to bring some order to it. "You should have called."

"I told you," Dylan whispered to Olin.

"We just wanted to see how you were doing," Connor said, ignoring the comment.

"I mean . . ." She made a face. The answer was obvious.

"Is there anything we can do to help?" Olin asked.

"You are doing something, aren't you? Don't you have any leads?"

"The phone was stolen," Connor said. "Looks like it was probably the same person who kidnapped Jerry. Detective Pierce is seeing if he can figure out where the man might have gone after he stole it."

"You don't seem optimistic."

Connor did not have the heart to say she was right, but he implied it with his response. "The man knew enough to evade the security cameras in the aquarium as well as those that recorded the theft. He also knew enough to turn the phone off when he was done with it."

"What about your case notes? Did you find anything there that might help?"

Connor shook his head. "I'm sorry. There is something we need to tell you about, though. Can we go into the living room?"

Dylan looked questioningly at him.

"We told Detective Pierce about the note. We need to tell Lucy, too."

"What note?" Lucy said.

Connor gestured toward the living room. "Please."

"Okay," Lucy said. "I guess." She led them into the living room and, perhaps instinctively, they all took the same seats they'd had before—Lucy on the sofa, Connor and Dylan in the floral-print chairs on the other side of the coffee table, Olin standing behind them.

The only person missing was Gretchen. "She's out doing some shopping," Lucy explained. "We need food, and I . . ." She paused as she fought back tears. "It's crazy to me how life just seems to go on for everyone else after something like this. I mean, I feel like the whole world should just stop, you know? My son's been kidnapped. And all those people out there, none of them seem to care."

Connor's heart broke a little for Lucy. It was, indeed, unfair.

Once she pulled herself together, she said, "What was this about a note?"

Connor told her everything he had told Stewart. Then, once he thought she was as ready as she could be to read the note, he pulled the photocopy out of his pocket and passed it over.

"What do you think it means?" she asked when she was done reading the nursery rhyme.

He explained as much of the symbolism as he felt comfortable sharing. The time—*one o'clock*. The *Hickory. Dickory. Dock.* calling card.

The only thing he left out was his speculation that "Done" might mean "Dead." Since it *was* speculation and had no practical application to their investigation, he didn't want to put that thought in Lucy's head. Best to let her hold on to hope for as long as possible.

Lucy folded the piece of paper back along its creases but did not hand it back. "I guess we're stuck waiting for the kidnapper to call, huh?"

"Looks like it."

"Do you mind sticking around for a while? At least until my mom comes back?"

"Sure," Connor said.

"We'll stay as long as you need us to," Olin added.

Although Lucy had refrained from crying earlier, she still wiped at her eyes. "Does anyone want coffee or . . . or a drink? I could use a drink."

"Coffee would be fine," Connor said. Olin and Dylan agreed.

She pushed herself off the sofa.

Connor gestured for her to remain where she was. "Stay there. I'll get it."

Lucy waved him off. "It will give me something to do." Then, leaving the photocopy on the coffee table, she disappeared into the kitchen.

While she was gone, Connor thought back to his conversation with Alex in the bar. "You know, we might have discounted Leon too quickly."

"What are you thinking?" Olin asked.

"Savannah isn't that far away. If he wanted to, Leon could get to Atlanta and back in less than a day. The trip takes only four hours each way. I don't know what time that note was left on my door. He could easily have come up here and left the note, then come back the next day to kidnap Jerry."

Olin circled around to the sofa and sat down. "It does fit his M.O."

"And he certainly has a bone to pick with you," Dylan added.

"With all of us," Connor corrected.

Dylan shrugged, as if to indicate that was, indeed, more accurate. "We should check into him further."

"Absolutely."

"Did Alex tell you where he worked?" Olin asked Connor.

"Surplus Storage."

Olin leaned forward, resting his elbows on his knees. "His boss would know if he was at work yesterday or the day before. Maybe we should make a call and see if we can find out—"

"No way," Dylan said.

"Or we could tell Detective Pierce—"

"That's even worse."

Olin threw up his hands. "Why is that a bad idea?"

"If anybody calls Leon's boss, there's a possibility he will tell Leon about it. Probably a good one. For sure he knows Leon has a record, and if he thinks Leon might be getting into trouble again, he probably won't want to keep him around."

Connor considered that. He looked at Olin. "She's got a point."

"What do you suggest we do, then?" Olin asked.

Connor did not have an immediate answer. Dylan pulled out her phone, tapped and swiped, then looked up at Olin with a devious smile.

Connor had a feeling he knew what she was going to say, and he was right.

"Surplus Storage is exactly what it sounds like." She turned her phone around so Olin and Connor could see the company's website on the screen. The main photo featured a drab, two-story building with text that read: "First month's rent on any unit is free."

"Places like that don't have a lot of staff roaming around," she continued. "They're pretty much empty most of the time. That makes them a great place to stash someone, if you ask me. Especially if they have an empty wing or maybe even an empty floor. They're giving away a month's rent, so they must have a fair number of available units. Even if I'm wrong about that, then all Leon would have to do is tie Jerry up and gag him, and he wouldn't make much noise. You could be in the unit right next to him sorting through your great-grandmother's heirlooms and you'd have no idea he was there."

"Those places have cameras, though," Olin said. "A lot of them."

"Nobody's going to be looking at that footage unless they have a reason to."

"Which takes us back to why we should call them. Even if Leon's boss does go talk to him afterward, there's nothing he can do about what's on tape."

Dylan shook her head. "Actually, it takes us to why we should go down there and check the place out for ourselves. That footage will be great evidence if they still have it, but you're assuming Leon wouldn't have erased it already. My guess is he would have access to that equipment. Probably everyone there does.

"It's also possible Leon may have locked the boy up somewhere else, in which case a conversation with Leon's boss could put Jerry in more danger. Who knows what Leon might do if he realizes we're getting close?"

"*If* he's our kidnapper," Connor cautioned.

"Right. Which is another reason to do this ourselves. Let Detective Pierce work his leads his way. If we find anything out, we'll tell him about it. If we don't, then we'd be wasting his time on a hunch, wouldn't we?"

Lucy returned before anyone could answer. She had a glass of red wine and three cups of coffee on a serving tray but had not brought any cream or sugar with her. Since she frequently made coffee in the office, she already knew how everyone liked it. She passed around the drinks and placed the tray on a side table nearby. Then she joined Olin on the sofa, glass of wine in hand. "What are you talking about?"

Connor did not want to keep another secret from Lucy. He filled her in on their theory. When he was done, he added, "We're going to go down to Savannah and feel it out." He had already clarified why they weren't taking the idea straight to Detective Pierce, and Lucy seemed to understand.

To his surprise, she also said, "I want to come."

Olin turned toward her. "I'm not sure that's a good idea. Frankly, I don't even think *we* should be doing this."

"He's my son. I want to come."

"Olin's right," Connor said. "This could be dangerous, and if anything comes up while we're away, you might need to be here to deal with it."

"Alone?"

"You've got your mom, and Detective Pierce. You won't be alone."

"It's not the same. My mom's not a PI. She means well, but all she does is make me more worried. And I don't know anything about Pierce." She glanced at the piece of paper Connor had given her, which was still sitting on the coffee table between them. "I trust you."

Connor caught the subtext: *Even though you kept that from me.*

"I'll tell you what," Olin said. "I'll stay."

Connor wasn't surprised by the offer. Although Olin no longer saw the world through a lens of binary options—black and white, good and bad, right and wrong—he had never fully embraced the criminal techniques Connor and Dylan often employed to find out what they wanted to know. Even when working as a team to search Blake's house, he made no secret about the fact that he wanted to get out of there as fast as possible.

That might have had something to do with the one time Connor and Dylan convinced him to break into a house on his own. Needless to say, it hadn't gone well.

Connor looked at Dylan. She nodded subtly to suggest she thought it would be for the best, and he understood why. They could do what they needed to without Olin, and it might be a good idea to have someone on the team in town—as Dylan would later put it—"just in case."

"All right," Connor said. He got to his feet, and Dylan followed his lead. "We should get going. I want to get down there right away in case we're right about this."

Connor probably did not need to say that, he realized. Certainly, Lucy wanted the same thing. What mother wouldn't?

"Thank you," she said, likewise standing. She looked like she was once again on the edge of tears.

He grabbed the photocopied note off the coffee table and returned it to his jacket pocket. Then, on his way out the door, he added, "We'll be in touch as soon as we know something."

CHAPTER 22

DYLAN MADE THE long drive from Atlanta to Savannah without stopping. However, an accident on I-75 cost them over two hours, making the trip even longer, and it was past six o'clock by the time they reached the city.

When they arrived at Surplus Storage, the lot was empty and the lights were off. If Leon was there, he wasn't anyplace they could see him.

Connor got out of the car and checked the sign on the door to confirm the business was indeed closed.

"Shut down at five-thirty," he told Dylan when he got back inside. "So if Leon was working today, he probably cleared out a while ago."

"I would think so."

She looked across the street at the strip mall on the other side. Anchored by a Publix, the parking lot was too busy to go into from the front, so she drove around the building looking for other options.

The only other door they found was sandwiched between two bay doors on the side of the building and faced a McDonald's. A long line of cars snaked through the drive-thru, which meant it wasn't an option, either. Not right now.

"We'll have to come back later," Dylan said.

Connor nodded. "I think you're right."

Dylan made her way to the closest hotel—a Comfort Inn that

promised a free continental breakfast and wi-fi—and they checked in to a pair of rooms on the third floor. The McDonald's closed at 11 p.m., which meant they could safely go back at midnight. Until then, they would just have to kill some time.

They did this first by eating dinner at a local restaurant called Mick and Son's, which was better than Connor thought it might be, and then by checking in with Olin.

"How's Lucy doing?" Connor asked, with the phone on speaker.

He was sitting on one corner of the bed in his hotel room. Dylan had taken a nearby chair so they could both participate in the conversation.

"Last time I saw her, she was still keeping it together. As well as you could expect, anyway."

"I take it that means you're not at her house anymore," Dylan said.

"I left an hour ago."

"You heard anything from Detective Pierce?" Connor asked.

"No, nothing. But he's more likely to call you than me."

Connor figured that was probably true, and since he hadn't heard anything either, he was inclined to assume the detective had not had much luck tracking the kidnapper by reviewing the footage from the security cameras around the area where the phone was stolen.

"I have been thinking a lot about Reid Wilburn's case, though," Olin added.

It took Connor a couple of seconds to place the name. Once he did, Connor remembered he was the man who had come into their office only yesterday, suspicious of his sister's real estate dealings. It seemed like so long ago after everything that had happened since.

"Franz Ludwig, in particular," Olin continued.

That was the man who had overpaid for several of Alissa's properties.

"Since I didn't have anything better to do, I started digging around the internet a little bit. Remember we were wondering if he might have sold any of the places back to Alissa? Looks like he did. I've found two he sold so far. Both were for far less than he paid for them. I can't say for sure they went to Alissa, but that would be my guess. Why else would he dump them cheap right after he bought them?"

Dylan looked at Connor. "If that's not the final nail in the coffin, I don't know what would be."

Connor was inclined to agree. It seemed pretty clear at this point Alissa was laundering money through Franz. The only question he still had was why.

"I might have a lead on that, too," Olin said. "There's an article in *Entrepreneur* that was published last year. Sort of like a feature on Alissa's company. In it, she talks about plans to expand internationally. Among the list of countries she was looking at, of course she mentioned some of the most popular and expensive locations: the UK, France, Switzerland."

Switzerland was also a popular destination for people looking to hide money, Connor knew. Although, with the UK and France also on her list, it was hard to be certain that was why she had included it.

"The one that stood out to me, though, was Colombia."

"Alissa said she was looking to expand into Colombia?" Connor asked.

"She probably mentioned a dozen or more countries in the article, but yes, that was on the list."

"Do you think it's drugs?"

"Could be," Dylan said. "If she's importing drugs from Colombia, she wouldn't draw as much attention if she had a legitimate reason to visit."

"We should find out if she's ever been there," Connor said.

"That might be a little beyond my skill set," Olin said.

Dylan leaned in. "I'll do it when we get back to Atlanta. If there's anything out there, I'll find it."

Maybe, Connor thought. They had all learned recently that even the dark web had its limits. If it didn't, they wouldn't have needed Alex to tell them Leon was out on bail. That said, it wouldn't hurt to look.

CHAPTER 23

WHEN CONNOR AND Dylan returned to Surplus Storage at nearly midnight, there was significantly less traffic in the area. The halogen lights that lit up the strip mall parking lot were still on, but with all the businesses closed, there was nobody there. The parking lot at the McDonald's was also empty.

Although Dylan probably could have parked directly in front of the loading dock without drawing attention, she took a spot in the lot behind the building just to be safe. That struck Connor as uncharacteristically cautious.

Perhaps she picked up on that because after she turned off the engine, she said, "We don't know how long this is going to take. If anyone happens to see the car, they won't think twice about it as long as it's parked back here."

She removed a leather case from the glove box and got out. Connor already knew that case contained her lock picks.

As they climbed the stairs to the loading dock, she unzipped the case.

All they had to do was get past the door, and they'd be good to go. Surplus Storage offered its customers twenty-four-seven access, which meant there wouldn't be an alarm system they needed to worry about. It also meant getting inside would be about as easy as it could be.

Or so they thought, until they got close enough to the door to see the access-card scanner mounted to the wall beside it and a solid red light above that.

Dylan cursed under her breath.

Connor did not have to ask whether she could get them past the scanner. There was only so much you could do with a set of lock picks. Then he had another idea. "The front door." When he had gone to check the door hours earlier, he had noticed it was armed with only a standard deadbolt.

"That's not ideal," Dylan said.

She was certainly thinking about the four-lane road within sight of the door. Even with the strip mall closed, that still put them at risk. But Connor suspected the traffic was lighter than she thought now.

He gestured for Dylan to follow him. "Trust me." He led her around toward the front of the building. When they were within sight of the road, he pointed at the only car they could see and, perhaps needlessly, said, "Car." He waited twenty seconds or so until they saw another one and did it again. Then a third time.

Then he pointed to the intersection on their left. "Also, most of the traffic seems to be coming from that direction. There's no good view of the front door from there. If we wait until the light turns red, you'll probably get a minute or so without any traffic at all."

Connor did not have to ask if that was long enough for Dylan to work her magic. He'd seen her get through a deadbolt with a pair of bobby pins in less time than that. At Blake's, she'd done it even faster.

Dylan seemed to get the point. While this option was not risk-free, the risk was minimal. She headed toward the door. "Let me know when the light changes," she called over her shoulder, pulling the picks she would need from her set.

Connor watched the intersection for another thirty seconds before it did. "It's go time!" He hurried over to join her.

Dylan worked the picks around in the lock while Connor kept an eye out for any cars coming from the opposite direction.

Fortunately, Dylan got past the deadbolt before the light changed or a single car passed. She yanked the door open. "Let's go!" Then she followed Connor inside and pulled the door shut behind them.

The light coming through the windows provided enough visibility to keep the lobby from being a black abyss they would have to stumble their way through but not so much that a passing motorist would be able to see them.

Connor looked around, taking in the lay of the land. An assortment of packing equipment was for sale throughout—boxes were stored in wall-mounted bins; packing tape and markers hung from racks; tape guns, dish dividers, and bubble wrap were stacked up on shelves—and somehow all of it seemed organized to encourage people to grab as many items as they could between the door and the register.

At the back of the lobby were two doors, one in front of the employee counter that was accessible to the public and one behind it that was not.

"That probably leads to the storage units themselves," Connor said, pointing to the closest one.

"Makes sense," Dylan said.

Connor made his way around the counter with Dylan behind him. Calling the computer that sat on top of it "a register" seemed to undermine the complexity of the machine. Although there was a cash drawer underneath it, the attached mouse and keyboard made it clear you could do a lot more with the machine than merely ring up a customer.

Which, considering the nature of the business, was exactly what

Connor expected. No matter how many items a customer might pick up on the way to the counter, the company's bread-and-butter was obviously renting storage units.

Connor was certain he would be able to use the machine to look up any units Leon might have rented. However, when he moved the mouse to bring the thing to life, he was met by a login screen.

He had neither the tools he would need nor the time to get past it.

"I guess we're going to have to go floor by floor," Connor said. It would be tedious, but they hadn't come all this way to give up now.

They went through the door they believed would lead them deeper into the building, where they were immediately met by a long hallway with storage units on both sides and fluorescent lights overhead. Each storage unit had a blue roll-up door with a latch that could be secured by a padlock on the right side. In a small alcove to their left, there was an elevator and a door with a sign above it that read "Stairs."

"I'll take this floor," Connor said. "You go upstairs. Call me if you find anything."

"You got it," Dylan said, and disappeared into the stairwell.

Although Connor did not have the same ability to pick a lock that she did, they also did not intend on opening every single storage unit. Since some were secured with combination locks instead of keys, they wouldn't have been able to, anyway. Instead, they had agreed on their way over that the best course of action, if they found themselves in this very situation, would be to bang hard on every door and listen for sounds of life on the other side. If Jerry was here, he could probably make enough noise that Connor would be able to hear him if he listened closely. Even if Leon had gagged him so that he couldn't scream.

However, the only sound he heard throughout his search was that of a door opening. Following one hallway to another, he had cleared almost the entire floor when it happened.

"Connor?" Dylan called.

"This way!"

The footsteps sped up and, soon enough, Dylan rounded the corner at the other end of the hall.

"I take it you didn't find anything," Connor said.

"No. You?"

"I've just got these last ones to check, but nothing yet."

Dylan helped him finish the floor.

At the last unit, Connor pounded harder than he had before and listened longer. Despite the odds, he hoped this last unit would provide them with the break they had been looking for. Once he was certain it wouldn't, he said, "We're going to have to find out where Leon lives. Maybe there's something there."

"There's no information online," Dylan reminded him.

"No, but . . ." Connor trailed off. He could feel an idea forming, a way to get the information they were after. Then, as he stared down the long hall of storage units, the solution suddenly occurred to him. It was so obvious, he could not believe he hadn't thought of it sooner.

Connor hurried back to the lobby with Dylan on his tail.

"Where are you going?" she asked.

"When Leon was hired here, he would have had to complete some paperwork. That's where we can get his address." He pushed through the door that took them back into the lobby and circled around to the one behind the counter.

When he had assumed the first door led to the storage units, he had also assumed this one led to an office. He had not said as much before because he didn't think it mattered. Now, it might be the only room in this whole building that did.

“Like a résumé or a job application,” Connor continued.

“A lot of that stuff is done online now.”

Connor paused with his hand on the doorknob and looked back at her. “Let’s hope that’s not the case here.”

He pushed the door, and it opened into the office he expected would be there. It was small and dingy, with a dented steel desk and a rat trap in one corner. But it also had a computer and a filing cabinet, and that was all Connor cared about.

He closed the door, turned on the light, and pointed to the filing cabinet. “Let’s start with the easy stuff. Maybe we’ll get lucky.”

CHAPTER 24

DRAKE HARTFIELD PULLED up to a modest single-story house and parked along the curb. He had been here a dozen times or so over the years. He knew from the address the place was not cheap. Nothing in this part of town was.

Still, this brick-front Cape Cod with flower boxes hanging from the windows and a patch of grass barely big enough to be called a yard did not reflect the standard of living Alec Garcia could have afforded. Drake was certain of that. After all, he knew how much the accountant had been paid.

Drake had never explicitly told Alec he was paying as much for his silence as he was for his skills. Until recently, he wouldn't have thought he needed to.

It's time to make sure that message hits home, he thought, getting out of the car and chuckling quietly at his own pun.

At this late hour, he knew Alec's wife and son would be asleep. It was a big part of the reason he hadn't stopped by earlier. The other part was that he could be confident the neighbors would be, as well.

He removed a baseball bat from his trunk, then casually walked down the driveway to the kitchen door at the back of the house and swung at the window inside it. Glass shattered. Alec's ADT system went off instantly. That would no doubt piss off the neighbors. It might even bring a few of them to their own windows.

He would be inside before anyone would see him, though. All he had to do was reach through the window, turn the deadbolt, and step over the threshold.

As Drake entered the kitchen, he noted the time on his watch. On average, it took an alarm company eight minutes to notify the police and the police another ten minutes to respond. Even if Sofia dialed 911 from her cell phone, he still had plenty of time to do what he came here to.

He called for Sofia to show herself. "You're only going to make this worse if I have to come find you," he said when she didn't.

He moved quickly from the dark kitchen to the dining room. There, he had a clear view of the living room and, beyond that, the front door.

Sofia would not be moving as fast as he was, Drake thought. She would have been disoriented when she awoke. Even if she correctly assumed Drake had broken into the house, she would have needed time to collect herself, to get her son. He might not have been able to hear her with the alarm screaming in his ear, but he knew she could not have gotten to the door yet.

Since the house was designed with the bedrooms accessible only from a hallway on the other side of the living room, he also knew she could not get to it now without going through him first.

Drake charged down the hallway to the first door and threw it open. Because he had been here so many times before, he knew that led to the child's bedroom. He flipped on the light switch, ready to scoop the boy up in his arms and carry him into Sofia's room, where he could punish them both for Alec's betrayal.

When he got to the crib, though, he saw it was empty.

Drake remembered what Alec had told him when he threatened Alec's family: *I've been expecting it for weeks now.*

Had they gone into hiding?

As he hurried out of that bedroom and headed to the next one, he told himself not to worry. They would be here. Sofia didn't have any family nearby. Alec had never spoken about any close friends. He worked too much to have any, and she was too busy with the kid. Besides that, Sofia's Mercedes had been parked in the driveway. Alec had bought it for her as a birthday present one year. Drake knew how much she loved that car. It was her pride and joy until her son came along. Sofia would not have gone into hiding without that.

Likely she had the kid in the room with her, Drake reasoned. Perhaps she had figured if a night like this ever came, they would be able to escape out the window.

Drake threw open the door to her bedroom and found it empty, too. The wrought-iron canopy bed was neatly made. No clothes were on the floor or the chair in the corner. There was nothing to indicate the woman had left in a hurry.

Still, his gaze shifted to a pair of large windows, one on each side of the bed. Both were closed. Drake made his way over to them to confirm that meant they were also locked, which it did.

At that point, there was little reason to check the rest of the house. Sofia might not have any close friends or family nearby, but there were plenty of hotels around Atlanta.

Alec was right—Drake was never going to find them.

Drake was still standing in front of one of the windows when he had this realization. The button-tufted armchair he had noticed upon entering was directly beside him. He grabbed it and heaved it across the room with frustration.

Had Sofia left her beloved car here as a ruse? A way to fool Drake into thinking she was still living at the house if he were to do a drive-by?

Maybe.

Then again, Alec drove a Hummer, and Drake had not seen his car when he arrived. Perhaps, no matter how much Sofia loved her Mercedes, she had left in the bigger vehicle so she could take more stuff with her.

Both of those possibilities occurred to Drake within less than a second. Of course, he did not have the time at that moment to figure out which of them was correct and decided it might have been a little of both.

Feeding his rage another serving of revenge, Drake toppled the dresser.

As he surveyed the damage to the room, he decided that although he might not be able to get to Alec's family tonight, he could still make this trip count.

Drake returned to the kitchen and scoured the drawers for a lighter. He knew there had to be one somewhere. Sofia loved her candles almost as much as she did her car—there were two on the nightstand, others on the dining room table, and still more on the kitchen counter.

What he found instead was a box of long-stick matches, which he decided would work just as well.

He grabbed a bottle of vodka from the cabinet, doused the curtains, the sofa, the beds. Then he set them all aflame and left the same way he had come in.

Drake looked at his watch again. He had been in the house for no more than four minutes. Fire spread fast. By the time the police got here, it would be impossible to put out without the fire department. And by the time the fire department arrived, the house would be engulfed in flames.

Sofia would never live here again.

Drake got back in his car and sped away. As he merged onto I-85 South, it occurred to him that even though Sofia did not have any family nearby, Alec did. He had a brother in Dahlonega, which was only about an hour north, and parents in Miami, which was still close enough to drive to.

Would Alec have sent Sofia to stay with them?

Maybe.

But aside from the city, he didn't know where any of them lived. Fortunately, there were people who could find that out for him, and, even if Sofia wasn't there, one family member would probably work as well as another. Especially after Alec learned his house had burned to the ground.

You think I'm going to stop? I'll never stop. I'll take everything from you like you're taking everything from me.

Alec would get the point. Shaving a few years off his sentence might have sounded good at first, but not at the cost of everything that mattered to him.

CHAPTER 25

THE FILING CABINET at Surplus Storage was better organized than Connor anticipated. He and Dylan found Leon's job application almost immediately. It contained his name, address, and work history, in addition to a few other incidental pieces of information Connor had no interest in.

He tapped the top of the second page, where the work history began, to draw Dylan's attention to it. "Look."

She did.

Leon had listed his most recent job as "Entrepreneur." This was not code for prison time. His employer would have known he had been incarcerated. Not only that, but based on his start and end dates, he'd stopped being an entrepreneur the month he was arrested. Instead, it was code for something else, and Connor and Dylan knew all too well what that was.

"Once a liar, always a liar," Dylan said.

Then Connor noticed the neat block print Leon had used when filling out the application. He pulled out the photocopied note, placed it and the application side by side on the desk to compare.

Dylan did not have to ask what he was doing, but after Connor had stared at the papers for a while, she did ask, "What do you think?"

"I don't know. Maybe."

"Let me look."

Connor stepped aside to make room for her, and Dylan spent as long studying the papers as he had.

"Well?" Connor asked.

She sighed. "I couldn't say for sure. There are differences. Leon may have been trying to disguise his handwriting."

"That's what I thought, too." Connor put the photocopy back in his pocket and typed the address into his phone. "At least we know where he lives."

"We'll check it out tomorrow when he's at work."

When Connor and Dylan got back to the hotel, they looked up the address so that they knew what they were in for.

The apartment complex where Leon lived was a massive, garden-style community that wrapped around a pool and clubhouse and was surrounded by a fence. Connor did not expect to find the man in a place like this. The complex was practically a fortress. He was certain that if it was in a better part of town, it would have been well outside of Leon's budget.

"How are we going to get past that?" Connor said, referring to the fence.

"Don't worry about it. I got it," Dylan responded.

"You know, there's not going to be a lock there you can pick your way through."

She looked at Connor like he was stupid.

"All right, then how are you going to do it?"

"After that wise-ass comment, I think you're just going to have to wait to find out."

And that was as much of an answer as Connor was going to get until they pulled up to the gate at 6 a.m. with Dylan in the driver's seat.

"So?" Connor asked.

She smiled, rolled down her window, and hit the buttons on the digital callbox. There was the click of a connection, and the line started to ring.

"You're not calling him—"

"Of course not."

The call rolled over to voicemail. Dylan hung up and repeated the process.

"What are you doing then?"

A man answered before Dylan could respond. He sounded like he had just woken up.

Dylan leaned out the window, getting as close to the callbox as she could. "We're here to pick up Frank for work."

"No Frank here."

The man hung up.

"What was that about?" Connor asked, hoping Dylan would finally clue him in on her plan.

"Social engineering. You know a thing or two about that, right?"

Connor did. Most of the hacking he engaged in involved good old ones and zeros, but there were a lot of hackers out there who would exploit human nature to make their way into a computer. Apparently, Dylan was doing something similar now.

"Do you really think that's going to work?"

"Somebody will let us in."

Dylan tried a third number. She repeated the lie, and again the person hung up.

"Are you sure?" Connor asked.

Dylan tried a fourth number. This time, when she said she was there to pick up Frank, the woman on the other end of the line groaned. Just when Connor was sure she was about to hang up, too, her voice was cut short by an annoyingly loud beep.

The twin gates that barred entrance began to open.

"I told you it would work," Dylan said. She pulled onto the property. "Actually, it was easier than I thought it would be."

They drove around the complex until they found Leon's building, and then parked far enough away that their car wouldn't draw his eye when he left for work.

Dylan pulled up on the parking brake, cut the engine, and slid the seat back to make herself comfortable. "Now we just have to wait."

CHAPTER 26

THE SUN CAME up, and still hours more passed. So far, Leon had not emerged from the building.

"What if he's not here?" Connor asked.

"We need to know for sure before we go inside."

"I could go to the front desk, say I've got a delivery for him."

"Empty-handed?"

"They won't ask."

"What if they do?"

"I'll say it's in the car and too heavy to carry up on my own. Regardless, if Leon's the kidnapper, the call will alarm him. He might even think it's a trap. He'll want to find out what's going on."

"If the police were closing in on him, they'd just come to his door."

"Maybe he'll think it's us. So what if he does? He's probably not keeping Jerry here. The walls in these sorts of buildings are too thin to hold somebody prisoner inside, and there are too many people around to risk moving somebody in or out against their will."

Dylan considered the plan. She nodded. "That might work. If he's our guy, he probably won't want to stick around after that. He'll probably go into hiding."

And he would probably take Jerry with him, they agreed—if he didn't try to get rid of the boy first.

"Either way, Leon will lead us straight to where he's keeping him."

Dylan playfully punched Connor's arm. "Look at you, putting a little social engineering of your own to work."

Connor shrugged and climbed out of the car. The office was located in the center of the complex. He walked straight in and did exactly what he'd said he would.

"He'll be right down," the leasing agent said when she got off the phone.

Connor thanked her and told her he would meet Leon outside. Then he returned to the car. He obviously did not plan on hanging around to meet with Leon, if Leon was, in fact, coming to the office at all. He might just up and leave.

The leasing agent would be confused if Leon showed up and Connor was nowhere to be found. But then again, so what?

Connor climbed back into the car. "Leon's here."

"Good," Dylan said. "Let's see what happens."

After a minute or two, a man exited a nearby building and approached the leasing office. Connor had no trouble recognizing him as Leon. He looked exactly the same as he had the last time Connor had seen him.

Dylan slid her seat forward. But neither she nor Connor said a word until Leon stepped back out of the office, looked around, and returned to his building.

Dylan started the car. "Get ready. He'll probably take off any minute now."

Only problem was—he didn't.

CHAPTER 27

ANOTHER TWO HOURS passed.

"It's been a long time," Connor said. "What if he never leaves?"

Dylan shrugged. What else were they going to do? He had to go somewhere eventually, and he was the only lead they had. "It *is* strange he didn't go after Jerry like we thought he would."

"You think he might be innocent?"

"I mean, that's what we're here to find out, right?"

Finally, Leon appeared.

Dylan spotted him first. "Look," she said, sliding down in her seat and pointing at the building.

Connor followed her lead, and they stayed like that, hunkered down in the car, until Leon climbed into an old beat-up Chevy and drove away.

"All right, we're going to have to make this quick," Connor said. "We have no idea how long he'll be gone."

Dylan agreed.

They were in and out in no more than fifteen minutes. When they were done, Connor did a quick walk-through to make sure the apartment looked like it had when they arrived. The place was small, and Leon did not have much to fill it with. Connor did not have trouble remembering where everything belonged.

Then Dylan used her lock picks to lock the door behind them and they returned to the car.

"So that's it," she said after she climbed into the driver's seat.

Connor understood what she meant. Although their search had been fast, it had also been thorough. Still, they'd found nothing.

"Maybe he's not our guy," Connor said.

"He's got to be. Or else . . ."

Or else we're out of leads, Connor thought.

That was a possibility neither of them was ready to face yet, but Connor could see it weighing on Dylan as they drove back to Atlanta and could feel it weighing on him, as well.

Somewhere between one small town and another, Connor's phone rang.

Dylan's head whipped around. "Do you think it's him?"

Connor assumed she meant the kidnapper. He pulled the phone out of his pocket and looked at the number. "No." Then he answered. "Hi, Rebecca. What's up?"

"You busy?"

"It's just . . . Kind of."

"More secret private investigator stuff?"

"Something like that."

"Okay, I'll be quick," Rebecca said. "You want to have dinner Friday night? I mean, you kind of screwed up the last one, so I thought you might want to make it up to me."

"I . . ."

"That was meant to be funny."

"It was."

"Good, because I went by the apartment a couple of times, and you weren't there. I wanted to do this in person so I could see your face, but eventually, I figured the phone was just going to have to do. You sure it was funny?"

"I'm sure," Connor said. "And, yes, I'd love to have dinner Friday night."

"Good. Consider it a date."

Connor felt his heart flutter, and he smiled in spite of himself. Then he looked over at Dylan, who seemed to be enjoying the call a little more than she should, and said, "I have to go. See you then."

"So," Dylan said, when he got off the phone, "you have a date."

"Yes."

Now she was smiling. "Good for you. Tell me about her."

Connor reluctantly did. He thought Dylan might tease him, but to his surprise, she was thoughtful and attentive, never once indicating she *might* try to push Connor's buttons.

"It's about time," she said when he was done. "You've been single for too long."

"What about you?"

"Yeah, but I like it this way. You weren't built for it. I can tell."

Connor felt like he had been doing just fine on his own, but since he didn't want to drag the conversation out any longer, he let it go.

When they got back to Atlanta, Dylan dropped him off at the office so he could get his car, and he returned to his apartment. He moved slowly through the lobby, hoping Rebecca might come in or out with her dog while he was down there.

It was silly, especially since they already had a date scheduled, but he couldn't help himself. He wanted to see her again, and sooner rather than later now that he knew he hadn't blown his shot with her.

Then it occurred to him that perhaps Dylan was right. Maybe he would be better off in a relationship. He couldn't imagine her hanging around the lobby of her building waiting for a guy.

He lingered another few seconds, then took the elevator up, fished his keys out of his pockets on the way, and followed the hallway to his apartment door.

Connor expected another quiet night at home, which would probably have been good considering how poorly he had slept in the hotel. He hadn't been able to stop thinking about Leon or Jerry or how he had been certain he was so close to putting this mystery behind him.

Instead, he was met by another note. This time, it was sealed in an envelope that was attached to a plain cardboard box somebody had left in front of his door.

The box was rectangular, about eighteen inches on its longest side, and three inches deep.

For the second time today, Connor became keenly aware of his own beating heart. Only this time it was not joy that sent the muscle fluttering. It was terror.

He stared down at the box for a while, wondering whether he should pick it up.

Connor and Dylan had driven past Surplus Storage on their way out of town just to see if Leon's car was there, and it was. Since they had not stopped again until they reached Atlanta, he didn't see how Leon could have gotten ahead of them. Was it possible he had come to Atlanta and left the box for Connor the night before?

It would have meant driving all night, but maybe that also explained why he had been in his apartment most of the day. Perhaps he was catching up on his sleep.

Connor reluctantly decided to pick up the box. It was not heavy enough to be a bomb. In fact, it felt almost empty. He carried the box inside, sat down on the sofa, and placed it on the coffee table in front of him.

He knew he needed to call Lucy and Detective Pierce right away. Still, he wanted to see what the note said first. The package might not be a bomb, but there were other things the kidnapper could have sent that would be just as bad, like anthrax or severed fingers from the victim.

Connor reasoned the package was no more likely to contain anthrax than it did a bomb. As far as Connor could tell, it would work against the kidnapper's interest to kill him. However, severed fingers were still a possibility. Fingers, or an ear, or . . .

He shivered at the thought of all the possible body parts the kidnapper might have sliced off to make a point and imagined the note that might have come with them: *You should have tried harder to find the boy.*

If that was indeed what had happened, Connor wanted to be able to prepare Lucy first.

He took a deep breath, removed the envelope from the box. Just as the box was lighter than he expected, the envelope was heavier. He extracted the note he had expected to find and, with it, a pair of keys. One looked like it belonged to a padlock, the other to a deadbolt.

Cupping both in his right hand, Connor frowned at them, trying to figure out what they might be for. Reluctantly, he accepted the reality that he would not guess his way to that answer. Like so many other mysteries about this kidnapper, their purpose would only be revealed when the kidnapper was ready.

He returned the keys to the envelope to keep them safe and read the note.

Ready to give up? Bring the box to 932 Amhurst Court. Do not open it. Come tonight, and come alone.

Connor was glad to see the message was not like the one he had imagined. Although it was alarming in its own way, and, with the keys, had brought a whole new set of questions, like: Why did the kidnapper want him to transport a box that he surely could have taken himself? What was in it? What were the keys for? And what was going to happen to Connor when he got there?

He wished he could rule Leon in or out once and for all. If Connor could say definitively whether he was involved, at least that might give them some idea of what they were up against.

Then he remembered his phone call with Rebecca. She had said she had been by his apartment a couple of times before she called. If the box had been here then, she probably would have mentioned it. However, he could not know that for certain without asking her.

Since that answer could have huge implications for their suspect list of one, he decided to make it the first of his three calls.

"You're not calling to cancel our date, are you?" she asked as soon as she picked up. "That would be rude."

If Connor hadn't been so deep in his own thoughts, he would have realized she was joking. "No, nothing like that. I just had a question for you."

"Okay . . ."

"When you came by my apartment earlier, was there a package there waiting for me?"

"No. Why?"

Connor hated to lie to Rebecca again. So far, he had avoided any conversation about Lucy's son by saying he didn't want to talk about the case. He wasn't sure that would be good enough here. If he did, Rebecca might correctly infer the package meant trouble for Connor. And if that was the assumption she made, she would also worry, no matter what Connor said afterward.

He didn't want to put her through that.

"It's not important. I was expecting a package from Amazon. The website says they already delivered it, but it's not here. I thought maybe you picked it up for me."

"You think somebody stole it?"

"I don't know. It's not a big deal. I'll reach out to them and get it straightened out. See you Friday."

Connor ended the call, placed the cell phone down on the coffee table, and once again stared at the package. There was still the possibility that it had been left by Leon. They had seen only his car at Surplus Storage when they left town, not him. He could have switched one vehicle for another in that parking lot and reached Atlanta before them. Or he could have left Surplus Storage after them, speeding past them on the interstate. Perhaps the box had been left only minutes before Connor arrived.

Connor shook away those thoughts. They were all so improbable, they bordered on absurd. There was only one reasonable conclusion he could draw from his phone call with Rebecca, and it was that their suspect list of one had just shrunk to zero.

CHAPTER 28

SOON, CONNOR'S APARTMENT was buzzing with more activity than it had since he'd moved in. Lucy had arrived with her mother, and Detective Stewart Pierce had brought with him a team of technicians. Of course, Dylan and Olin were also there.

Gathered in the living room, they had all agreed he needed to follow the kidnapper's directions if they wanted any chance of getting the boy back.

"But you're not going alone," Stewart had said.

Lucy, who had been sitting nervously on the sofa, suddenly looked alarmed. "What? We can't send somebody else in there with him. Who knows what might happen to my son if we do that?"

"It will be okay. The kidnapper's not going to see them. We're going to set up a perimeter around the building and mike Connor up so we can hear what's happening. The kidnapper won't have any idea. Once it's safe, we'll move in."

The building they were talking about was one of a dozen warehouses in an industrial part of the city. There was little around it other than a Pepsi plant and a Mexican restaurant called Pico. Connor knew this because he had scouted the area using Google Maps after he had made all his phone calls.

While they were talking, a group of technicians gathered up the box and everything that had come with it, then took it all down to their mobile lab to examine.

"You're sure he won't see them?" Lucy asked.

"I'm sure," Stewart said.

She stood up and started pacing—at least, as much as anyone could pace in that small and crowded room. Then she spun around to face the detective again. "I have a better idea. Why don't we just find out who owns the place? That should tell us everything we need to know, shouldn't it?"

"That's a good question," Dylan said.

Connor was inclined to agree. However, before he could say anything, Stewart shot down the idea. "I had somebody looking into that on the way over. The place is owned by Newsom Enterprises. They're a big player in the commercial space. Industrial, in particular. Whoever is using that warehouse is renting it from them. It's already after eight o'clock—too late to get a name. We'd have to wait until tomorrow for that, and I don't think that'd be such a good idea. The kidnapper obviously believes Connor would get the package today, so we're taking a big risk if we don't follow through on his instructions. At the very least, I think we need to stay engaged."

That information framed Lucy's question in a new light. While Connor figured it would be difficult to buy a building with a fake name, it wouldn't be nearly as hard to rent one. That meant, even if they got a name, they couldn't assume it would lead them anywhere.

After he said as much, Dylan asked, "What about the box? Maybe once the technicians are done with it, we should open it up. Maybe there's evidence in there we could use."

Stewart shook his head. "Bad idea. Somebody is probably expecting Connor to hand him that package when he gets to the warehouse. He might be able to tell if it's been tampered with. That could put the whole operation in jeopardy. We're better off sticking with the original plan."

Lucy sighed. "All right. Just get my boy back. Don't screw this up."

Then more technicians taped a mike to Connor's chest and tested the audio.

Once everyone was in place and the technicians had confirmed through a series of X-rays and other tests that the package did not contain anything hazardous, Connor made the drive from his apartment to 932 Amhurst Court.

Stewart had assured him somebody would always have eyes on him, that he would always be safe. Although it sure didn't feel like it. On the busiest streets, no car stayed behind him for very long. On the quietest ones, there was often not a single car within sight.

He pulled up to the warehouse, still seemingly alone, and was met by a large chain-link fence with razor wire along the top. There were no lights on in or around the building, which meant the only real visibility he had came from his headlights.

He got out of the car and looked around. The moonlight illuminated a construction site on the opposite side of the street. Welded steel beams rose out of a bed of cement and loomed over the property like the skeleton of some giant beast. Closer to the road, there was a construction trailer and a sign Connor could not read in the darkness.

Other warehouses had dotted the road upon his approach, but there were none beyond it—this was the end of the street—and with large swaths of undeveloped land between them, Connor suspected this warehouse would feel as isolated during the day as it did now. Even with the construction.

"I hope you guys are close by," he said for the benefit of the microphone.

In response, he got the only answer he expected, which was none.

He had to keep moving, he told himself. He had to trust Stewart's men were out there. Since he would have come even if they weren't, that was easier than Connor would have expected.

He stepped toward the gate to open it and saw it had been secured by a padlock. *Finally found the use for the first key,* he thought.

He pulled both keys from the pocket of his jeans, selected the only one that might fit, and tried his luck. The key turned easily. Then Connor hung the padlock on the chain link and pushed the gate open.

The warehouse somehow seemed more foreboding now that nothing stood between it and Connor. There was no way he was driving his car onto that lot. If the kidnapper came along behind him and locked him inside, he'd be screwed. Not only would he have to find a way over the razor wire (which he would have to do, regardless), but he'd also have to make it back to the main road on foot.

That seemed like a horror movie in the making.

Sure, he had this microphone taped to his chest and supposedly there were police out there somewhere watching him, but he still felt like he was alone, which made it more of a risk than he was willing to take.

Connor removed the box from the backseat and cautiously made his way onto the property. As he stepped farther from the car, the sound of the engine faded, making it easier to hear the crickets around him, which in turn reinforced his feeling of isolation.

He slipped the box under one arm and pulled his gun from the shoulder holster. Connor did not think the kidnapper intended on killing him. But since he didn't know what the man *did* intend to do now that Connor was on the property, he decided he had better be ready for anything.

Taking shallow breaths, he made his way the last thirty feet to the main door. A halogen lamp hung over the lone cement step in front of it, and a small window inside it revealed only darkness.

Something about this didn't feel right. Was someone sitting there in the dark waiting for him? Perhaps that wouldn't be any stranger than anything else the man had done so far, but Connor didn't like it. If this was any other case, if the kidnapper did not have Lucy's son, Connor would have turned around and called it quits right then.

He placed the box on the ground and fished the second key out of his pocket. It slid easily into the deadbolt. Then he licked his dry lips, raised the gun to his shoulder, and turned the key.

Here we go.

He jerked the door open, stepping to the side as he did so that he would not be an easy target if the kidnapper started shooting from within that darkness. But there was no rat-a-tat-tat of gunfire, no smell of smoke drifting out of the doorway. In fact, all he heard was the creak of old hinges, and all he smelled was the mustiness of an unused space.

Still, Connor was slow to step away from the protection the side of the building provided. When he did, he peered once again into the warehouse. This time, his view was not limited by the small window he had looked through before. However, even with the headlights of the car behind him and the halogen lamp overhead, it wasn't much better.

The light that made it through the doorway revealed only a dusty cement floor and was quickly swallowed up by the darkness that seemed to close in from all sides.

"Hello?" Connor shouted.

His voice echoed back to him, but he received no other response.

He tried again. "I'm here. Alone. With the box. Where are you?"

Still nothing.

Connor began to wonder if the kidnapper was just screwing with him, if the man had no intention of having someone here to meet him or providing any additional instruction when he arrived. That certainly wasn't beyond the realm of possibility. From the moment Connor had realized the man who had left the note on his door was the same man who had abducted Jerry, he knew the kidnapper was not right in the head.

Connor also wasn't leaving until he was certain that was the case. He would be kicking himself for years if he missed another note directing him elsewhere or a clue that might provide Jerry's location.

"I'm going in," he said, again for the benefit of the microphone.

He stepped over the threshold and felt along the wall for a light switch. When he found it, he flipped it up, but no light came on. He tried again twice more.

Then he noticed a faint, high-pitched whirring sound that seemed to quickly grow in volume and intensity. Connor had never heard anything like it. Nonetheless, he knew immediately what it was.

"Oh, shit."

He scrambled back out the door but was barely a foot away from the building when the bomb went off.

CHAPTER 29

THE POWER OF the blast blew Connor off his feet. He hit the ground hard enough to knock the wind out of him and rolled over to see flames engulfing the warehouse. He could hardly believe he was still alive. Seemed like the cops could hardly believe it either.

When the bomb exploded, lights came on all around Connor. Undercover police cars that must have crept onto Amhurst Court behind him sped into the warehouse parking lot. Officers who were hiding in the shadows of the construction site charged across the street.

Now, they were closing in on the warehouse, some trying to see if there was anyone inside while others crowded around Connor, asking if he was all right.

"I'm fine," Connor insisted. "Really."

Olin pushed his way through the officers. "Give him some room, all right?" He reached out a hand to help Connor to his feet, which Connor gratefully accepted.

He spun Connor around, checking him from all sides. "He's fine, all right? Not a single burn mark that I can see," he told the officers. He turned back to Connor. "Anything hurt?"

Of course, Connor thought. His chest was sore. The cement had scraped up his hands and his chin. That wasn't what Olin meant, though. He wanted to know if Connor had broken any bones, so he settled for a simple, "No. I'm okay."

He found his gun six feet away and returned it to its holster.

Then he thought about the box he had brought with him. He looked toward the cement stoop where he had left it, only to see that the blast had blown it away from the door. Along with other debris that littered the parking lot, the box was on fire, barely identifiable as flames consumed it from all sides.

Suddenly, there was another voice. Lucy's. She was screaming, charging for the warehouse door. She looked like she was about to go straight in—flames be damned—in search of her son.

A group of police officers closest to the warehouse grabbed her and held her back.

Then Dylan and the detective were there, too.

"Don't let her in!" Pierce shouted.

"We're not!"

"We need to clear the site! There could be another bomb somewhere! Everyone step back! Get off the property—now!"

"Come on, Connor," Dylan said, placing her hand on his shoulder and urging him to follow the detective's instructions.

Connor didn't hear her. All of his attention was on Lucy. He could imagine how horrible this must be for her. He wanted to go to her, to say something, if only to tell her it would be all right.

With all the officers around her, though, he would not be able to get to her, and maybe that was for the best. She wouldn't listen to him, anyway. Nothing was going to make her feel better until she had her son back in her arms.

"Connor," Olin said, now urging him off the property as well.

"I shouldn't have flipped on the light switch," Connor said in response.

"What?" Dylan asked.

"That was when the bomb went off. If I hadn't flipped on the light switch . . ."

"You couldn't have known that."

"If Jerry was in there . . ."

"Don't talk like that," Olin said. "Now, come on. We need to get away from the warehouse."

Connor finally began to walk but kept his eyes on Lucy until the officers surrounding her got her moving away from the warehouse.

"We should get you all out of here," Pierce said. "We can regroup later to—"

"No. I'm staying," Connor said, shaking his head.

"Excuse me?"

"I need to know what happened." In truth, he had to know if they were going to find Jerry's remains.

Then he thought again about the note—*Hickory Dickory. Dock.*—and about the phone call—*"I want you to try to find him."*

Connor and his friends had not been able to trace the kidnapper to a former client, but the man clearly had a bone to pick with Connor. Had this been his plan all along? Did he know Leon was out on bail? Had he set Connor up to waste time investigating Leon to make him feel like a failure before also burdening him with the guilt of Jerry's death?

The mouse was Done.

But why? Why would he do that?

Connor realized Pierce had started talking again.

"After what you've been through—"

"I'm as much a part of this investigation as you are," Connor interrupted. "I'm staying."

Pierce sighed. "Fine." He shot a look at Olin and Dylan. "What about you two?"

"If Connor's staying, I'm staying," Dylan said.

"Me, too," Olin agreed, as they all stepped onto the street.

"All right, but we've got to get Mrs. McBeal out of here."

Connor looked around. "Where's her mom?" The last time Connor had seen Lucy, her mom had been with her.

"She's still at your apartment. I'll call her and let her know that I'm having an officer drive Lucy home."

Once the police were off the grounds, the fire department moved in. They extinguished the flames from a safe distance, and a bomb squad searched the building to make sure there weren't any other explosives the police needed to worry about.

Along with most of the officers, Connor and his friends watched it all happen from the safety of the construction site across the street. After Lucy's outburst, there had been a lot of speculation about whether the boy was inside, and Connor hoped like hell he was not.

"Don't listen to any of that," Pierce said. "We're going to be able to get inside soon, and we'll take it from there."

While the bomb squad worked, Pierce put Connor through a series of questions with the intention of understanding what happened after Connor arrived at the warehouse. After all, the microphone taped to Connor's chest could only get them so much, especially since the little bit of conversation it had recorded had all come from Connor.

As the hours passed, the uniformed officers cleared out, replaced by a forensics team that went in when the bomb squad was done to make sense of the remains.

With Pierce at his side, Connor was allowed beyond the threshold, as long as he agreed not to touch anything. Dylan and Olin waited at the construction site to limit the foot traffic within the building.

As Connor crossed the parking lot, he kicked the charred remnants of the box he had brought with him, and it crumbled to ash. If there had been any evidence inside that box that might have helped them find the kidnapper, it was gone now.

Inside the warehouse, the forensics team had set up large lights to illuminate the space. It was bigger than it looked from the outside, and the mangled remains of now unidentifiable machines were scattered throughout—twisted metal plates, severed steel rods, bits of rubber that perhaps had come from timing belts obliterated in the blast.

Connor walked around the single large room, looking for any signs that Jerry had been there. Although he did not want to be the first to find a bloody stump of an arm or something else equally gruesome, he had to know.

The mouse was Done.

Halfway through Connor's search, a member of the forensics team, dressed in a white jumpsuit and rubber gloves, approached Pierce carrying some sort of electronic device that was about the size of a bar of soap. Wires hung out of it like the guts of a squashed animal, and Connor could see buttons on one side of the device. However, it was blackened from the blast and split in two, and he could not identify what the device was with any more certainty than he could the machines that had occupied this space.

"Sir, we found the detonator."

"What is it?" Pierce asked, apparently equally confused by the remains of the device.

"A walkie-talkie."

Now that Connor knew what the device was, he could recognize it. "You can use a walkie-talkie to detonate a bomb?"

"You can use all kinds of things," the technical said. "Cell phones are the most popular, but you can use garage door openers and even some toys."

Pierce nodded thoughtfully. "The bomb was detonated remotely."

"It looks that way."

Connor was relieved to know that he had not triggered the device by flipping on the light switch, but he still intended on finishing his pass through the warehouse. If Jerry was here, it was still his fault. Although many walkie-talkies had a range of five miles or more, he was certain the kidnapper must have been close when he detonated the bomb. He had told Connor not to bring the police and was probably watching for them. The bomb was payback for not following the directions Connor had been given.

"Let's see if we can get the serial number off that thing," Pierce said. "Maybe we can find out where it was purchased."

CHAPTER 30

PIERCE ALSO TOLD Connor he would track down the name of the person renting the warehouse tomorrow, but Connor did not have high hopes that the name would be legit. He also did not have high hopes that the serial number on the walkie-talkie would produce a lead more meaningful than any other they had investigated.

This kidnapper seemed to know exactly what he was doing.

As far as Connor could tell, there was only one piece of good news that had come from the warehouse—and that was what they *didn't* find: a body.

Which meant there was still a chance they could get Jerry back alive.

Thank God.

Connor was too wound up to sleep, so when there was nothing left to do at the warehouse, he went with Dylan and Olin to Sue's Diner, where they sat at their usual booth and drank too much coffee for way too long. They did not bother proposing theories about the man behind the crime. They did not discuss possible clues or avenues of investigation. The well was dry. All they could do was take comfort in each other's company and hope this would all be behind them soon.

When Connor got back to his apartment, it was almost dawn.

Another note was waiting for him. So was another box.

Connor scooped them up and carried them inside, this time without hesitation. He dropped them on the coffee table, phoned Olin, then conferenced Dylan into the call.

"I've got another package," he said, putting his phone on speaker.

"Already?" Olin asked.

"Is there a letter?" Dylan added.

Connor peeled the envelope off and could tell from the weight that it, too, contained more than a piece of paper.

He slid the note out and found another key. This time, there was just one. He placed the key on the coffee table and read the note aloud.

> *Do you think any of this is a coincidence? I am with you. I am inside the police department. I know everything. You need to follow directions better. Let's try this again. Take this box to 1343 Highgrove Avenue, apartment 2D. DO NOT BRING THE COPS. DO NOT OPEN THE BOX. This will be your last chance.*

After Connor finished, nobody spoke for several seconds. Finally, Olin broke the silence. "What are we going to do?"

"Well, I'll tell you what we're not going to do," Dylan said. "We're not going to go to the cops this time."

Despite the explosion at the warehouse, Connor thought Olin might disagree, but he remained silent.

Then Connor thought about the first box the kidnapper had delivered and the evidence it might have contained. "Should I open it?"

"Absolutely," Dylan said. "If there is anything in there that might help us find the kidnapper, we don't want to lose it a second time, right?"

"Whoa," Olin said, finally objecting. "Hold on. Connor almost got killed the last time we didn't follow the kidnapper's instructions."

"We need to tell Lucy," Connor said. "This is her son we're talking about. We can't make this decision without her."

They all agreed that was the best course of action, so Connor got off the phone with Olin and Dylan and called Lucy to see how she wanted to proceed.

"How do you think I want you to proceed? I want you to do what he says. I want you to get my son back." She sounded like she had been crying. Connor wasn't surprised. She had been devastated after the bomb went off and, even though she had been told her son wasn't there, she only seemed more upset with every passing minute.

"All right, I got it. No police. Box stays closed. I'll head over there now."

Then, for the second time that night, Connor made the trip to a mysterious address at the kidnapper's behest.

CHAPTER 31

CONNOR FOLLOWED THE turn-by-turn directions his phone provided to 1343 Highgrove Avenue. The streets were even more deserted now than they had been the last time he had gone to meet the kidnapper. In fact, at just after 5 a.m., they were probably as deserted as they ever got.

Connor traveled whole blocks on streets that were crowded during the day without seeing another car. He felt like he was entirely alone. He had felt this way when he'd driven to the warehouse, also. Only, this time, he really *was* alone. There was no microphone taped to his chest, no police lying in wait. He had his gun to protect himself, but there was nobody to help him if he needed it.

When the phone told him he had arrived at his destination, he parked along the curb in front of a rundown three-story apartment building. It reminded him of a similar building he had visited when he had been angling to get the picture of a man who was stalking his client, Jax Hart.

That building had been in such a state of disrepair that he could only imagine the many code violations an inspector might find. At the time, Connor didn't think it could get any worse. This one, however, looked like it was about to fall in on itself.

He made his way to the front door with the package in one hand, pulled the key the kidnapper had given him from the pocket of his jeans and tried to fit it into the lock. No luck. Then, just for the hell of it, he gave the handle a push, and the door swung open.

The key must open the apartment, he thought.

Connor looked inside to see what he was getting himself into. A number of graffiti artists had spray-painted the walls. Mold was creeping along the ceiling and the baseboards. Eviction notices had been taped to the two doors closest to him, and Connor suspected there might be more.

This was not the kind of place Connor wanted to find himself, no matter what time of day it was.

"This is for Lucy," he mumbled, stepping inside and vowing to be quick.

Connor followed the hallway to the stairwell at the end. The floors creaked, which he worried might bring him unwanted attention, but he made it from one end of the hall to the other without incident.

The handrail rattled when Connor grabbed it, like it might pull straight out of the wall at any second. He let go and bounded up the stairs two at a time, hoping he would not need it.

He found apartment 2D halfway down the hall and once again pulled the key from his pocket. He slid it into the deadbolt and turned. The lock screeched. Connor gritted his teeth.

When the lock had turned as far as it would go, he slid the key back into his pocket, placed his hand on the knob, and took a deep breath. The general condition of this building (along with the eviction notices) suggested it might not be entirely occupied, but there were certainly enough people here that someone could get killed if another bomb went off.

He told himself to relax. He had done everything the kidnapper had asked him to do.

Before he could let his nerves get the best of him, Connor pushed the door open and was met by a single room with a hallway beyond it.

Unlike at the warehouse, the light coming through the doorway was enough for him to see all four walls.

At first glance, the room appeared empty. Just a sad space with paint peeling at the corners and large, mysterious stains on the carpet. Then Connor realized that in one of those corners there was a camera mounted to the wall, and in another, a cell phone lying on the floor.

The apartment would have looked like it belonged in the same horror movie the warehouse did even without those details, but they took the creepy factor up tenfold. Connor could imagine the door closing behind him when he went inside. He could practically see a clown with an uneven smile stepping out of that hallway, perhaps armed with a knife or, more likely, a threat.

You have fifteen minutes to find your way out if you want to survive.

Connor pushed the thought out of his mind. Nobody in the real world would go to that much trouble to kill someone. If the kidnapper wanted Connor dead, he could have waited until Connor had made his way farther into the warehouse before detonating the bomb.

Nonetheless, Connor stood where he was for a long time, ready to run if he heard the high-pitched whirring sound that had preceded the last explosion or saw the subtle movement of shadow from the hallway that might suggest there was indeed a clown lying in wait.

After a minute or more, the phone in the corner began to ring. Connor watched it until it stopped.

Strange, he thought, then decided it must have been a wrong number.

A few seconds later, though, the phone started to ring a second time. Again, Connor watched it until it stopped.

Once might have been a wrong number. Twice likely was not.

The phone started to ring a third time.

Finally, Connor realized the call must be for him.

He stuffed his fear down into a small box in the back of his mind, drew his Glock, and stepped inside. The person on the other end of that line was likely the kidnapper, he reasoned. If this was how he wanted to communicate, Connor had no choice but to answer.

He cleared the door in two steps and spun around, gun out, to make sure there was no one behind it. Then, with the phone now ringing for a fourth time, he put the package by his feet, switched the gun to his left hand, and picked up the cell.

The phone was an old Motorola with physical buttons and a screen that had been obscured with a black magic marker, making it impossible to get any useful information about the device. Connor couldn't even tell which network it was using.

He pressed a button to answer and another to put the phone on speaker. "Hello?"

"Turn to face the camera, would you? I want to see you when I'm talking to you."

The words were delivered in the same deep, raspy voice Connor had heard the first time he had spoken with the kidnapper. At the time, he had assumed that had been the result of too many cigarettes. Now, in the absolute silence of this apartment, he thought there was something artificial about it. Something digital. As if the man was using a synthesizer to disguise his voice.

"Did you hear me?"

Connor turned to face the camera.

"Show me the box."

Connor picked up the box and held it up for the camera.

"Turn it around," the kidnapper said.

Connor did as instructed.

"Did you open it?"

"No."

"Good. Now, let's talk."

Connor put the box back on the ground by his feet.

"There's a man named Drake Hartfield," the kidnapper continued. "Do you know him?"

Connor tried to remember. The name sounded familiar. "I'm not sure."

"I'm surprised. He's been in the news a lot lately."

Then it came back to him. "Isn't he going to trial for tax evasion?"

"Drake is going to trial for a lot of things. He's a bad man."

Connor did not know exactly what Drake had done, but all of the financial crimes in the world did not add up to kidnapping, as far as he was concerned. However, this did not seem like the best time to point that out, so he kept his mouth shut and waited for the kidnapper to speak again.

"I want you to do something for me," the kidnapper finally said.

"What is it?"

"Drake has a wall safe in his penthouse. A Shield DCX 2700. You got that?"

"Yes."

"Repeat it back to me."

"A Shield DCX 2700. So what?"

"He has over thirty million dollars in bearer bonds in that safe. I want you to rob him."

Connor could hardly believe his ears. As the shock of the request rippled through his body, he looked down at his feet, then around, as if there had to be somebody else here, as if surely this must be some sort of game or trick.

"Eyes on me," the kidnapper said.

Connor turned back toward the camera. "You have to be kidding."

"I'm absolutely serious."

"I can't do that."

"On the contrary, you can. You and Dylan and Olin can do it without getting caught, too."

"I'm not robbing anyone."

"He lives in a building called the Pearlman. You have two days or I'll kill the boy."

"*Two days?*"

"If you take the phone, I'll kill the boy."

"Please. Even if that was something I could do, I couldn't do it in two days."

"If you disable the camera, I'll kill the boy."

"Something like that has to be planned."

"If you go to the police, I'll kill the boy."

"Seriously—"

"I *am* serious, Connor. You've got one shot to get this right. Don't fuck it up. I will let you know what to do with the money when it's time."

Then the kidnapper hung up. Although Connor could not see the screen, there was nothing stopping him from using *69 to call the man back. As far as he was concerned, he was not done with this conversation.

When the kidnapper didn't answer, Connor waved his arms in the air like he was landing a plane, then pointed at the phone.

It didn't make any difference. The kidnapper still didn't answer.

Frustrated, Connor threw the phone across the room as hard as he could. It hit the wall with a *thud* and fell to the carpet.

Connor had no intention of robbing Drake, regardless of whether the man deserved it.

Instead, with the threat of Jerry's death hanging over his head, he vowed to redouble his efforts. He would find the boy, no matter what it took. And he might as well start by finding out what was in the box the kidnapper had asked him to bring.

He used his house key to slice through the packing tape holding the box together on one end and peered inside to see a stack of papers. He pulled them out. They were standard 8.5 by 11 sheets, available at any office supply store and—for that matter—most pharmacies and grocery stores.

Connor looked into the box once more to make sure it was empty, then dropped it on the floor. He flipped through the pages. There were roughly one hundred in all, and all of them were blank.

What in the world?

He flipped through them again to make sure he had not missed anything.

Connor could think of only one reason the kidnapper would ask him to bring a box of blank papers to this address. He wanted to see if Connor would open it.

DO NOT OPEN THE BOX.

The man was testing him.

Or maybe it was an excuse to get Connor alone.

DO NOT BRING THE COPS.

Certainly, the kidnapper suspected Connor's phone could be monitored by the police after the first call.

Or maybe he was just screwing with Connor. There was no way to be sure.

Connor let the papers fall to the floor and, gun drawn, began a search of the apartment. He imagined that the kidnapper was still watching him on the camera and that there might be more cameras in other rooms, but he didn't care. Let the man watch.

Connor assumed the room he was standing in now was meant to be the living room. He moved slowly into the hall and saw four doors leading off it, two on each side. He cleared them one at a time—closet, kitchen, bedroom, bathroom. All of them were empty. Not a single article of clothing in the bedroom or the closet. Not a dish in the cupboard. Not even a toilet paper roll in the bathroom or another camera to watch him anywhere.

He put his gun back in his holster and returned to the living room. The phone was still there, sitting on the floor. If he wanted to leave the apartment with evidence that might lead him to the kidnapper, that would be it.

Of course, Connor couldn't take it. Even if the man had written his name on the back of the device, he couldn't take it. The kidnapper would kill Jerry if he did, and there was no way he could get to any evidence he might find on that phone fast enough to stop him. So Connor did the only thing he could: he left.

CHAPTER 32

CONNOR CALLED OLIN and Dylan from his car once he was back on the road. He wished he had thought about the software the police had installed on their phones when they spoke earlier. He would not have openly discussed the second package he had received from the kidnapper if he had.

He reasoned the police weren't monitoring him twenty-four/seven. After they had installed the software, they had told him how to use it if he wanted the police to listen in on the call. Still, he suspected they could hop on any call they wanted just by virtue of the fact that the software was there. Since he didn't want to risk having another conversation he would rather they not overhear, he kept these calls brief.

With limited preamble, they basically boiled down to this: "Meet me at my apartment as soon as you can. I have something I want to talk to you about."

By the time Olin and Dylan arrived, Connor was running on fumes. He'd been awake for more hours than he cared to count at this point and had brewed a strong pot of coffee to keep him sharp.

They gathered in the living room, each with a mug. Connor relayed the series of events that happened when he delivered the package to the apartment.

"Do you think he'd really kill Jerry?" Dylan asked, leaning against a wall with her cup clasped in both hands.

Connor collapsed onto the sofa. "I don't know, but I think we have to assume he will. He's after thirty million dollars."

Olin sat down beside him. "Maybe we should tell Detective Pierce. Pretend we robbed Drake. How would the kidnapper know the difference?"

"The police aren't going to turn over thirty million dollars in bearer bonds to a kidnapper. Where would they even get it from?"

"They could fake it."

"We have less than two days," Connor reminded him. "They're not going to be able to generate fake bearer bonds that fast. And I doubt they'd do it, even if they could."

Dylan took a sip of her coffee. "All right, what leads do we have on this guy? We've got to know something about him by now, right?"

But that was the problem—they didn't. Nothing useful, anyway. It wasn't like the police would round up every man in Atlanta with a beard and hold them until somebody broke.

Dylan dragged a chair in from the dining room and sat down on the other side of the coffee table. She leaned forward, resting her elbows on her knees, and looked seriously at Connor and Olin. "I hate to say it—"

"Then don't," Olin interrupted.

He seemed to know where she was going, but that didn't come as much of a surprise because Connor suspected he did, too.

"I think we need to rob the safe," Dylan continued.

"If we do that, we're no better than he is," Olin said.

Connor wasn't sure if Olin meant Drake or the kidnapper, but decided the statement was true in either case.

Dylan raised a hand to silence Olin. "Hear me out. We're going to keep trying to track him down in the meantime. But if push comes to shove, we need to do whatever has to be done to get Jerry back. Besides, it's not like we're going to let him keep the money. When we make the exchange, we'll put a tracker in the bag so we can find him later. That way we'll be able to find out who he is, for sure. And once we know who he is, all we have to do is work backward to build our case. By the time we're done, we'll have a solid collection of evidence to give Detective Pierce."

"Sorry," Olin said, "you said we're not going to let him keep the money, but I missed the part of your plan where you told us how we're going to get it back."

"Once we know who he is, that shouldn't be any harder than getting the evidence against him."

"Not necessarily," Connor said. "He could cash the bonds in, transfer the money to an offshore account. It'd be gone forever then."

Dylan rolled her eyes and threw up her hands. "Ugh. Fine. Then it's one criminal stealing from another, and either way, the kidnapper ends up in jail."

"So will we if we get caught," Olin said.

"This has been a tough night," Connor said. "Let's not make any decisions right now." His gaze cut directly to Dylan. "Especially not any that could land us in jail."

"We do stuff that could land us in jail all the time," Dylan said.

Technically, that was true. How many places had they broken into? How many computers had they hacked? Comparatively, though, they were minor crimes, done only to track down information that would help them right a greater wrong.

Connor did not bother to explain this. Dylan already knew as much. Perhaps, he figured, she saw the kidnapping as the greater wrong.

"Besides," she continued, "we don't know that Drake would go to the police. I bet there's a good chance those bearer bonds are stolen."

"Maybe," Connor said, "but we can't make that assumption. And either way, if anyone catches us, it's still a crime. Let's give Pierce a few hours to see what he can find out about that warehouse. We might get lucky."

Connor still did not have high hopes that the name on the rental contract would prove to be a real person, but the lead had taken on greater significance now that they were looking at grand theft. They needed to play that out.

CHAPTER 33

DETECTIVE STEWART PIERCE began calling Newsom Enterprises every fifteen minutes starting at 8 a.m., waiting for somebody to answer. Between calls, he finished getting dressed, then went down to the kitchen to toast whole wheat bagels for himself and his wife. His brother, Allen, had been on his laptop in the living room when he got home, and was still wandering around the house at 4 a.m., so he wouldn't be up anytime soon.

As the bagels popped out of the toaster, he slathered them with cream cheese.

His wife was still upstairs getting ready for work. She would spend every minute she had trying on outfits like she had never worn them before and fixing her makeup long past the point of perfection. She would grab her bagel on the way out the door and eat it in the car.

Since Stewart knew this, he wrapped it in a paper towel and left it on a plate on the kitchen island. He also filled a thermos with coffee and left it beside the bagel.

Then Stewart took a seat at the breakfast table and ate his own bagel at a leisurely pace. His day would be hectic enough. With calls to Newsom Enterprises every fifteen minutes, it already felt like it was. As far as he was concerned, he could take five minutes to eat in peace.

Or some semblance of peace, anyway.

While he ate, he could not help replaying the explosion at the warehouse in his mind. Like he had in his dreams, he saw it over and over again, winding his nerves ever tighter and compounding his concern for Lucy's son.

What the hell did the kidnapper want?

It sure didn't seem to be money. If that was what he was after, he would already have demanded it. Instead, he seemed to be using the abduction to manipulate Connor. Why?

Stewart believed Connor did not know the answer to that question. Not yet, anyway. He hoped sometime soon something the kidnapper said or did would jog loose a memory that would help them figure it out.

That was a big part of the reason he had agreed to share information with Connor.

He did not trust the PI—he didn't trust anyone except for his wife—but after Alex had told him about the note Connor had received and his history with Alex himself, Stewart couldn't take the risk that Connor might continue to keep information from him.

He placed another call to Newsom Enterprises. Again, it went to voicemail.

He rinsed his plate, put it in the dishwasher, and shouted up the stairs to tell his wife he was leaving.

"Hold on!" Melinda called back. She hurried down the stairs, both hands raised to her left ear as she tried to get the clasp on the back of a diamond earring.

Stewart knew she was annoyed. Melinda only came down to talk to him in the morning like this when she was. But even if that wasn't her M.O., even if she usually came down for breakfast and talked about the weather and gave him a kiss when he left for work, he would have known. He could hear it in her voice, see it on her face.

She wasn't just annoyed. She was pissed.

"You've got to do something about Allen," she whispered when she reached the first floor. "You've got to ask him to leave."

Melinda did not like to be the bad guy. Ever. She wouldn't even do it at Darrin Nickle High School, where she worked as a guidance counselor. *Every kid has a future*, she said. Every kid had potential. Never mind that a good school wouldn't care about your potential if your grades were poor, and life would just as soon serve you up a future that landed you in prison as it would one that landed you in a palace.

She only wanted to bask in the positive.

Normally, Stewart was fine with that. He didn't mind being the bad guy. But this was different. They were talking about his brother. And although he'd had enough of Allen as well, he couldn't ask his brother to leave.

"I'm serious. I want him out of here tonight."

"Come on, be reasonable. He hasn't found an apartment yet."

"He hasn't been looking," Melinda snapped, loud enough for her voice to carry up the stairs. She looked toward the second floor, worried Allen might have heard her. Then she lowered her voice and added, "He's never going to look. As long as he's staying here for free, what reason does he have?"

Stewart sighed. "We need to give him some more time."

"We're not giving him more time."

"I'll tell him he's got until next Friday, okay? That should be long enough for him to find something."

"And you know what will happen when next Friday comes? He'll have another excuse for more time. It will never stop."

"That's not going to happen."

Melinda pointed her finger at Stewart. "I want him out of here tonight, you hear me?" She charged toward the garage door. "Tonight! Or it will be just the two of you in this house tomorrow morning!"

Melinda had raised her voice now even more than she had before. This time, she did not cast her eyes up toward the second floor.

Perhaps she was too angry to realize how loud she was talking, Stewart thought. Regardless, she had reached her limit. If Stewart wanted to hold onto his marriage, he was going to have to get Allen out of the house before Melinda came home from work tonight.

CHAPTER 34

CONNOR GOT A few hours of fitful sleep in his bed. Dylan took the sofa, and Olin curled up with a blanket and a pillow on the floor; they were both too tired to drive home. When Connor awoke, he slipped on a fresh pair of jeans and a black tee-shirt, then went into the living room to wake them.

"Guys."

Dylan opened one eye and groaned as Olin rolled over to face him.

"I have an idea. The kidnapper is going to have to go back to that apartment at some point to retrieve his camera and cell phone, right? I mean, he's not going to just leave them there for somebody to find."

"If he hasn't gone to get them already," Dylan said.

"Fair point. If he hasn't, though, he will sooner or later." Connor pulled the key the kidnapper had given him out of his pocket. He tossed it in Olin's direction, and Olin, despite the fact that he had just woken up, caught it. Connor expected as much. If it had come hurling through the air at *him* first thing in the morning, it no doubt would have hit him square between the eyes if it had not missed him entirely, but Olin had an instinctive hand/eye coordination that had come from years of playing baseball in high school and college.

"I'll give you the address. Go by the apartment and see if the equipment's still there. If it is, just park yourself outside of the building and watch for anything unusual."

"Like what?"

"Well, there's nothing else in the unit, so if he comes back for the equipment, he won't stay long. Also, if he's not carrying the stuff right out in the open, he'll probably have a backpack or some other kind of bag. Trust your instinct. You'll know if you see something."

"And if I do?"

Connor did not think this part had to be explained, but since Olin asked, he said, "Follow him. Maybe he'll lead you back to Jerry."

Olin slowly made his way to his feet. "What are you going to do while I'm gone?"

"I'm going to see if I can find out who the apartment was rented to. I know Pierce is checking on the warehouse, but it's still worth looking into."

"You're thinking that if he used a fake name on one, he might not have used a fake name on both," Dylan said.

Connor shrugged. "People make mistakes. We can't assume anything right now."

"Maybe I should go with Olin. The kidnapper could have changed the lock on the door since last night."

"Why would he? He'd have to have called a twenty-four-hour locksmith to do that. Seems like it would be a lot easier to just go in and take the camera and the phone if he wanted to hide the evidence. Besides, I have something else I want you to do."

Dylan raised an eyebrow.

Connor disappeared into his bedroom and returned moments later with his laptop. "While we're gone, I want you to put your web skills to work. See what you can find out about Drake. Whoever wants us to steal that money has to be somebody close to him. There couldn't be that many people who know about the bearer bonds."

While he spoke, he set the computer up on the small dining room table.

"The way I figure it, we've got today to figure out who this guy is. If we don't . . ." Connor was not yet ready to say they would have to rob Drake's apartment, but Dylan was right: robbing a thief was a lesser evil than letting an innocent child die.

"I think it's the only choice we have," Dylan said, acknowledging the unspoken thought. Then she moved from sofa to table and began clacking away at the keyboard.

"I'll call you if I find anything out," Olin said on his way out the door.

Minutes later, Connor left behind him.

CHAPTER 35

STEWART FINALLY GOT hold of a receptionist at Newsom Enterprises who routed him to someone in the leasing department who, in turn, told him they could not provide the name of the lessee over the phone.

"How am I supposed to know you are who say you are? Anybody could call and say they're a cop. We can't just give that information out."

Under normal circumstances, he would not even have tried to call the company, since that was exactly the response he would have expected to receive. But he thought that after the explosion at the warehouse last night, they would be more accommodating.

It had already been nearly forty-eight hours since Jerry went missing. According to the statistics, that meant the odds of finding the boy alive were dwindling quickly.

He hoped that whatever unfinished business the kidnapper had with Connor would keep the window of opportunity open a little longer, but he knew that would probably amount to hours, not days. Every kidnapper eventually cut ties and ran if they weren't able to get what they wanted, and that almost always meant killing their victim.

If that wasn't enough to put him in a bad mood, the conversation with his brother before he left certainly was. Allen had griped when Stewart pounded on the door to the guest bedroom and told him to go away. He'd griped even louder when, instead, Stewart let himself inside.

"You got today to leave," Stewart said, standing halfway between the door and the bed. "I'd suggest you get out there and start looking for something."

Allen, who was still bleary-eyed and covered with only a sheet, pushed himself up against the headboard. "What?"

"You heard me."

"You're going to do this to your own brother?"

Stewart saw no point in explaining to Allen that his wife had given him an ultimatum. Especially since part of him agreed with her. Stewart wanted to help his brother, but he didn't want Allen taking advantage of him. And that's all that was happening anymore.

There was no great cryptocurrency plan, and if there was, it wasn't going anywhere but onto the growing pile of failures that defined Allen's life.

"You heard me. You got until five o'clock. I don't care where you go, but you can't stay here anymore." He turned around to leave. At the door, a moment of compassion crept over him. He turned around and said, "Listen, I really do hope everything works out for you."

In response, Allen said, "Fuck off."

Although Stewart had the good sense to walk away, the desire to say something equally crass was still gnawing at him when he reached Newsom Enterprises. It had put him in a foul mood that was even worse now that he found himself closing in on a house so far out in the suburbs it was practically rural.

The place belonged to a man named Peter Farnsworth. According to Newsom Enterprises, this was the man who had rented the warehouse.

With long stretches of land between Peter's house and his neighbors', a boy could stand out here screaming his lungs out and still not be heard. It was the perfect place to stash a kidnapping victim.

He found the house by the numbers on the mailbox, then got out to open a rusty steel gate that was attached to a wooden fence on both sides. The gate was secured by a simple latch, which made getting onto the property a breeze.

After he had driven the car onto Peter's land, he stopped to close the gate. He didn't want to alert anybody who might enter the driveway behind him. The dirt road from the gate to the house meandered through a wooded area that looked like it was barely wide enough to allow his car through in some places. Even though it was unlikely anybody was going to drive up behind him, the trip would be slow going. One phone call from the gate to the house, and Peter could slip away before Stewart even got to the door.

However, the dirt road was not as narrow as it appeared to be for the entirety of the drive. Once Stewart got around the first bend, the trees gave way to large, open fields where horses grazed without giving him a second thought (or a first, for that matter).

He parked in the roundabout in front of a 1920s farmhouse. The two-story structure was painted white and accented with black shutters. It looked good, regardless of its age. It looked, now that Stewart thought about it, like the kind of place he wouldn't mind living in when he retired.

Somehow, that only made him more annoyed.

He slammed the car door without thinking about it, climbed the two steps to the front porch, and knocked.

An elderly man in a pair of jeans and a pressed, white dress shirt answered the door. He had a confused look on his face. "Can I help you?" he asked, a deep Southern drawl permeating every syllable.

Stewart looked him over. The man he had seen on the CCTV

footage at the aquarium might be impossible to identify in another context. With his face hidden by the beard, sunglasses, and baseball cap, he could literally have been almost anyone. Even this man, Stewart decided.

He flashed his badge. "I'm looking for someone."

"Yeah?"

"A boy."

"Oh." The old man pushed open the screen door that still separated them and looked questioningly at the detective.

"Are you Peter Farnsworth?"

"I am."

"You're renting a warehouse down on Amhurst Court."

"I am?" Peter said, this time phrasing the two words as a question.

"Don't play games with me."

"I'm not playing games with you."

Stewart looked at the old man hard and saw his brother. These two were cut from the same cloth—always scheming, always trying to pull one over on you. Stewart could just tell. He took a deep breath, trying to keep his cool. "Mind if I have a look around?"

"What for?"

"You going to let me look around or what?"

The screen door closed. "I don't think I am. What do you need to look around my place for, anyway?"

Stewart saw him going for a hook-and-eye latch. If Peter managed to secure the screen door, that would be the end of the conversation. There would be no way he was getting inside without a warrant. But if he got the screen door open *before* Peter slid the hook into place—well, then, who knows? Perhaps in his official report, he could claim Peter *had* let him in. After all, Peter wouldn't be the first person to change his mind after he agreed to let an officer search the premises. People usually acquiesced, whether or not they had something to hide, because they thought it made them look innocent. Maybe they even thought the police were bluffing. Regardless of the reason, so many of them seemed to believe they could call off the search whenever they wanted. What they didn't understand was that the police had the legal right to keep going if they had probable cause—and since probable cause was subjective, a search was hard to stop once it had been started.

Stewart grabbed the handle on the screen door, jerked it open, and stepped inside. "I'm just going to have a look around, all right?"

Perhaps as a reflex, Peter stepped back. "I said you weren't welcome." He pointed at the door. "Get out."

Disregarding the command, Stewart charged from one room to the next, giving each a quick scan before moving on. He opened every door along the way, even if he suspected it led to nothing more interesting than a pantry. When he was done here, he planned on knowing for certain whether Jerry was on the property.

Stewart had made it from the living room to the dining room to the kitchen before Peter grabbed his arm. "Hey! You deaf? Get the hell out of my house!"

Stewart swung around, jerked his arm free. "I'll go when—"

Peter shoved him. "You'll go now."

Stewart slammed Peter into the kitchen wall so hard that the family portrait hanging on it fell to the floor, landing face down with the sound of glass shattering. Stewart had gotten a look at that picture for barely a second before it fell, but that had been long enough for him to know Peter had a wife and two children. Although the children were small in the picture, Peter was also much younger. They would be grown and out of the house by now.

As far as the wife—who knows? They might be divorced. She might have passed away. Or she might just be hiding somewhere deeper in the house with a shotgun, ready to blow Stewart's head off if he got too close to Jerry. Since there was no way to be certain, he didn't dwell on the possibilities.

With Peter pinned to the wall, Stewart reached around to the leather pouch attached to his belt and withdrew a pair of handcuffs. He locked one cuff around Peter's right wrist and the other around the refrigerator door handle. That probably wouldn't hold forever, but it would hold long enough for Stewart to finish searching the house.

"What do you think you're doing?" Peter shouted.

"I told you I'm going to have a look around."

Peter's face turned red as he shouted about government overreach. This was an invasion of privacy, he insisted. A trampling of his rights.

Stewart ignored all of it. He drew his gun and went room by room through the rest of the house. He had not found Jerry (or a woman with a shotgun) by the time he reached the basement stairs.

He flipped the light switch, but no light came on. Peter was shouting louder now. Stewart wondered if that was because he was getting closer to the boy. The basement would be the ideal place to keep him.

He pulled his cell phone from his pocket, clicked the flashlight button, and began his descent. He went slow, gun out, flashlight aimed everywhere the barrel was. His heart was beating fast.

When he reached the dusty cement floor, though, he realized the unfinished space offered nowhere to hide a child.

He cursed under his breath and returned to the main floor of the house. Once he was within sight of Peter, he cut the man off mid-sentence. "You have the right to remain silent . . ."

Stewart uncuffed Peter's left wrist from the refrigerator and slammed the man against the wall again when Peter tried to take a swing at him. Then he cuffed Peter's wrists together behind his back while he finished reciting the Miranda warning.

If Peter had not put up a fight, Stewart would not have had anything to charge him with. But assaulting a police officer was enough to get the man into an interrogation room, and, right now, that was the best he could hope for.

Even if Peter was not involved in the abduction directly, his name had been on the lease for the warehouse. He had to know something. After a few hours in an interrogation room, Stewart might just be able to convince him to trade that information for a reduced sentence.

CHAPTER 36

OLIN ARRIVED AT the address Connor had given him. The apartment building was even more grimy and disgusting than he had imagined. He entered through the front door, reluctantly grabbing the handle and using his jeans to wipe away the filth he imagined had transferred from the door to his hand once he was inside.

Like Connor, he counted himself as lucky when he reached the stairwell at the other end of the hall without encountering any of the residents. Normally, he would chastise himself for that way of thinking, tell himself there was no reason to assume the people who lived in this building were any better or worse than those who lived anywhere else, but in *this* building—and especially in *this* neighborhood—that sort of thinking would be nothing less than naive.

While he was able to use his shoulder to get into the stairwell, to get out he once again had to grab a handle, which made him just as sick this time as it had the last.

He found the apartment. Ready to get this task over with, he slid the key Connor had given him into the lock and turned it. Connor had called fifteen minutes earlier to tell him he should not open the door all the way in case the camera was still there.

Olin imagined that Dylan would have responded with a "Duh," but since that wasn't his style he had settled for "Good idea," and "Thanks."

He pushed the door open only wide enough to peek inside. If Connor's description of the room was accurate, the camera should have been within sight. Since it wasn't, he pushed the door open a little farther. Still no camera.

Olin had a bad feeling they were too late. He pushed the door open all the way. Yup, it was definitely gone. He did not see a phone anywhere in the room, either.

He called Connor to let him know.

Connor wasn't surprised the camera and phone were gone. Dylan had said she thought they might be before he and Olin left for their respective tasks. As soon as she had proposed the possibility, Connor knew it made sense. Why would the kidnapper leave them there any longer than he had to?

Hell, for all Connor knew, he might have been watching from another apartment in the building. If that was the case, he could have grabbed the equipment and gotten out mere minutes after Connor had left.

Nonetheless, it had still been worth a shot. Just like checking the name on the lease was (which he also suspected might be doomed to failure).

The apartment building was owned by a company called Quality Living that had another two dozen just like it, all in equally sketchy parts of the city. The company was, as far as Connor could tell, the true definition of a slum lord.

Even its corporate headquarters wasn't much better.

Tucked away in the corner of a strip mall, it was not easy to find. Especially since the only sign Connor found identifying the company was hanging behind a large, tinted display window.

Connor stepped inside. An old-fashioned bell clanked against the glass. A man sitting at one of two aging and chipped desks turned to look at him. He was wearing a thick pair of glasses and a powder-blue tie with a brown stain on it that happened to match his jacket. He ran his hand across the top of his head, straightening a combover that was so sparse Connor did not at first realize it was there.

"Can I help you?" he said, as he stood and approached the waist-high wall that separated the public and private spaces.

Connor flashed his PI license, hoping to make the conversation quick. "I need to ask about one of your apartments."

"Look, everything's up to code. If you—"

"It's not that," Connor said, although he doubted everything was indeed up to code. "I need the name of somebody renting one of your units."

Connor thought that if the man gave him the name at all, he would at least ask why Connor wanted it. Instead, he returned to his computer, placed his hands on the keyboard, and said, "What's the address?"

Connor gave it to him.

The man hunted-and-pecked his way through a series of screens. It was painfully slow. "Peter Farnsworth," he said. "Anything else?"

Connor figured it had been so easy to get the name because the man didn't want Connor looking any closer at Quality Living than he was already. Perhaps code violations weren't the worst offenses he would find if he were inclined to look deeper. He decided to try to push his luck a little further. "How long has he been there?"

The man turned back to the screen. "Two weeks."

Then Connor thanked him and left. He doubted there was anything else the man could tell him that he couldn't find out on his own, and he wasn't interested in being there any more than the employee was interested in him staying.

Two weeks, he thought as he stepped back through the door and that old-fashioned bell clanged against the glass again. At least that was something. That and the name. If it matched the one Detective Pierce found on the warehouse lease, they might finally be on to something.

CHAPTER 37

ON HIS WAY back to the station, Stewart called out a team to search the grounds around Peter's house. There was a lot of land out there. While he was confident Lucy's son was not in the house itself, there might be a shed or a storm cellar or some other similar structure where Peter was keeping him.

"You think I took that boy?" Peter said after Stewart got off the phone.

Stewart didn't answer. He wanted to wait until they were in the confines of an interrogation room to confront Peter. He wanted to be able to look the man straight in the eye. He wanted to harness all the anger he had been holding back after his brother had told him fuck off and direct it at this scumbag. He wanted to scare the hell out of him.

The rest of the way back to the station, Peter kept declaring he was innocent. He said he had no idea who Stewart was looking for.

Stewart didn't buy it. He had gotten Peter's name and address from Newsom Enterprises. There was no doubt Peter was renting the warehouse, which meant there was no doubt he was involved.

At least, that's what Stewart thought until he relayed those same facts to Peter in the interrogation room and Peter, sitting nervously at the table with his wrists now cuffed in front of him, asked, "How do you know it was me?"

When Connor got back to his apartment, he found Olin sitting at the dining room table with Dylan. He expected as much. With the kidnapper's equipment gone, there had been no reason for Olin to wait for the man to return.

Dylan turned from the computer to Connor when he stepped inside. "You find anything?"

He shrugged, then joined them at the table with a half-smile. "Got a name. Peter Farnsworth. Rented the place two weeks ago."

"Don't get too excited," she cautioned.

"I know. But it might be something. I'm waiting to see what Detective Pierce finds out about the warehouse. How are things going here?"

"The best lead I've got is a man named Alec Garcia. He was Drake's accountant for a long time. Seems like they're close. You go far enough back in Alec's Facebook timeline, and you'll find pictures of them on vacation together. I don't mean down to Florida, either. I mean like Milan, Paris. There are pictures of them on a private plane. Alec's wife is in some of them, too, along with another woman I can't place. Drake's single, so she was probably his girlfriend. If his photos are any indication, he seems to have had quite a few. She hasn't been in any pictures in a long time, so I don't think she's consequential. But Alec—seems like he might be the kind of person who would have known about the bearer bonds."

"So maybe we have something."

"Maybe. Alec is in jail. If he's involved, he'd have to be working with somebody on the outside. I suppose that could be . . ." Dylan snapped her fingers as she tried to remember, then looked at Connor. "What's his name?"

"Peter Farnsworth."

"Right. Him."

"You think you can find a connection between Alec and Peter?" Olin asked Dylan.

"I don't know. They could have been in jail together. Let's see."

Stewart thought about Peter's question: *How do you know it was me?*

He had assumed that if the name the kidnapper had given Newsom Enterprises was fake, it would not have led back to a real person. But maybe that wasn't true. The kidnapper might well have wanted a name that could be associated with a real social security number in case they needed to run his credit.

He thought about how easy it had been to get onto the property. Peter had a gate, but it was secured by only a simple latch. If you had kidnapped a child, wouldn't you at least use a padlock?

Then Stewart thought about his interaction with Peter at the house. Stewart had assumed that his reluctance to let the detective inside was further evidence of his guilt, but Stewart had also accused him of renting a warehouse he claimed he had not rented. If that was true, was it so unreasonable he might not have wanted to let the detective inside? Might he not think that if he had been falsely accused of one thing, he could be falsely accused of another?

If Stewart had not been so angry with his brother (and even a little angry with his wife, if he was being honest with himself), maybe he would have considered those possibilities. Now that he had, he needed to know for certain whether his accusations held water.

"Stay right here," he said. Then he left the room, slamming the door behind him.

Standing in the hall outside, he pulled out his cell phone and called

Newsom Enterprises once again. And, once again, the receptionist routed him to the leasing department.

"Can I help you?" a man said when he answered.

Stewart recognized the voice and knew he was speaking to the same person he had spoken to when he had visited hours earlier. "It's Detective Pierce," he said.

"Oh. Hi, Detective. What can I do for you?"

"Did you ever meet Peter Farnsworth?"

"No. Why do you ask?"

Stewart sighed. "I've got a man in custody here. I'm trying to find out whether he is actually the guy who signed the lease on the warehouse."

"Well, we have a copy of Mr. Farnsworth's license on file, if that will help."

"You do?"

"It's part of the leasing process. We have to know who we're renting to, after all."

"Why didn't you tell me that when I was down there?"

"You didn't ask."

Stewart took a deep breath, trying to control his anger. "Yes, that would help. Could you email me a copy of it?"

"Sorry, no can do. We have rules about that. Those photos contain PPI. That stands for 'protected personal information,' in case you don't know. I could get in big trouble if I emailed something like that."

Stewart knew exactly what PPI was and wasn't surprised by the answer. In fact, if he wasn't so worked up, he wouldn't have even asked.

"If you want to come down here," the man continued, "I'd be happy to show it to you."

Making the drive back to Newsom Enterprises would take more time than Stewart felt like he had right now. He needed another way to compare the photo in the license to the man he had in custody.

Then Stewart had an idea. *He* didn't need to be the one who made the comparison.

"What if I send you a picture?" he asked. "Can you tell me if it's the same man in the license?"

"Sure, I suppose I can do that."

"Great." Stewart copied the man's email address down into his phone, hung up, and went to retrieve a copy of Peter's mugshot.

Dylan clicked around the web for a long time, looking for any connection she could find between Alec and Peter. Like everything else about this case so far, she was not able to find anything useful. Peter Farnsworth had never been in jail, nor did he travel in the kinds of circles that would have put him in touch with Alec when Alec had been free.

Peter had been a physician's assistant for nearly thirty years before he retired and moved to the far edge of the suburbs, where he lived now. He had two children, both of whom were in their thirties and living in different parts of the country. His wife had died two years earlier. These days, his entire social calendar seemed to consist of checkers on Wednesday nights at the Parkfield Community Center and an aerobics class for senior citizens at a nearby YMCA.

Connor and Olin had both pulled chairs over so they could see the screen.

Dylan let her hands fall away from the keyboard and rotated in her chair so she could face Connor. "I don't think this is our guy."

Just then, Connor's phone rang. He knew Pierce's number well enough by now that he recognized it when he looked at the Caller ID.

He clicked to answer and put the call on speaker.

"Any word from the kidnapper?" the detective asked.

"No," Connor lied. "Not yet."

"Well, after last night, he'll probably call soon. I don't think that's the last we're going to hear from him."

"Were you able to find out who was leasing the warehouse?"

"That's a dead end," Pierce said. "The guy used a fake ID."

"You sure?"

"Absolutely. I got the guy's name from Newsom Enterprises and paid him a visit. He didn't seem to know anything about it, so I had the leasing agent compare his picture with the ID they have on file. Photos don't match."

"But with the beard and sunglasses—"

"No beard or sunglasses in the ID on file."

Connor thought about the voice synthesizer he had noticed last time he'd talked to the kidnapper and wondered if the beard might have been fake, as well.

"Unfortunately, a lot of their leases are done electronically," Pierce continued. "The kidnapper could have matched the stolen name with a fake picture. Either way, we're going to try to get the photo on the six o'clock news. Just in case. Maybe, if we're lucky, somebody will recognize him."

"What name did he use on the fake ID?"

"Peter Farnsworth. Why?"

Connor felt the little bit of hope he had vanish. Since the kidnapper had used the same name on both leases, there was no point in chasing that lead down any further.

He was equally sure the picture would be a dead end. Not just because the detective seemed to think it might be, though. He knew that Peter—mostly thanks to his kids—had dozens of photos online.

They were all over Facebook and Instagram, which he had seen because they were the main sites Dylan had used to piece together the details of his life. But none of Peter's pictures online looked like those you saw on a driver's license. In fact, very few people had pictures like that on the web, which not only explained why the kidnapper had matched a name and a photo that didn't belong together, but also led him to the conclusion that the picture had likely come from one of those websites that specialized in stock photography. It certainly wouldn't be the kidnapper—he had been too careful to make a mistake like that—but it likely wouldn't even be somebody who knew him.

"Why did you want to know the man's name?" the detective asked again, snapping Connor back into the moment.

"Just curious," he said, and hoped the detective did not question his response.

For a second or two, it seemed like he might. Then the detective moved on. "Anyway, in the meantime, let me know if the kidnapper calls back," he said, by way of ending the conversation.

Connor said he would and hung up.

Dylan pushed the laptop away from her. It was as clear to her as it was to Connor there was no point in spending any more time researching Peter.

In fact, there was probably little reason to bother researching anybody else, even if they had a name. The clock was ticking fast. More than eight hours had passed since the kidnapper had given Connor the ultimatum.

"I think we're going to have to do it," he said, looking from Dylan to Olin as he addressed them both.

Dylan sat up a little straighter. "You mean . . ."

Connor could hear the excitement in her voice. He didn't

particularly like that. This was not a task to be relished. But stealing from a thief wasn't the worst thing they could do, he reminded himself.

He nodded.

"Are you sure?" Olin asked. "This could mean big trouble for us. Maybe we could go down to the jail and talk to Drake's accountant."

"And say what?" Dylan asked. "Peter and Alec might not have known each other, but that doesn't mean Alec isn't involved. He could still be the mastermind behind this crime. And if he's not, he might say something to Drake about it."

"He's testifying against Drake. Why would he say anything?"

"We don't know what he's going to say on the stand. He could plan on lying."

"The prosecution isn't going to ask him questions they don't already know the answers to."

"It's still too risky," Connor agreed. "Dylan's right. We don't know what their relationship is right now. Even if he doesn't like Drake anymore, he still might warn him."

"Why?" Olin asked.

Connor shrugged. "Perhaps he would be worried about what would happen to him if he didn't. Even if Alec isn't behind all this, Drake might think he is. Guys like that have contacts in all kinds of places. Sometimes even in jail. Maybe Alec felt safe enough testifying against him, but that doesn't mean he would want Drake blaming him for stealing that much money. That's the kind of thing that could get him shanked, for sure."

"*Shanked*?" Dylan asked.

"Stabbed. Whatever. The point is, if he tells Drake, Drake will move the money."

"Or hire additional security," Dylan said.

"Both of which would be bad for us. Face it, Olin, we're out of options. This is starting to look like our only chance to get Jerry back. I think we're going to have to take it."

Olin did not look convinced.

"Drake's a *bad* guy," Dylan said. "He's being charged with a wide range of crimes from fraud to tax evasion, but it seems like the police suspect him of much more. They think he might have perpetrated a whole series of high-profile thefts that have never been solved. He might have even killed a few people. They can't get him for any of that, though, so they're getting him for what they can. We're not doing anything to him he doesn't deserve."

"We could end up in jail."

"Do you want to tell Lucy her son is dead because you were afraid to go to jail?"

Connor knew the answer to that would be no. Still, he waited for Olin to say it.

Eventually, he did. Then, after another long hesitation, he added, "All right. I guess I'm in. But we're going to do this smart. No screwing around. No shooting from the hip. I want a plan."

"What are you looking at me for?" Connor said.

"You know how you can be."

"We'll have a plan."

"I mean, this thing needs to be down to the second. I'm not going to jail."

"We'll have a plan," Connor said again, this time more firmly. Then he remembered something, and his face lit up. "In fact, I might even know what it is."

CHAPTER 38

WHEN CONNOR DID not immediately lay out his plan, Dylan asked, "Well, what is it?"

Connor hopped up from the table and began to move toward the door. "I need to go check on something. While I'm gone, you two go see if you can get your hands on a Shield DCX 2700."

"What's that?" Olin asked.

"If the kidnapper's right, that's the safe Drake has in his apartment. We're only going to have minutes once we get inside. Dylan, you need to figure out how you're going to crack that thing once we do."

"I can do that."

Connor swung the door open. "While you're out, get some cell phones for us, too. Pay cash."

"Why?" Olin asked.

"We're going to need burners. Pierce had the police install listening software on all of our phones, remember?"

"But they can only listen in if we let them."

"That's what Pierce said. If you don't want to get caught, then we probably shouldn't assume he was telling the truth. Even if he was, these things leave a digital trail. We don't want to hand them evidence that proves we were at the building when the robbery occurred."

Connor figured Olin should already know about the digital trail cell phones left behind. They had used that very technology to track

Dylan's whereabouts years earlier. Then again, it had been years. It probably wasn't top of mind, and either way, there was no harm in telling him again.

Olin nodded. "All right. Makes sense."

"Good. When you guys get the safe and the cell phones, come back here. We'll work out of my apartment until we're ready to go. I'll be back as soon as I can."

"Stop being so cryptic," Dylan said. "Where are you going?"

"I'm going to scout the building. We need to know exactly what we're up against." And with that, Connor was out the door.

CHAPTER 39

IF YOU HAD told Connor a year ago he would one day find himself planning a heist worth millions, he would have told you you were crazy. Sure, he'd broken the law plenty of times, but he'd never done something so brazen.

Connor headed to his car at the back of his building. He was only feet away when he pulled his keys out of his pocket, pressed the unlock button, and fumbled, dropping them on the ground.

With a small sigh, he reached down to pick them up. As he did, he saw something stuck to the bottom of his rear bumper. Although he had never examined the car from this angle, instinct told him that what he was looking at had not been present when the car had rolled off the assembly line.

Strange, he thought as he moved closer to get a better look.

He examined the item first by touch and then by kneeling low enough so that he could actually see it. A small silver disk with a white rim and Apple's logo in the middle. He knew immediately what it was: an AirTag.

Designed with all kinds of useful purposes in mind, an AirTag could help you keep track of your keys or your wallet or your luggage. Basically, anything you wanted. For that reason, criminals had started using them for an even broader array of activities, like tracking cars they wanted to steal.

If Connor drove a Mercedes or a BMW, he might suspect that was why the AirTag had been put there. But nobody would be interested in stealing his CR-V. At least, not anybody who would go to the trouble of tracking it with an AirTag.

That meant there could be only one reason for it. The kidnapper was using it to track his movements. It was how he knew when Connor would be out, how he had known when Connor was getting close to the warehouse or the apartment. He could even have used it to know whether Connor was getting close to finding the boy.

The thought that the kidnapper had been monitoring him this whole time made him sick, angry. He thought about using his keys to pry it off the vehicle. Then, just before he moved forward with that plan, he reconsidered.

If he left the AirTag where it was, the kidnapper would know that he was going to the Pearlman to case the building. That, alone, wouldn't buy them any time, but it might keep the kidnapper from losing his cool, from doing something horrible to Jerry that could not be undone.

Besides, now that Connor knew the AirTag was there, he might be able to use it to his advantage.

He climbed into the driver's seat and called Dylan.

She answered immediately. "Yeah?"

"When you get out to your car, check your bumper for an AirTag."

"Seriously?"

"The kidnapper put one on my car. My guess is he put one on yours and Olin's too."

"That son of a—"

Connor could tell from her voice she was already starting to move. He had not asked if she and Olin were still in the apartment and could not wait for her to finish the rant she was about to start. He couldn't take the risk that Dylan might already be on the street in front, only feet away from her own vehicle, where she no doubt intended to remove the AirTag like he nearly had. "Leave it, if it's there," he interrupted.

"What?"

"If he doesn't know we know, we can use this later."

Dylan huffed.

"Trust me."

"*Fine.*" Dylan hung up.

Connor looked down at his phone and considered calling her back. She had not told him whether there was an AirTag on her car or not. Then again, it didn't matter right now. He could find out when he returned to the apartment.

In fact, he probably should have had the whole conversation when he got back to the apartment. He should have known she wasn't going to handle the news well, and now Olin was going to be stuck riding around with a pissed-off Dylan for the next few hours.

"Sorry, buddy," he mumbled as he backed the car out of the parking space and got his head back into the game. There was nothing he could do about Dylan's mood now, and he had more important things to think about.

Connor could feel his nerves tightening the muscles in his neck as he approached the condominium building. He felt like he had been in fifth gear since he woke up. The nervous energy that was making his brain work overtime to put a plan in motion had been ratcheted up even higher when he found the AirTag, and that would not serve him well.

He needed to slow down. Be calm.

Calm, cool, and collected, he thought as he parked in a metered spot a block away from the building. If that was not what people saw when he stepped into the lobby, they might take notice—and not in a good way.

Hey, remember that twitchy guy who showed up yesterday? Maybe he had something to do with the robbery.

The front of the building was made entirely of glass. On the other side of it, Connor saw a lobby that looked exactly like it had in the pictures online: a leather seating area, a marble desk with a receptionist behind it, and modern chandeliers hanging overhead.

Connor reached for the door and, as he did, a doorman opened it from the other side.

"Welcome to the Pearlman," the doorman said, blocking the entrance. He looked Connor up and down, perhaps judging the tee shirt and jeans he was wearing. "Are you here to see someone?"

Connor mustered up a look of disdain. "I'm here to buy a condo," he said as confidently as he could. "Now, if you'll excuse me."

The trick worked.

Once the doorman stepped out of the way, Connor meandered his way through the lobby, pretending to take it all in. In actuality, he was looking for security cameras. He counted four in total, discreetly positioned behind tinted glass canisters along the ceiling. Between them, they appeared to cover every inch of floor space.

Connor decided he could safely assume the rest of the building was covered, as well.

He let his gaze fall back to the doorman and frowned. "It's not as nice as I was expecting."

The doorman looked insulted, which was exactly what Connor

wanted. Only a rich, pretentious asshole would talk like that, and rich, pretentious assholes did not break into condos.

Connor turned and headed straight for the front desk. As he did, he looked around once more, this time for the restrooms, and saw a sign directing him to an alcove beyond the elevators.

The receptionist smiled at him.

"Excuse me," he said, now giving all of his attention to her. "I was wondering if you have any units for sale."

"We have a few. They are listed with Pembroke and Associates."

"Great. If I gave you my email address, could you send me over their information?"

"Sure."

Connor gave her an email address he had set up using Gmail on his phone before coming inside.

The receptionist tapped at her keyboard for a minute or so. "Done."

Connor thanked her and left. This time, he noticed, the doorman did not bother to open the door.

CHAPTER 40

WHEN CONNOR RETURNED to his apartment building, he stopped by Rebecca's to ask a favor.

"I thought I wasn't going to see you until Friday," she said with a smile.

Then he told her what he wanted, and the smile faded. "More secret private investigator stuff?"

"I'm afraid so."

Rebecca crossed her arms over her chest and sighed. "All right, I'll help you. But I want to know what all this is about when you're done."

"I'll tell you what I can. When can it be ready?"

She shrugged. "Six o'clock."

"Great. I'll stop by later and pick it up."

Once again, he couldn't decide whether he should kiss her, so once again, he did not.

When he reached his apartment, he found Dylan sitting cross-legged on the wooden floor, staring at a safe that was about three feet on all sides. "You sure that's it?"

Olin, who was sitting on the floor beside her, nodded toward the dining room table. "Your phone's over there." He was obviously referring to the burner, since Connor's phone was in his pocket.

"What do you mean?" Dylan snapped, circling back to Connor's question. "Of course I'm sure."

"I guess I expected something bigger."

"If the kidnapper's right about what's in this thing, Drake wouldn't need a lot of space. You could carry over one hundred million dollars in bearer bonds in a briefcase if you wanted to." Dylan's voice had an edge to it that did not seem to match the tone of the conversation.

"Did you find an AirTag on your car?" Connor asked her.

"Just where you said it would be."

Connor looked at Olin. "What about you? Did you check your car?"

"When we got back," Olin said.

"And?"

Olin nodded.

"Good."

"I still think we should just pry those things off," Dylan said.

"I told you. We're going to be able to use them to our advantage."

"How?"

Connor pulled an AirTag of his own from his pocket and sat down. "I bought it while I was out," he said. Then he explained his plan, ending with the email he had received from the receptionist at the Pearlman, the IP address he would be able to get from it, and the security cameras mounted throughout the lobby.

"You think that's going to work?" Olin said when he was done.

"You're the most cautious one here. Do you?"

Olin took a moment to consider the plan, perhaps scrutinizing it in ways he had not when Connor had explained it. Eventually, he nodded and said, "Yeah. I think it will."

Connor already had a good feeling about his plan, but he knew that if Olin bought into it, it was as good as it could be. Not that there weren't risks. There were plenty of them. But there was no way to rob a unit in the Pearlman without taking *some* risks.

"Of course, a lot of this is riding on you, Dylan. Do you think you can get us past that safe or not?"

She took a deep breath. "Maybe. Not the way I thought I could, though. There's no way I'm going to be able to find my way to the combination by touch alone. At least not quickly."

"That safe might not be big, but it's formidable," Olin said.

Dylan looked at the time on her phone. "Speaking of which, I need to go. I found someone online who can get me what I need to give us a shot. I'm supposed to meet him in thirty minutes."

By "online," Connor assumed Dylan meant the dark web. After all, where else would she find someone who would sell her the tools to crack a safe?

She stood up. "Besides, sounds like you've got some work of your own to do while I'm gone."

Connor did, indeed. He moved from the floor to the table, where his laptop was still sitting. Olin, who was nothing but a spectator so far in this crime, moved with him.

CHAPTER 41

CONNOR HARDLY SLEPT that night, even with the IEN news anchor monotonously droning on in the background. He kept replaying the plan in his head. There were no guarantees this was going to work. Dylan still had not managed to break into the safe, and she had damaged it to the point that there was no longer a reason to keep trying. He would just have to hope that she was right when she said that, although she hadn't done it, she had figured out how.

And that wasn't the only new obstacle they had encountered.

Still, they only had today to pull this off. They did not want to take the risk that the kidnapper might decide to cut his losses if they postponed since they all knew what that might mean.

Dylan and Olin were supposed to show up at 11 a.m. True to form, Olin arrived three minutes early. Also true to form, Dylan arrived twenty minutes late. It did not look like they had slept any better than Connor.

They sat around the dining room table, drinking coffee and talking through the plan one last time. Then Connor called Detective Pierce on the off chance the photo on the news had produced a lead. Since it had not, he logged into his laptop, reviewed with Olin what he would need to do, and left with Dylan.

They took Connor's car to the Pearlman, where Connor once again parked on the street. He looked at the time on his burner. 11:57 a.m.

Dylan waited in the car, a large backpack by her feet, and Connor walked the last block to the lobby entrance. The same doorman was there. This time, he must have known Connor had an appointment, because he opened the door and stood aside without saying a word. Although his expression said plenty.

Connor barely acknowledged him as he stepped inside. He looked around a space that seemed as vast and impressive as the first time he had seen it. The only person within sight besides the doorman and the receptionist was a woman sitting in a chair to his left. She was wearing a gray and white suit and was staring intently at something on her phone.

Connor figured she must be Leslie Shade, the real estate agent from Pembroke and Associates who represented the units in this building.

"Mrs. Shade?"

Leslie looked up from her phone. Now that Connor could see her straight on, he could tell she looked exactly like she did online. Long black hair hung to her shoulders. A sharp jawline. Sculpted nose. Makeup so carefully applied it almost looked painted on.

"Mr. Tucker?" she asked.

"Tucker" matched the surname on the fake email address Connor had given the receptionist yesterday, and he had decided he should stick with it. A lot was going to happen before Connor left the Pearlman. The fewer clues he could leave behind that he had been here, the better.

"Pleased to meet you," Connor said.

A disarming smile stretched across her face. She stood up and shook Connor's hand. There was a bit of small talk about why Connor wanted to move in and what appealed to him about the Pearlman. Connor responded with answers that were specific enough to sound convincing but did not open up a lot of avenues for follow-up questions.

Then Leslie held out a hand, directing Connor to the elevator.

The condominium was what Connor expected it to be. Polished hardwood floors, marble countertops in the kitchen and bathroom, and stainless steel appliances. "All of it top of the line," Leslie pointed out as she placed her purse on the small wooden table by the door.

Connor doubted anyone would dispute that. Still, he would be hard-pressed to say it was worth the price tag.

Halfway through the tour, they reached the master bedroom. The space was staged with a canopy bed and a pair of matching side tables, all of which looked like they might have once belonged to a king.

Leslie made sure to point out the view, told him the windows faced north so he would not have to deal with direct sunlight in the morning or the evening, and asked if he had any questions.

He shook his head, and Leslie turned to step back into the hall.

Throughout the tour so far, she had ushered him into and out of rooms ahead of her, meaning he was always within her line of sight. This, he realized, might be his only opportunity to do the single most important thing he needed to do before he left the apartment.

Connor pulled the small black device Rebecca had made for him from his inside jacket pocket and tossed it behind the bedroom door. Since this was the only room with carpet he had seen so far, he did not have to worry about it making any noise when it landed.

Connor checked the clock on his burner when he finished the tour. 12:23. He realized he was fixating on the time in a way that didn't matter yet, but he still couldn't help himself. Perhaps because soon it would matter a great deal.

"So, what do you think?" Leslie asked now that they were back in the living room.

"It's nice." Connor glanced once more around the space. "I'll think about it."

"Well, don't take too long," Leslie said, as she led him to the door. "These condos go fast."

He smiled. "I'm sure they do." Then, on the way out, Connor discreetly reached into his jacket pocket again, found the second item Rebecca had given him, and pushed the button on the device.

12:26.

They waited for the elevator together in silence and rode down together in silence. When they reached the lobby, Connor asked, "Do you have a restroom I can use before I go?"

"There's one over there," Leslie said. "Would you like me to wait?"

"It's not necessary."

Leslie nodded. "Okay. Let me know if you decide you would like to move forward."

Connor assured her he would and then stepped into the bathroom. He pulled out his burner to call Dylan.

12:28.

"Three minutes and counting," he said when she answered. "Get ready."

CHAPTER 42

THE NEXT THREE minutes seemed to take an impossibly long time. When they were up, the minute that followed moved even more slowly. Connor was beginning to wonder if the device Rebecca had made for him had worked. Then the fire alarm went off.

Just as it should have.

This little bit of trickery was inspired by the remote-activated smoke bomb Rebecca had made to get out of a history test years earlier. He figured since she'd made one before, she would have no trouble making one again, and it looked like he was right.

Connor pulled out his burner and called one of only two numbers programmed into it: Olin's.

Olin was sitting on Connor's sofa watching a baseball game on ESPN when his burner rang. He muted the TV, clicked to answer, and was already on his way to the dining room table by the time he spoke. "Ready?"

"Yes," Connor said. "Do it now."

Olin hung up. He sat down in front of the laptop. On the screen was a black window with a blinking cursor. Next to it was a small piece of paper with a series of handwritten commands for Olin to enter at just this moment.

Although the interface did not look like much, it was in fact a direct tunnel into the Pearlman's security system. While Dylan was out getting the equipment she needed to break into the safe, Connor had used the IP address associated with the email the receptionist had sent him to find a way into the building's network. Olin had seen him do stuff like this before. It was as amazing to watch as it was tedious. Hour upon hour of seemingly meaningless strings of text entered into a screen just like this, with equally arcane responses from the machine.

Olin placed his hands on the keyboard, hesitated. He was about to become an accomplice to a crime that might just go down in history as one of the largest thefts of all time. If Dylan was wrong, if Drake did go to the police, Olin might find himself in jail for the rest of his life.

Then he reminded himself that it was stealing from a thief, that it was for a greater good, that Connor and Dylan were counting on him, and he started typing.

Connor stood close to the bathroom door, listening for the roar of angry and confused residents leaving the building. Because of the piercing alarm, though, he never heard any.

After thirty seconds or so—long enough for Olin to enter the commands into the computer, disabling the CCTV—he pulled the door open an inch to take a peek. The residents he was waiting for were already swarming out of the stairwell. Leslie was nowhere in sight.

Good. So far, everything was going exactly as it should have been.

Connor pushed his way into the stairwell, apologizing and claiming he forgot something in his unit.

Aside from the restrooms and the security cameras, there were a couple of things Connor had taken note of when he'd scouted the lobby the day before. In particular, he had noticed the scanners in front of the stairwell and by the elevators. The intention was to keep anyone who didn't live here from getting upstairs. Even Leslie, who probably had cause to be in this building frequently, wasn't getting upstairs without a temporary badge from the receptionist.

However, Connor noticed, she hadn't needed to use the badge to come back down. He'd expected this, as well. Many security systems seemed to assume that once you were inside, you belonged.

Thus, setting off the smoke bomb got him into the stairwell. The stairwell would get him to the penthouse. And once the fire alarm stopped, the elevator would get him back down.

Connor looked at his phone again when he rounded the landing for the ninth floor.

12:36.

He did his best not to think about how many floors he still had to climb. At least the foot traffic was starting to thin a little bit.

Another seven floors up, and he walked right past Drake Hartfield. Connor recognized him from their research online. He was sure this would happen sooner or later if Drake was in the building. Drake looked at him, perhaps wondering what Connor was doing heading up when everyone else was heading down, but Connor did not make direct eye contact. If Drake or anyone else had asked, he would have repeated his story that he was going back to grab something important from his condo.

The explanation was weak, at best. But with everyone moving, there wouldn't be any follow-up questions. And with the CCTV out of service, there would be no way to prove that the man people saw in the stairwell was actually Connor.

Besides, Drake—who mattered most—was also the least likely to ask.

Connor had been after two things when he hacked into the Pearlman's network. The first was access to the CCTV. The second had been Drake's email address. It wasn't unusual for a building like the Pearlman to keep those on file in case they needed to notify the residents about upcoming maintenance or any number of other items that might affect their daily lives. Like a fire drill. Connor was sure Drake was mildly annoyed by the inconvenience, but he also figured that as long as Drake thought it was a drill, he wouldn't bother removing the bearer bonds from his safe before leaving the building.

Connor didn't know the address the Pearlman would normally use to send those emails, but he'd dummied up something that looked official and hoped for the best.

Since Drake's hands were empty, it must have worked.

Connor's legs began to ache as he trudged his way from one landing to the next. By the time he reached the top floor, he was sweating and out of breath. He had not seen anybody else coming down the stairs in a while now.

He stepped out of the stairwell and found himself in a small room that contained only two other doors. One was for the elevator. The other was the for the penthouse.

At least there wouldn't be any confusion about which unit they needed to break into.

Now all he had to do was wait for Dylan.

Although he had not heard anybody behind him, he knew she had to be only seconds away. He grabbed the doorknob and turned it on the off chance Drake had left the condo unlocked. No luck.

Then, right at that moment, Dylan came through the door, also out of breath.

Neither of them tried to speak. Especially not with the fire alarm blaring overhead. Instead, as they each worked to catch their breath, they nodded, and through a series of hand gestures, Connor indicated the door to the condo was locked.

Dylan shrugged out of the backpack, removed two pairs of gloves from inside it, and handed one pair to Connor. After they put them on, she pulled her lock pick set out of the pocket of her jeans and went to work.

This would be the easy part. He'd watched her get past so many doors at this point, he figured she could do it blindfolded.

Connor hoped that once they were inside the condo, the alarm would not be so loud.

Dylan worked the picks around in the lock until it turned. She offered a thumbs-up and opened the door.

This condo made the one Connor had seen earlier look like it belonged in the dilapidated building where the kidnapper had delivered his demands. Not only was it massive (it had to be, since it occupied the entire floor), but there was not a single corner cut anywhere. Although Connor did not know much about design, he could tell everything here was expensive. The furniture. The finishes. Even the decorative light switch covers that—he looked closer—just might have been solid gold.

Dylan closed and locked the door behind them, then turned to the home security system mounted beside it. A blinking red light told them it was armed. As loud here as it was in the hallway, the fire alarm drowned out the accompanying *beep, beep, beep* that warned them they had only seconds to deactivate the device before it would call the police.

This obstacle was likewise expected, and Dylan already had a way to deal with it. The technique wasn't one she had employed before because normally when they broke in, the intention was to leave without anyone knowing they'd been there. Since that wasn't going to happen here, there was no reason to be subtle.

Dylan dropped the backpack by her feet, unzipped it, and rifled through the equipment she had brought until she found a hammer. Then she spun it around and slammed the claw against the alarm panel repeatedly until the plastic split, the circuit boards underneath cracked, and the screen went dark.

This primitive way of dealing with an alarm was commonly referred to as "crash and smash," and could be very effective as long as the system was destroyed before the alarm called the security company.

12:49 p.m.

They set about finding the safe. The kidnapper had neglected to tell them exactly where it was located. But they did know it was a wall safe, and they could assume Drake would want easy access to it, so they started by removing the wall art to see what they might find.

In a condo of this size, that was no small task, and when they were done, all they had found was drywall.

Next was the furniture. Anything that had been backed up to the wall and was easy to move was fair game. Especially anything that did not look like it would draw the attention of a common thief. That was also a bust.

Connor knew by now the fire department would already be in the building, searching the unit Connor had toured for the blaze that had triggered the alarm. After all, Connor had learned while planning the heist that these days the firemen did not always have to go floor by floor, clearing every inch of a building. Many modern high-rises like this had smoke detectors that could point you straight to the location where the fire had occurred. The reasoning was self-explanatory: The quicker a fire department could get to a fire, the less damage it could do.

After the firemen determined there was no danger (which they had also likely already done), they might even find the custom smoke bomb Rebecca had made for them. It did not look like any smoke bomb Connor had seen before, so they probably wouldn't know what it was. But if they did, would they suspect the fire alarm had been triggered to create a diversion? Would they call the police? Or would they report their findings to the Pearlman's management and let them decide how to handle it?

There was no reason to think a smoke bomb on one floor would lead them to assume the penthouse was being robbed. Nonetheless, since these were all questions Connor couldn't answer, it made their search for the safe that much more urgent.

12:57 p.m.

Dylan began opening every door she could find—cabinets, closets, pantries—while Connor turned his attention to the built-in bookshelves in the living room. He pulled the books off the shelves in groups and let them fall to the floor only to find nothing behind them.

He wanted to scream. Perhaps there wasn't a safe here at all. The kidnapper's information might be bad. If that was true, Connor and Dylan had taken this risk for nothing. Worse than that, the kidnapper might think they had decided to make off with the money themselves, which would mean Jerry was never coming home, no matter what they did.

Connor slammed his fist against the wall in frustration. A deep thud reminded him that between the two-by-fours that framed the rooms, often the only thing behind drywall like this was insulation.

They were already looking for a wall safe. What if it was entirely enclosed within the wall? What if the safe was not intended to be accessed easily? If the bearer bonds were stolen, maybe Drake was holding on to them as a sort of safety net. Didn't criminals like Drake always have a backup plan in case they needed to run?

Connor grabbed the hammer Dylan had dropped and began a quick walk-through of the apartment. Fortunately, this part of the search didn't take long. The open floorplan that had made it possible to see clear from the front door to the private outdoor space on the opposite side of the unit meant there weren't a lot of walls that could be discreetly modified for the purpose of concealing a safe.

The best candidate for something like that would probably be the bedroom closet, Connor figured. It was large enough that Drake could have moved one of the walls in a couple of feet and likely no one would notice. If he was handy, it might have even been a job he could have done himself. There would be no trim to match. All he would have had to do was nail a couple of two-by-fours into the floor and the ceiling, hang the sheetrock, and paint over it.

Connor had spent the summer between his junior and senior years in college helping a house flipper with a remodel. That was a difficult summer for a lot of reasons, not the least of which was that it was the summer his mother and father were abducted.

Regardless, he had learned from working with Austin, his boss at the time, how easy a modification like that could be.

Connor made his way to the closet in the master bedroom. He had been in here before but had not given any thought to the way the space had been designed. Built-in shelves, complete with custom racks, lined the longest two walls. The shelves seemed to house primarily shoes and sweaters, the racks suits and dress shirts. Nothing was mounted to the narrow walls on either end of the closet.

At the time, that had not struck Connor as significant. Now, it seemed like a poor utilization of the space. Unless, that is, you had a safe hidden behind one of them.

CHAPTER 43

DRAKE MILLED ABOUT on the sidewalk with a hundred or more other people, all waiting to be let back inside. Thank God this had not happened during the evening or on a weekend. If it had, there would be at least five times as many people out here.

He looked at his watch, wondered how long the drill would take. Then two fire trucks rolled up with sirens roaring and parked along the curb.

Drake had an uneasy feeling about the email he had received. If this was just a drill, why would there be fire trucks here?

Two of the firemen hopped off the truck and ran into the building, while more began hooking up hoses to nearby fire hydrants.

Drake turned to a woman in a floral-print house dress standing beside him. He had seen her in the building several times, but she was old and unattractive, so he had never paid her much attention. "Excuse me, did you receive an email yesterday telling you there would be a fire drill today?"

Her ancient brow furrowed. "I don't know. I don't check my email very often. As far as I can see, it's just another way for companies to send me junk mail. My kids sure don't send me anything. I wonder if they even know what my email address is. I—"

"Thank you," Drake said, cutting her off. He had no interest in hearing her life story. Especially not when he was starting to suspect the email he had received might have been part of a con targeting him.

Drake turned to a man on his right and asked the same question. This was not somebody Drake had seen around the building, but he assumed the man had to be a resident since he was standing here.

The man shook his head. "No, nothing like that." Then he pulled a phone out of a holster attached to his belt. "Hold on. Let me check just to be sure. Maybe I missed it." He scrolled through his emails. "Strange that fire trucks would show up for a drill," he mumbled.

Once the man had confirmed that he had not received a similar email, Drake looked back at the building. His concern compounded. Suddenly, he realized this was about someone getting into his safe. He was sure of it.

Drake rushed across the street, holding his hand out to stop the traffic that was fighting its way around the fire truck. Horns blared. He could feel his weak heart pounding.

Feet from the entrance, a fireman who had been unspooling a hose hopped off the truck, blocking his path. "What do you think you're doing? You can't go in there."

"I need to—"

"It's not safe. Whatever you need to do isn't worth losing your life over, is it?" He pointed to the rest of the residents waiting on the other side of the street. "Go back over there. We'll let you know when it's okay to go back in."

Drake resisted the urge to push past him. He knew that if he succeeded, they would chase him down and drag him out. They might even call the police to bring him under control if that's what it took. Drake didn't need that sort of attention right now.

He returned to the designated area and stared anxiously at the building. While he waited, a memory emerged. A man in the stairwell. Avoiding eye contact. Going up while everyone else was going down.

He remembered a woman, too. She was carrying a backpack and had been perhaps three floors behind the man. She did not avoid eye contact. In fact, if he wasn't mistaken, she might have smiled at him. No, not just smiled. Laughed. Like a small chuckle.

Since Drake had thought it was a drill, he didn't wonder too much about them at the time. He assumed they simply knew about the trial and the charges he was facing. But now that he was sure somebody was after his safe, they were at the top of his list of suspects.

He did a quick calculation about how long he had been gone. One way or another, he had to get back inside, he decided.

Drake approached the building again, this time from the side, where no firemen were present. There was one door here. Gray, with no peephole. Very utilitarian, he thought. It probably would have opened into a service hallway, except that the deadbolt was locked.

His access card could not get him past that, so he moved on.

As he circled around to the back, he wondered who might have told those two about the safe. There weren't a lot of people who knew about it. It had to be Alec, he reasoned. Was this revenge for torching his house?

He decided it had to be. Using a fake fire to clear the building would have been a good idea even if Drake had not recently burned down Alec's house, but this was straight-up symbolic. Alec was sending him a message, and it was going to cost him. If those two thieves got away with Drake's money, he wouldn't just go to Dahlonega to torture Alec's brother—he would go there to kill him, and he would do the same to Alec's parents in Miami.

There was no price high enough Alec could pay for something like that.

But his plan did not hold together more than a minute. As he was climbing up the stairs to a small loading dock used by residents moving in or out of the building, his phone rang. It was his lawyer.

"Did you burn down Mr. Garcia's house?" Patrick Erwing asked, as if the memory of that fire had invited the phone call.

Drake could tell from the tone of Patrick's voice he was angry. Even if he hadn't been, Drake knew better than to answer that question. Their relationship might be subject to attorney–client privilege, but he didn't think it was a good idea to confess to a crime, no matter who he was talking to.

Patrick apparently agreed, because as soon as he asked the question, he said, "Never mind. Don't tell me. But you're in a shit-ton of trouble. The police have revoked your bail. Dollars to doughnuts they'll be by the Pearlman soon looking for you."

Drake did not ask how Patrick knew that. The lawyer had people from all over the government sharing secrets with him—most likely for cash. It was an extension of his "liberal view of the law."

Drake cursed and hung up. There was nothing else to say. He wasn't going to sit around here and wait to be taken back to jail. It was finally time to run. The only problem with that was he had to get back to his condo first. He needed those bearer bonds. No matter how much money he had in the bank right now, he wasn't going to be able to withdraw enough to take him very far. And once the police found out he had fled, those accounts might well be frozen, meaning the little he got now might be all he would get.

He grabbed the handle of the nearest door and pulled. It didn't open, either.

Screw this.

Drake returned to the front of the building, determined to get inside no matter how the fire department felt about it. Turned out, that wasn't going to be a problem, since they were already letting residents back into the lobby. The problem, instead, was getting to the top floor. With a swarm of occupants crowded around the elevator, all trying to board, it could be a while until he got his turn, no matter how many residents he tried to push out of his way.

A handful of people—likely those who lived on the lowest floors—were taking the stairs back up instead. Although it was a long climb to the top, he wasted no time deciding that was his only realistic option.

CHAPTER 44

CONNOR NOTICED ONE side of the closet was closer to the door than the other. There could be logistical reasons for that, but Connor decided to trust his gut. He slammed the hammer into the drywall over and over until he had created a hole big enough to get his hands through. After that, he grabbed the drywall and began to pull. A large chunk tore away with relative ease.

It quickly became clear that there were more than a few inches of space behind this wall, and that there was no logistical reason to explain it. If anything, it appeared to be an extension of the master closet.

Connor leaned in through the hole and saw the safe on the floor.

The fire alarm stopped.

Connor knew they were running out of time, but now they had much less than he thought they had before. Residents would start coming back into the building any second. That would include Drake.

The only thing they had working for them now was that it would take a while for the one elevator to get everybody back up to their condos. Some people would choose to take the stairs, but Drake would not be one of them, which meant he'd probably get stuck in the lobby for some time. The climb had almost killed Connor. It wouldn't be any easier on him.

Working harder, faster, he shouted for Dylan, and she was at his side moments later, helping him pull down the sheetrock.

Once the front of the safe was exposed, Dylan ran into the living room and grabbed the backpack. She dropped it on the floor beside Connor, where chunks of sheetrock were piling up as he continued to clear away more of the wall.

Dylan removed a drill with a nine-inch bit attached. "Get out of the way!"

Connor stepped back. His ears were still ringing from the fire alarm. He figured Dylan's were, too, which might have been why she was shouting.

She placed the drill on the floor beside her, examined the safe to see if it was bolted to the ground, then dragged it partway out of its hidey-hole, grunting the whole time. The safe was a lot heavier than it looked. Even with Olin's help, she'd had to stop more than once when she'd brought a model like it into Connor's apartment.

Once she had enough space to squeeze behind the safe, she drilled a hole in the back of it. There was no reason to go after the lock itself, she had previously explained. This safe, like many, had a cobalt sheet protecting the wheel pack. Even with a diamond tip, the motor on the drill would wear out before she ever got through it. There was likewise no reason to try to go through the face beyond the perimeter of the cobalt sheet because this safe featured a sheet of glass within the face that would trigger a secondary locking mechanism if broken.

Dylan had found out the hard way that, once that happened, she would not be able to get the safe open no matter what she did. Hence, the method she was trying now was little more than theory.

Dylan had drilled a hole in the back of her test safe. She had also managed to snake a borescope through the hole and, using the attached viewer, find the locking mechanism she would need to look for when they found themselves confronted with the real thing. But since she had already triggered the secondary locking mechanism, also known as a relocker, she was not able to try her hand at finding the combination.

All she knew for sure was that it had to be four digits, and that she would have to alternate between turning the dial left and right as she moved through the combination.

"It will be fine," she had assured Connor. "All I have to do is line up the notches and the fence will fall into place. It's not that much different from picking any other lock, and this time I'll be able to see what I'm doing."

Connor had to admit that she certainly sounded like she knew what she was talking about, but since she hadn't done it before, he was still worried.

This was the moment of truth.

Dylan positioned the borescope so that she could see the locking mechanism on the small monitor and moved around to the front of the safe, where she could try her hand at the combination.

1:06 p.m.

She moved the dial slowly. On the borescope monitor, Connor could see several metal dials. Dylan stopped when a groove in the dial—which Connor assumed must be the notch she was referring to earlier—was lined up directly underneath a metal rod—which he also assumed must be the fence—and started turning in the other direction.

She repeated this process until the notches on all four dials were directly underneath the fence. She took a deep breath, looked at Connor. "Here we go."

Connor nodded. "Do it."

It was 1:08 p.m. If this didn't work, they were going to have to leave without the bearer bonds. They had already been here much longer than Connor expected they would.

Dylan pushed down the handle on the face of the safe. Perhaps to her surprise as well as Connor's, it moved.

She pulled the door open. "We did it!"

Inside, they found a disorganized stack of documents that was at least nine inches deep. There was no gold, no jewelry, no rare artwork, or other collectibles. Just the papers. Those on top were clearly the bearer bonds. Connor did not know if the safe contained other items, like a birth certificate or a deed to the condo, but they did not have the time to sort through the contents to figure that out. They were going to have to take it all.

He dragged the backpack closer and transferred the papers from safe to bag while Dylan packed up the borescope. She tossed it and the drill into the backpack as well.

Then Connor stood up and swung the backpack over his shoulders. "Let's get out of here."

They raced from the bedroom to the living room. Suddenly, the sound of a gunshot echoed like a cannon around the apartment and the sliding glass door at the rear of the unit shattered.

The apartment had two leather sofas, positioned in an L formation. Connor dove behind one, Dylan the other. A fraction of a second before he did, he had seen a man standing in the doorway to the condo. Connor had moved too fast to recognize who it was right away, but as he reconstructed the image in his mind, he realized there was only one person it could be: Drake Hartfield.

Connor was certain Drake had seen where they had gone. If he started firing into the furniture, he could easily kill them both. However, there was only a limited number of bullets in the gun he was carrying, and odds were he didn't have a spare magazine on him. If he did fire into the furniture, he might well spend them all without hitting either target.

In fact, Connor was pretty sure that was the only reason they were still alive.

Just as it wasn't in Drake's interest to fire into the sofas, it also wasn't in his interest to come charging into the room. He did not know whether either Connor or Dylan was armed, and he wouldn't be able to fire at one without turning his back on the other.

"I know what you're here for," he called. "Give me the bearer bonds, and I'll let you leave."

Connor doubted that was true. Drake wouldn't have come in shooting if he was willing to negotiate. But, he realized, the demand might give them the opportunity they needed to escape.

He took off the backpack.

Wide-eyed, Dylan shook her head.

Trust me, he mouthed.

He removed the bearer bonds and the drill, indicated what he intended to do next, and gestured for Dylan to ease her way toward the far end of the sofa.

Dylan nodded her understanding and began to move.

"Don't make me start shooting," Drake said.

Connor tossed the backpack over the sofa he was behind and moved to the end of it. Peeking under the sofa, he watched Drake's feet move slowly toward the backpack. As he did, he tucked the stack of documents under one arm.

Any second now.

Then he saw Drake's hand wrap around the backpack, and he tossed the drill across the room. It hit the wall and clattered as it fell to the floor.

Drake spun toward the noise and fired again.

As he did, Dylan ran up behind him, kicked him hard in the back.

Drake fell to the floor and, before he could regain his bearings, she also kicked the gun away.

"Now!" she shouted.

Connor raced out of the apartment behind her. He imagined Drake was already moving again, going for the gun, planning to kill them if he got the chance. But he knew better than to waste time looking back to find out if he was right. That would only slow him down.

CHAPTER 45

CONNOR SCRAMBLED DOWN the stairs behind Dylan. He had made it nearly seven stories before he was certain Drake wasn't going to try firing into the stairwell. Although that didn't mean he wasn't back there somewhere.

When they neared the bottom, they once again ran into residents going the opposite direction. They pushed their way through, but the congestion still slowed them down a lot more than Connor would have liked. At least he could take comfort in the knowledge that, if Drake was back there somewhere, he would be slowed down by the same crush of people.

At the ground floor, they took the emergency exit that led them from stairwell to street and ran at a full sprint back to the car, nearly trampling a man they hardly noticed in the process.

"I'll drive!" Dylan shouted. "Pass me the keys!"

Dylan ran around to the driver's side as Connor fished them out of his pocket. A quick double-tap on the unlock button and they were inside.

She started the car and threw the gearshift into reverse. Although a screen on the console had come to life, providing her with a view from the rear camera, she nonetheless spun in her seat so she could see the car parked behind her. Tapped the gas. The brake. And was just about to swerve out of the spot when Connor yelled, "Wait!"

"What?"

He pointed at the envelope that had been stuck under his windshield. "Get that before we lose it."

"Are you kidding? That's just junk—"

"It's from the kidnapper."

"Are you sure?"

He nodded. The envelope looked exactly like the other ones the kidnapper had left for him.

With a huff, Dylan opened the car door, swiped the envelope off the windshield, and tossed it to Connor. Then she slammed the door shut again and pulled out of the parking space as cars honked around her. She swerved through traffic, putting as much distance as she could between them and the Pearlman. As good as she was in situations like this, Connor still flinched when she cut between vehicles. Twice, he was certain that if she didn't slam into another car entirely, she was going to take off a mirror.

She never did.

Once they were half a mile away, Connor was starting to feel a little safer. Dylan was, too. He could tell from the way she was driving. Instead of speeding and swerving between cars, she was now blending into traffic, drawing less attention to the CR-V.

Connor had been so consumed with their escape (and so concerned Dylan was going to crash), he had almost forgotten about the thirty million dollars in bearer bonds sitting in his lap. Not to mention the letter from the kidnapper.

He had been surprised to see it tucked under his windshield wiper. Now he remembered the AirTag stuck to the bumper of his car and decided it made perfect sense. The kidnapper was keeping tabs on him. He had probably been nearby when Connor entered the Pearlman the last time, too.

"What's it say?" Dylan asked.

Connor opened the envelope and pulled out a note. "'*Take the money to 1343 Highgrove Avenue. Leave it on the living room floor.*'"

"Where?"

"That's the apartment he sent me to before."

"What about Jerry?"

Connor turned the note over to see if there was anything else on the back. "He doesn't say."

"We're not giving him the money unless he hands over Jerry."

"Agreed, but I think the apartment needs to be our next stop, regardless."

"Do we need to go by your apartment to get the key?"

Connor knew they did not. He was wearing the same jeans he'd had on yesterday, which meant the key should be in his right front pocket. He checked to make sure it was still there. It was. "No."

Dylan sped up again. "All right, let's go put this behind us once and for all."

CHAPTER 46

ALTHOUGH DYLAN WENT fast, she was not driving like a stunt double in a *Fast and Furious* movie. Connor no longer had to worry they might end up in an accident. He pulled his burner out of his pocket and called Olin.

"Hello?"

"Turn the cameras back on."

Connor did not have to explain what Olin needed to do to make that happen. The commands to type into the computer were written down on the same piece of paper as those Olin had used to turn the cameras off.

"Okay," Olin said.

"And I want you to meet us at the apartment you went to yesterday. Take the rental."

"He's already made contact?"

"He has."

"Okay," Olin said again.

"Get there as soon as you can." Connor hung up. The robbery was complete, but their plan was not. The kidnapper was not going to get away with this scot-free. Renting a car was part of making sure that happened.

Dylan had picked it up that morning, which she claimed was most of the reason she was late. Connor still thought she would have found a way to be late anyway, but thought it best not to tell her that.

After he hung up, he reached into the backseat and grabbed the briefcase Olin had used when he was working as an accountant, hauled it up into his lap, and shoved the nine inches of paper inside. As he did, something slipped out of the stack and tumbled onto the floor by his feet.

Connor locked the briefcase, returned it to the backseat to get it out of the way, and reached down to pick up the item he had dropped.

He had not even gotten his fingers on it by the time he realized it was a US passport. The name inside said it was issued to one Herbert Buckley. The man in the photo was Drake. If this money was intended to be some sort of escape fund, certainly this was the ID he intended to use to flee.

Since there was nothing Connor could do with this information right now, he shoved the passport into the glove box.

The kidnapper's apartment was closer to Connor's building than to the Pearlman. Olin was already there by the time they arrived. He had backed the rented blue Nissan Sentra into a parking space behind the building. When Connor and Dylan pulled into the lot, he climbed out.

The three friends met halfway between the two vehicles.

Connor had a death grip on Olin's briefcase. "Probably best if I go in alone," he said.

"Are you sure?" Olin asked.

Connor nodded. So far, the kidnapper had not wanted to deal with anyone else. At this late stage, there was no reason to assume that would have changed. "I'll call you if I need you. In the meantime, just keep your eyes open for anything unusual."

Olin and Dylan climbed into the Nissan Sentra. If the kidnapper entered the lot, he would almost certainly look for Connor's CR-V, but the Nissan would be no more significant than any other car here. They would have plenty of time to duck out of sight.

Although there was a door that led directly into the building from the parking lot, Connor entered the same way he had last time. He didn't like being here with thirty million in bearer bonds. He certainly wasn't going to take the risk that the door facing the parking lot might lead him into a rarely used part of the building where a couple of ill-intentioned strangers might be loitering. As it was, he barely considered the main hallways safe enough to use.

Connor hurried from the front door to the stairwell at the opposite end of the hall. He once again noticed the graffiti covering the walls; the mold creeping along the ceiling and the floorboards. The eviction notices taped to doors—only now, there seemed to be more of them.

When he took the stairs, he remembered how the handrail rattled the last time he grabbed hold of it. *A good tug and it might come straight out of the wall*, he had thought. He did not bother to grab it again.

Although Connor did not remember the apartment number, he recognized the unit by the eviction notice taped to the door opposite and the paint peeling around the frame. He reached for the key in his pocket, slid it into the lock, and turned. Then, shielding his body with the wall, he swung the door open. If the kidnapper responded with gunfire, intending to kill Connor, at least the wall would provide him some protection.

But that did not happen.

Still, Connor stayed where he was for a good minute before daring a glance into the apartment. It was not quite as empty as it was when Olin had visited. Apparently, the camera was back. No cell phone this time, though. Instead, he saw an envelope sitting on the floor. It did not have his name on it, but it was nonetheless clearly intended for him.

He stepped into the apartment, placed the briefcase on the floor, and picked up the envelope. From the feel of it, he could tell that it did not contain a key or any other item that would weigh it down.

Connor removed the single sheet of paper inside and let the envelope fall to the floor. Like all of the other notes the kidnapper had left, the message was brief.

The boy is in Greenwood Park. You have ten minutes to get there if you want to see him alive. Leave the money.

Connor knew the park. Getting there in ten minutes would be nearly impossible.

He glanced at the camera. The little red light on it suggested the kidnapper was watching. He thought about pleading for more time. Although he would not be able to hear the kidnapper, he suspected the kidnapper could hear him. Then he realized there was no point. The kidnapper had given Connor only ten minutes for a reason: he did not want Connor hanging around the apartment after he had delivered the money.

As soon as Connor put those pieces together, he raced out of the apartment, down the stairs, out the front door, and around to the parking lot in back.

Dylan saw him coming and opened her door to get out. Olin followed suit.

"We have to get to Greenwood Park," Connor shouted as he came to a stop only feet from the Nissan's grill. "That's where the kidnapper has Lucy's son. The kidnapper said if we're not there in ten minutes . . ." He did not want to stop talking, but he was out of breath.

"Slow down," Dylan said. "We knew something like this could happen. We talked about it."

That was not exactly right. They had discussed an exchange. They had assumed they would get Jerry when Connor handed over the bearer bonds. After they got him, the plan was for Olin to drive the boy home while Connor and Dylan staked out the apartment to wait for the kidnapper.

He would be monitoring Connor's car using the AirTag stuck to the bumper, but there would be no way he could know about the vehicle Dylan had rented. Nor would he have any reason to assume she had rented one. Most people would do exactly what Connor had almost done when they found the AirTag—rip it off the bumper. So long as it was still broadcasting, the kidnapper would believe he still had the upper hand in this exchange.

Then Connor realized Dylan was right in the only way that mattered. They did plan to split up. They might not be taking Jerry directly from the apartment, but that did not mean their whole plan had to fall apart.

Dylan held out her hand. "Give me your keys. I'll go get Jerry."

"Shouldn't that be my job?" Olin said.

"I'm a faster driver." She turned her attention back to Connor. "Now give me the keys."

Connor didn't care who stayed with him. He just wanted to make sure the odds remained in their favor. If he had to go up against the kidnapper in a fight of any sort, he wanted somebody to have his back. God knows what might have happened if he had been alone in Drake's condo when Drake returned.

He handed his keys to Dylan. Then she took off without another word and he turned his attention back to Olin. "You know she'll get there faster than either of us would."

CHAPTER 47

CONNOR AND OLIN climbed into the rental car to wait for the kidnapper.

Once they were inside with the doors locked, Connor dialed Dylan's burner from his own, put the call on speaker, and placed the cell phone on the dashboard. If anything happened on either end of the line, they needed to be ready to react as a group. With Jerry's life on the line and the kidnapper coming for the bearer bonds at any moment, seconds lost could be disastrous.

Dylan answered on the second ring.

Connor listened to the engine roar as she navigated the traffic around her. He imagined her slipping between cars with even more daring than she had when he was on board and worried whether his CR-V would survive the trip.

Suddenly, he saw a car turning into the parking lot and all thoughts about his CR-V evaporated. It was some sort of old, boxy Ford. That much he was sure of by the emblem on the grill. The model, however, remained a mystery. Not that he cared at that moment.

"Duck," he said, sliding so far down into the seat that he could no longer see over the dashboard.

Olin did as instructed. "You think that's him?"

With his back almost entirely flat against the seat, Connor shrugged as well as he could. "I guess we'll find out."

Connor waited a little while longer, then pushed himself up enough so that he could see the door that led from the parking lot to the building. There was a man heading toward it. He was thin, lanky, wearing a green tee-shirt and blue jeans. With his hands in his pockets, he looked left and right repeatedly.

He was clearly nervous about something, but whether this was the kidnapper, Connor couldn't say. If it was, he had ditched the beard, the sunglasses, and the cap, thus becoming unrecognizable.

"So?" Olin asked.

"I don't know. Let's see if he comes back with the briefcase."

He pulled his own cell phone out of another pocket and turned it on. While he had not wanted it broadcasting his location when he was at the Pearlman, he couldn't see any harm in it pinging a tower here.

Once the phone came to life, he clicked an app called "Find My" and selected the AirTag they had hidden inside one of the pockets of the briefcase. Dylan had suggested they use a tracker to find the money after they made the exchange with the kidnapper, but until Connor had seen the AirTag attached to his bumper, he wasn't sure what sort of tracker he was going to use.

The AirTag was an obvious solution, and a little bit of poetic justice.

"How are you doing over there, Dylan?" he asked.

"How do you think?"

"How close are you?"

"Five minutes. Maybe less."

Connor looked at the time on his phone. Dylan had left six minutes ago. It had taken perhaps a minute to get out of the building. But if the man who had stepped inside was the kidnapper, then that meant Jerry was at Greenwood Park alone.

Although the kidnapper had proven he could detonate a bomb

remotely, Connor doubted he would leave the boy alone with any such device strapped to him. Something like that would certainly draw attention. It was the middle of the day, after all.

Actually, any condition the kidnapper had left Jerry in would have drawn attention, wouldn't it? It's not like people would ignore a child bound with rope any more than they would ignore one with a bomb strapped to his chest.

Was this whole thing a trick?

Connor could feel the muscles in his neck begin to tighten. He hoped Jerry was not already dead, dumped in a river, or buried deep in the woods.

"Let me know as soon as you get there."

"Duh."

Connor looked back at the map on his phone. The AirTag did not seem to have moved, but he also doubted the device would register any change in location that occurred within the building.

Suddenly, the door that led from the parking lot to the building opened and the man in the green tee shirt stepped out. This time, he was indeed carrying the briefcase Connor had left.

They had finally found their kidnapper.

As Connor and Olin slid back down in their seats, Connor exchanged the Find My app for his camera and did his best to take a picture of the man without drawing attention. He showed it to Olin. "In case he gets away."

Olin did not ask what they would do with the picture if they needed it, and the truth was, Connor didn't know. They couldn't show it to Detective Pierce without explaining how they got it, and if they did not find the man among Lucy's social media contacts, the picture would probably be useless. It certainly wasn't clear enough for a reverse image search online.

But there was no guarantee the kidnapper would not ditch the briefcase somewhere, so they had to take every opportunity they could to make sure he didn't disappear into the wind.

Connor moved his burner from the dashboard to one of the cup holders, speaker up, so it wouldn't slide off, then followed him out of the parking lot, making sure to put plenty of distance between the two cars. He didn't want to take the risk that the kidnapper might see him. On the neighborhood streets immediately around the building, that meant depending a lot on the AirTag. Once they reached Carole Drive, though, Connor was able to use the three lanes of heavy traffic going in each direction to hide in plain sight.

Eleven minutes had passed since Connor had exited the building. Dylan still had yet to say she was at the park.

"Tell me you're close," he said into the burner.

"Pulling up now," she replied.

Greenwood Park was not very big. In fact, it was little more than a play area for children with several surrounding benches. If there had been an explosion, Dylan would already know about it.

Connor changed lanes, shifting his position relative to the kidnapper's vehicle, which he hoped would make him harder to spot. Then he directed his attention back to the phone. "Do you see him?"

Dylan did not answer for several seconds. Connor heard a car door open and then close.

"I see him!" she finally said. "I see him!" She shouted the boy's name.

Connor could tell she had broken into a run.

"Is he okay?" Olin asked.

"Yes, he's fine. He's just sitting here on a bench. He's okay."

Connor sighed with relief. The tension in his neck subsided a little.

"Hey, hey, hey," Dylan said, her voice some distance from the phone. "Everything's all right. Don't cry." Then, to Connor: "I'm going to take him home. Make sure you don't lose that son of a bitch."

CHAPTER 48

CONNOR HAD NO intention of losing the kidnapper. They may have gotten the boy back, but their job wasn't done until they had the bearer bonds, too. This—as Dylan had put it—*son of a bitch* was not getting away with the money. Connor was not going to let him turn them into accomplices in his crime.

He followed the old Ford to an apartment building half an hour away. From the outside, this building seemed only marginally better than the one they had just left. It was, he noted, surprisingly close to Lucy's house.

Could this man be an acquaintance? Maybe even a friend? Somebody who knew Lucy worked for Connor and had set out to leverage that relationship?

Maybe that would make sense if this was an ordinary kidnapping, but it didn't fit here, since the kidnapper would also have had to know about the bearer bonds, and that seemed like too many coincidences.

Connor wished once again he had his gun with him. Whatever he was about to face in that building would be easier to handle if he was armed. This time, though, he said it aloud, and when he did, Olin replied, "I brought it."

"What?"

Olin opened the glove box. "Yeah. Right here. I understand why you didn't want to take it into the Pearlman, but I thought it might be handy to have afterward, so I brought it."

Connor almost smiled. He reached over and grabbed the Glock. "Let's go get that money back."

Olin did not have a gun of his own, but he had a brute strength and a willingness to use it that Connor did not. So long as it was two against one in there, they should be just fine.

Olin nodded and followed Connor to the main entrance.

Connor, who was still holding the gun in his right hand, grabbed the handle on the door with his left and pulled.

Now that they were inside, he realized the differences between this building and the one they had just been at were greater than they first appeared. Here, there was no graffiti covering the walls, no eviction notices taped to doors, no mold creeping along the ceiling or baseboards.

Olin looked down the long hallway. "Now what?"

Connor's first instinct was to suggest they start knocking, but that plan came with problems he wasn't sure how to handle. Most notably, the fact that the kidnapper might simply decline to answer, in which case, they would have no way of knowing whether he was there or not.

Connor did have one more card he could play, though. The same AirTag he had used to follow the kidnapper here could take him to the precise location of the device once it was within range of the phone's Bluetooth. That was about thirty feet.

He explained the idea to Olin.

Olin nodded. "Okay. Let's do it."

Since Connor would need both hands to fire his gun, he unlocked his phone, pulled up the Find My app again, and passed the device to Olin.

As they moved down the hall, they paused briefly in front of each apartment. The phone did not find the AirTag on the first floor, so they went up to the second, where they planned to repeat the process.

They were barely out of the stairwell when the DIRECTIONS button on the app switched to FIND, indicating the AirTag was now within range of the iPhone's Bluetooth.

Olin held up a hand as he stopped moving, and Connor got the message. Then Olin tapped the digital FIND button. The screen faded to black and little white dots swirled around it as the two devices connected. Once they did, the dots then transformed into an arrow pointing them toward an apartment on Connor's left. The screen also advised them that the AirTag was eighteen feet away.

They followed the arrow to the door and the iPhone now reported the AirTag was only six feet away.

"All we have to do is get inside and grab the briefcase," Connor whispered.

"Yeah, but how are we going to get inside?"

Connor had thought about that. They could try turning the knob to see if the door was unlocked, but if the knob squeaked or the kidnapper happened to be looking, he would know someone was there. If he didn't suspect it was Connor, he would certainly suspect it was the police. Either way, they would lose the element of surprise.

Their only choice was to go in fast, loud. And the only way to do that was to go in shooting.

Connor knew Olin wouldn't like that plan, which was why he did not bother to explain it before dropping to one knee and firing at the lock. He pulled the trigger three times in rapid succession with the barrel aimed up toward the ceiling to minimize the odds he would hit anybody inside.

Olin jumped back. "*Are you fucking crazy?*"

Back on his feet, Connor kicked the door open and charged into the apartment, the gun now held out in front of him. Since Connor and Olin were now technically accomplices in the kidnapper's crime, this confrontation would not end the way similar confrontations had ended in the past. There would be no call to the police. There would be no sending the bad guy to jail. Not today, anyway. Since they now had a picture of the kidnapper and an address, they might find a way to build a case against him in the future that did not also ensnare Connor and his friends. For the moment, though, Connor just wanted to get out of the building with the bearer bonds in hand.

At least that would be justice of some sort, he figured.

As the door rebounded off the wall, the kidnapper hopped up from a table deeper in the apartment. He looked toward Connor, surprised and ready to run.

"Stay where you are!" Connor shouted, aiming the gun at him. "Stay right where you are." He was not sure he could pull the trigger if it came to it, but that was not the reason he had bought the gun in the first place. He had bought it for the same reason he was using it now: to intimidate.

The briefcase was on the floor to Connor's right. Easy enough to grab—if it weren't already open and empty.

Connor looked back at the table where the man had been sitting. He now realized the bearer bonds were stacked up on top of it in two piles, one face up, the other face down.

The kidnapper had been counting his haul.

Then he realized something else, something he should have realized when he took the man's picture. This was the same person he had nearly trampled when exiting the Pearlman with Dylan. Perhaps only moments from leaving the note on Connor's car.

Connor wasn't surprised he had not made the connection earlier.

The picture was fuzzy, and he had other things on his mind—like Jerry's wellbeing.

Besides, now that he had made that connection, what did it matter? There wasn't anything he could do with that information.

"Back away from the table," he said.

The kidnapper raised his hands and did as instructed. He looked like he would kill Connor if he got the chance.

"Olin!"

Olin was still standing in the hall with his mouth hanging open. Although he had brought Connor the gun, he had not yet recovered from the sight of Connor firing into the door.

"Olin!" Connor said again. "Get the bearer bonds."

Finally, Olin started to move.

When Connor turned his attention back to the kidnapper, he realized the man had taken several steps away from the table. But he wasn't trying to run like Connor had first thought. He was moving toward the coffee table, where he had a Glock of his own.

"Hey! I said stay where you are!"

The man once again froze, hands raised in the air.

"I swear, if you make one more step toward that gun . . ."

Olin scurried around Connor and grabbed the bearer bonds. On his way back, he also grabbed the briefcase. He did not, however, make it out of the apartment like Connor had expected. Instead, as he straightened, with the bearer bonds tucked under one arm and the briefcase in his opposite hand, Connor heard another voice, this one a woman's.

"If you shoot him, I'll shoot Olin. Drop the bearer bonds and get out of here."

Connor knew who it was without turning to look, but he did anyway. "Lucy?"

She also had a gun. Hers was aimed directly at Olin and, unlike Connor's, was only inches from her target's back.

Connor kept his weapon aimed at the kidnapper but stepped deeper into the kitchen, which was adjacent to the front door, so that he could keep both him and Lucy in his sights. Then, aiming the weapon over the bar that divided the kitchen from the living room, he asked Lucy, "What the hell's going on?"

He did not have to wait for her to answer before the pieces started falling into place. If Lucy was here, she had to be in on the crime.

"It's not as bad as it seems," Lucy said.

The kidnapper looked from Connor to Lucy. "What are you doing?"

It was the first time Connor had heard the kidnapper speak. He realized he was right when he had assumed the man was using a digital synthesizer to disguise his voice. Which meant he was also probably right when he had assumed the beard was fake. This man had gone to great lengths to disguise his identity.

Since Lucy was here, Connor knew he hadn't done that just because of the money. He was close to the family, which might have made him easy for the police to find if he himself had not. And when Lucy spoke again, Connor found out just how close.

"Jerry wasn't in any danger," Lucy said. "He was with Antonio the whole time."

"Lucy!" the kidnapper shouted.

Connor had heard Lucy talk about Antonio before. He was her husband. The man who had drifted from one sales job to the next. The man who could no longer handle the stress of raising a child.

The man who had been inching his way toward the gun on the coffee table.

"We just needed a little money," Lucy continued. "That's why Antonio left. We just needed to take some of the stress off the family."

"Lucy! Shut the fuck up!"

"You understand. You have to understand. I mean, you guys don't always do what you're supposed to." She glanced at the stack of bearer bonds to make her point. "But you always do what you do for the right reason. That's all we were doing here. We just wanted to be a family. What can be more right than that?"

Antonio clenched his fists and shook them violently but didn't dare move with Connor's gun pointed at him. "Goddammit!"

Connor thought about how she'd sought them out, how she'd made a point of getting the job as their secretary. He remembered what she had said when he asked her why she wanted the job: *That's easy. I like what you do. I like how you do it.*

She had been planning this from the beginning. She must have been.

Connor's gaze cut briefly to Olin. Lucy still had her gun pressed to his back. Despite the stress that had caused beads of sweat to pop up on his forehead and transform his expression into something Connor hardly recognized, he could tell Olin had drawn the same conclusion.

"Just let us go, okay?" Lucy said. "Nobody got hurt. Nobody needs to know about this."

"Somebody could have."

"You mean the bomb at the warehouse? That was just meant to scare you. We had to get you to the point where you would be willing to do what we needed you to do."

"Lucy, you have to shut up! What the fuck's the matter with you? Just pull the damn trigger and let's get the hell out of here!"

At that moment, Connor realized two important things.

The first was Lucy did not want to be on the run. Olin was standing directly in front of her with the bearer bonds under one arm; it would be easy for her to grab them and disappear. Connor obviously wasn't going to fire at her with Olin in the way. That probably had something to do with Jerry.

The second was that Antonio would kill them if he got the chance.

"Come on, Connor," Lucy said. "I know how you operate. Drake was a thief. He's killed people. You can't be upset about stealing from a guy like that."

Connor was already aware of both of those things, and they didn't change his calculation. Now that he knew the truth, he could no longer say the crime had been for the greater good. However, he wasn't ready to make such a declaration yet. Although Lucy might not want to find herself on the run, she certainly did not want to go to jail. If she felt cornered, she might make her own calculation about the lesser of two evils, and it might not tilt in Connor's favor.

He needed to get the upper hand.

He also wanted to find out how she knew about Drake. Not just the safe, either. The murders, too. That hadn't been published anywhere Connor had seen. If it was true, it only further emphasized the point that she and her husband must have inside information.

"How do you know all this about Drake?"

"Antonio—"

"Goddammit, Lucy!" Antonio lunged for the gun on the coffee table. Whatever Lucy was about to say, it seemed like it was going to be one step more than Antonio was comfortable with. He got off two shots before Connor could convince himself to pull the trigger. The first was aimed at Connor and missed. The second was aimed at Olin.

Connor might not have been able to fire when Antonio started to move, but he sure as hell wasn't going to let Antonio shoot his friend.

As Antonio fired the second shot, Connor fired one back.

Two bodies went down.

Neither one of them was Olin.

In the second or two it took for the situation to get out of control, it had also ended. Antonio was on the floor, lifeless. The bullet had landed center mass. *Straight into the heart*, Connor would later think.

On the other side of the room, Lucy was also on the ground, both hands to her throat as she choked up blood.

"Call an ambulance!" Connor shouted, dropping to his knees to see if there was anything he could do to help her.

Olin fumbled with his phone as he pulled it out of his pocket, dialed 911, and did his best to keep his voice from shaking as he asked for help.

Connor could tell Lucy wasn't going to make it. The bullet had torn through her carotid artery. Unless the paramedics were standing right outside, she'd be dead long before they got here.

Still, he stayed with her until she passed.

CHAPTER 49

WHEN FRIDAY ROLLED around, Connor took Rebecca to an Italian restaurant that was well out of his budget and told her the parts of that story he felt like he could.

In the longer version Pierce had heard, the kidnapper had called back demanding a ransom. Lucy had said she didn't want to get the police involved because she didn't want something else to go wrong, but she also didn't have the money to pay him. Olin, however, did. He had inherited a small fortune when his parents passed away. Apparently, he had been the target the whole time.

Connor secretly put an AirTag in the briefcase they used to deliver the money and followed it to Antonio's apartment. They had no idea that Lucy was involved until she put a gun to Olin's back. Then the shootout ensued, exactly as it had happened.

The police, of course, never located any money in the apartment, and Connor's only response was to say he had no idea what had happened to it. It wasn't like he'd had eyes on Antonio the whole time. Maybe the man had hidden it somewhere. (In reality, while he had been on the phone with the detective, he'd had Olin take the bearer bonds down to the car with the intention of anonymously sending them and the passport they had found to the police at a later time. Although Connor wasn't sure the DA's office would be able to use the former in their trial against Drake, he was certain they could use the latter.)

That theory turned out to be more plausible than Connor had first thought. In the days between the standoff and Connor's dinner with Rebecca, he had learned from one of Dylan's trips into the dark web that Antonio was Alec Garcia's brother—a fact that might have been obvious if Lucy hadn't kept her maiden name. And if anybody knew how to hide money, Alec did.

He also learned from Pierce that the police had found a small remote trigger in Lucy's purse that they believed had been used to detonate the bomb at the warehouse. Until that moment, Connor did not know how Antonio had managed to time the explosion with such precision. Now it made sense. Lucy was, after all, watching him from across the street.

She had probably put the AirTags on their cars, too, Connor figured.

Gretchen, who did not seem to know about Antonio's relationship to Alec or what her daughter was involved in, was devastated. Not only was her daughter dead, but Gretchen's memory of Lucy would be forever tarnished by that last selfish act.

She was, however, able to fill in more details about her daughter's life and the decisions that led up to the crime.

According to Gretchen, Lucy and Antonio had moved from Dahlonega to Atlanta several years earlier in search of new job opportunities. However, that had not panned out like they hoped it would. Lucy borrowed money from her mom to put a deposit down on the house she was living in only days earlier, thinking it would provide the bedrock they needed to build more prosperous lives. However, all it did was put additional pressure on Antonio, which quickly grew into more than he could handle.

As Lucy had indicated, this crime—almost certainly conceived of by

Alec—was intended to be their way out of that mess.

Connor would never know why Alec had turned on Drake. Maybe it was simply because he knew Drake would turn on him after he made a deal with the prosecution.

Regardless, Connor's crime had put Drake back in jail faster than he might have been otherwise. Apparently, when residents in the Pearlman heard Drake firing at Connor and Dylan, they'd called the police. Although the police were likely already on their way, since Drake's bail had been revoked, the gunshots brought them there faster.

Naturally, all the news said about it was that Drake had been arrested outside of the Pearlman.

It turned out Drake wasn't the only one to go to jail, either.

Connor felt like they had gone as far as they could with Reid's case. Especially since, even after digging around on the dark web, Dylan had not been able to find out for sure whether Alissa had been to Colombia. So, with Olin and Dylan at his side, Connor reported their finding to her brother. Alissa was involved in money laundering, almost certainly, he told Reid. Possibly drugs, as well.

After Connor delivered the news, he asked what Reid was going to do.

"I don't know," Reid said.

Friday morning, though, Connor found out. The same news feed that let him know about Drake's arrest had let him know about Alissa's. Whether she would go to jail was anyone's guess at that point, but at least she was going to trial.

And after Connor returned with Rebecca to the apartment building, he finally got that kiss he was after.

JOIN THE READERS CLUB TO FIND OUT WHEN THE NEXT BOOK IS AVAILABLE

PLUS GET AN EXCLUSIVE COPY OF *THE LAYOVER*

Connor Callahan is back in this exclusive novella that takes place three years after his parents were abducted and prior to his first case in Atlanta. When he sees a man discreetly tag a stranger's suitcase with a black magic marker, he sets out to discover what is going on. It's a decision that will thrust Connor into a conflict far more dangerous than he could have imagined, and when it's over he will know one thing for sure: You're not always safer on the ground.

When you join my readers club, you will immediately get a free and exclusive copy of *The Layover*, not available elsewhere.

I usually e-mail once or twice a month with things I think you'll find interesting, such as behind-the-scenes stories, new releases, and fan discounts. Of course, you can unsubscribe at any time.

Join the readers club by signing up at

read.reagankeeter.com

AFTERWORD

Dear Reader,

Thank you for purchasing this book. I hope you enjoyed reading it as much as I enjoyed writing it. There are a whole bunch of other great Connor Callahan thrillers out there and more on the way. I encourage you to catch up on them all, if you haven't already. You can also get an exclusive Connor Callahan novella when you join the readers club. Just go to my website or keep reading for more information.

If you liked the book, I would also appreciate it if you took a moment to leave a review and tell your friends. Help me spread the word! You can also follow me on all the major platforms. Just pick the one you like the most.

Thanks for taking this journey with me, and if you're looking for more thrillers to read, check out my standalones, as well.

I look forward to many more years of reading together!

Best wishes,
Reagan

What's coming next from Reagan Keeter?

Join the readers club to find out about upcoming titles, special offers, and giveaways. You will also get to take advantage of all kinds of other goodies, like the exclusive Connor Callahan novella, *The Layover*, you will receive as soon as you sign up.

Go to read.reagankeeter.com to join the club.

Follow Reagan Keeter on BookBub

Connect with Reagan online:

Facebook
Twitter
Goodreads
reagankeeter.com
reagan@reagankeeter.com

THE REDWOOD CON

EXCERPT

For a special sneak peek of Reagan Keeter's standalone suspense thriller *The Redwood Con*, just turn the page.

Elise Whitman

ELISE CHARGED INTO HER apartment, trying not to think about what she had done tonight. Her Pomeranian followed her to the window, jumping on her leg, yapping to get her attention. She patted the dog on the head. "Not now, Chloe." Then she pulled her phone out of her purse to see if she had a message from Liam. She didn't. She cursed herself for not waiting to hear from him before calling the others and sent a text.

I need to see you.

Gripping her phone in one hand, she crossed her arms over her chest and waited.

Elise had only lived in this apartment for three months. It was small, hastily decorated. The quasi-retro furniture from Value Interiors wasn't her. Still, she'd come to like the place a lot. Part of it was because, at twenty-eight, it was the first apartment she'd ever had in her name. The other part was the location.

From the window, Elise could see the quiet, tree-lined street that ran in front of her building. The old three and four-story condominium buildings lining most of it were charming. The neighbors were friendly, and she could walk to a grocery store and a coffee shop.

She hoped that after tonight she wouldn't have to leave. She hoped that by being honest with Liam her life would become something new and better than it was now. But if he didn't take the news well, she knew she'd have no choice. She'd pack up the things she could as soon as everyone was gone and disappear.

She looked at her phone again. Still no response. It had only been a minute, but she didn't have time to wait, so she sent two more messages, back to back.

I'm serious.

I need you to come over right now.

Then Elise got a bottle of Smirnoff from the kitchen to calm her nerves. She didn't have any glasses, so she filled a mug to the brim, took one big gulp. She placed the mug on the coffee table and paced the room, rehearsing what she was going to say. She'd only get one shot at this. She'd better make it count.

And, of course, she looked at her phone again.

Come on, seriously?

What was taking so long?

She sent another text to Liam: *Why don't you answer me?*

Finally, she got a response: *I'm on my way. We need to talk.*

Although Elise could tell she'd gotten under his skin, she didn't care. What mattered was he was coming over. After tonight, the last thing he'd be thinking about was those messages.

She returned to the window. If she craned her neck, she could almost see the entrance to her building. She thought it would be a good idea to keep a lookout, know who showed up first. But her mind wandered, back to what she would say and how she would say it—"Liam, you're in danger"—and when someone knocked on the door, sending Chloe into a tizzy, she had no idea who it was. Since she was expecting company, she didn't bother to check the peephole. She just tossed her phone onto the coffee table and turned the deadbolt.

Liam Parker

LIAM SAT AT THE lone poker table in Midwest Design's private room. The space was small but elegant, with polished hardwood floors and walls made of smooth brown tile. A combination of inset lighting and modern, ornate sconces cast the space in a warm glow. The only way in or out was through a door that opened onto the company's darkened public spaces.

At this hour, there were very few people in the building. The doors to the street were locked. A lone security guard manned the lobby nine floors below.

The night had started with six players. The two who remained at the table with Liam were Emily Stewart, a regular, and a new guy he had taken to calling "the Grunter." Their dealer, according to the nametag pinned to his tuxedo vest, was Jacob.

Emily had stately features and short, black hair plastered to her head with large quantities of gel. Having already folded, she could do nothing with the jack that appeared on the river but scowl at it. Liam wasn't sure if that look meant the card would've helped her or hurt her—his guess was the former—although it didn't matter either way. Once you're out, you're out.

Now he had to convince the Grunter to do the same. With a pair of twos, bluffing his way through this hand was about the only way to win it.

Liam doubled down on his bet.

The Grunter rolled his shoulders around in his tailored sports coat. He looked from his cards to those on the table and back. He shifted a toothpick from one side of his mouth to the other. Then, as Liam had come to expect, he grunted.

"All right," Jacob said, "play it or fold it. Make a move." Jacob was smiling and Liam could hear it in his voice. He didn't intend to aggravate the Grunter, he was just gregarious. He'd introduce himself to every new player, welcome back every old one, ask about their work, their family, and their pets.

Still, aggravate the Grunter he did.

"Shut up." The Grunter looked at Liam and Liam winked, trying to unnerve him. It almost worked too. The Grunter closed his cards into one hand, tapped them on the table like he did when he was about to fold, and hesitated. The corners of his lips curled down and his nose wrinkled up as if he smelled something rotten. "No," the Grunter mumbled. He scooped up a stack of chips and threw them into the pile. "You got shit."

Liam didn't know what to say. The Grunter was right. Still, he felt like he needed to say something. But his phone vibrated in his pocket, distracting him. He pulled it out, saw a text from Elise: *I need to see you.*

Before he could settle on his next move, two more texts came in rapid succession.

I'm serious.

I need you to come over right now.

He ground his teeth together. *Fine.* Elise wasn't going to give up until she got what she wanted, and the Grunter wasn't going to fold. Sometimes the closest you can get to a win is to quit. He placed his cards face down on the table and got to his feet.

"You're out?" the Grunter asked.

"I am."

The Grunter threw one fist into the air and laughing with a sort of hee-haw chuckle. "Boom!" He tossed his cards onto the pile of chips—a four of hearts and an eight of spades. "I don't know what you had, but it couldn't have been worse than that."

He was right. It wasn't. A pair of twos would've beaten him. *But,* Liam thought again, *once you're out, you're out.* So, as Emily groaned and the Grunter gleefully stacked up his chips, he did his best to smile and walked away from the table.

He cashed out and said goodbye to Ava Perez, the owner of Midwest Design. She nodded to one of the two men standing guard by the door and the man opened it. Liam navigated his way around the tables where designers and clients would huddle during the day, looking at photos, fabrics swatches, and sketches, and took the elevator to the underground garage.

He trekked the thirty feet through the cold to his Tesla, got in, and started the engine. Before he could put the car into drive, his phone vibrated again. Elise, no doubt. He took the phone out of his pocket and read the message.

Why don't you answer me?

He typed: *I'm on my way. This isn't working. We need to talk.*

Before hitting SEND, though, he thought about the morning they'd spent down at the lake, sitting on the beach and watching a sailboat ease its way across the dark horizon. They were on the tail end of their first date. Dinner at Alinea had turned into drinks at Eno, which had, through a series of events long since lost to the bottle, turned into quiet conversation near the water.

They'd learned a lot about each other that night; they'd both grown up in Oak Park and in households they would be hard-pressed to call middle class, their moms went to church and their dads liked fishing, they both worked in advertising, both liked '70s rock, and neither one of them cared that discussing politics was taboo.

He deleted the line "This isn't working." Elise might interpret that to mean he planned on breaking up with her, which wasn't the case. Elise was something special. But they did need to talk. She had to start giving him some space.

Liam traded his parking spot in the garage for one on the street near Elise's building. The midrise had a fob-activated security door but, unlike his building, no concierge, and most people paid the security protocol little mind. So it was no surprise when a young woman on her way out held the door for him.

The elevator rose to the fourth floor in fits and starts, then opened onto a long, narrow hallway that forked at each end. The paint was fresh, but the lights along the ceiling bathed the walls in a grayish-yellow that could make you think otherwise. From the look of it, the carpet hadn't received the same care. Worn thin, Liam suspected it had seen a decade's worth of traffic since it had last been replaced.

He headed down the hall to Elise's apartment, Unit 423, and knocked. Per usual, Chloe started to bark. The Pomeranian wouldn't quiet down until Elise opened the door and the dog got to sniff his shoes. Only thing was, she didn't open the door.

After thirty seconds or so, Liam knocked again. "Elise! Open up. It's Liam."

When that didn't work, he tried to call, waited an impossibly long time for her voicemail to answer, and didn't bother to leave a message.

Something was wrong. Even if Elise was mad, she'd at least open the door to tell him.

He turned the doorknob, not expecting much, and the door glided away from the frame. Chloe trotted into the hall, gave his loafers a sniff, then started panting.

Stepping deeper into the apartment, the Pomeranian at his side, Liam grew increasingly uneasy. "Elise?"

The apartment wasn't much bigger than the one he'd been in when he'd married his ex-wife. Liam could see most of it by merely rotating his head ninety degrees. The floors were an oak-strip laminate and the walls were the same color as those in the hall.

Elise was good about keeping things where they belonged and refrained from cluttering the space with things she didn't need. Liam would have been able to tell right away if anything were amiss.

The bathroom door was closed and, less than a minute later, it was the last room to check. Liam knocked, listened, heard only the sound of running water. As he stood there, he remembered Elise telling him once she didn't leave her front door unlocked. There were bad people out there, she'd said. "You never know what could happen."

Screw this. Liam flung the bathroom door open. He thought he was ready for whatever he might find on the other side.

He wasn't.

Liam Parker

ELISE WAS LYING IN the bathtub. Her thin face was slack, eyes closed, mouth open. Her head hung to one side, resting against the tiles running from tub to ceiling. The mascara around her left eye was smeared down to her cheek. The faucets were on, the water spilling onto the floor and red from her blood.

It took only two steps for Liam to cross from the door to the tub. He was muttering, asking for help, from God, from anyone. He reached into the water, scooping his hands under her armpits so he could drag her out. Liam didn't care that her blood was soaking into his clothes. He didn't even notice. He shouted her name, hoping she'd react, maybe say something or open her eyes or give him some sign she was still alive. Because she could be. The water was warm. She was warm. Maybe it wasn't too late.

He lifted, twisted, fought against her weight and the water. Her clothes, black slacks and blouse, clung to her body. She slipped out of his grip and back into the tub with a splash.

That was when he saw the cuts to her wrists. Telltale signs of a suicide.

It didn't make sense. Elise wasn't suicidal. But there was no time to think about that now. He needed to call 911. He should have called them as soon as he'd found the body, but he wasn't thinking clearly.

Liam went for the cell in his pocket, only to realize he'd left it in the car. He looked around, trying to figure out what to do. He remembered seeing Elise's iPhone sitting on the coffee table. He grabbed it, pressed the home button. It asked for a passcode.

Liam didn't have time to start guessing combinations. He dropped the phone and ran back into the hall, pounded on the nearest door. No one answered. He tried another. When no one answered that one either, he ran for the stairs. They were cement and narrower than they should be. Keeping one hand above the chipped rail so he could grab it if he fell, Liam took them fast. Starting at the top of each flight, he went two or three steps and jumped to the next landing.

He bolted out of the door leading into to the lobby and nearly ran into an old woman. She was hunched over and wearing something blue with white flowers on it. Her eyes popped open and she screamed. Liam suspected it was the sight of all the blood. As he'd hauled Elise out of the water, it had gotten onto everything, but was most visible across the front of his chest where it had stained his white dress shirt.

He didn't stop to explain or ask for help. He simply weaved around the stranger and kept going. He could hear her screaming until he exited the building and he wasn't even sure she'd stopped then.

His car was close. As he ran toward it, he fished the keys out of his pocket, pressed the unlock button. The lights flashed. His breath swirled in front of him. The cold seeped through his wet clothes and into his skin.

Liam reached in through the passenger door and grabbed his cell from the center console. Standing in the road, hands shaking, he unlocked the device and saw a small red dot on the corner of the phone icon with the number twelve in it. When he'd pulled it out of his pocket to read the first text from Elise, he'd seen a notification announcing he'd missed a call from her, but hadn't given it any thought. Ava had a strict "no calls" policy. His ringer had been on silent, and one missed call was no more significant than the message that had followed it. He cursed himself for not noticing the actual number of calls at the time, wondered if it would have made any difference, and dialed 911.

"Nine-one-one. How can I help?" the operator asked.

"My girlfriend needs assistance." Liam gave her the address, and told her about the blood.

He was barely off the phone when a police car, lights flashing, rounded the corner at the end of the block.

Thank God.

He flagged down the black-and-white and the cop rolled down his window. The driver had a meaty face that crowded in on his small eyes. His partner was lean and cloaked in shadow. Before either of them could speak, Liam said, "You're here for Elise, right? Elise Whitman? Where's the ambulance? She needs an ambulance right away."

"Relax. It's coming."

The paramedics did what they could, but Elise was gone, and the apartment immediately transformed into a crime scene. Liam hadn't been allowed back into the unit since the first officers arrived. With the apartment's new status, he wasn't even allowed to wait outside her door.

"We need to make some room," the meaty officer said, ushering Liam down the hall, past those ugly yellow walls that now looked even uglier.

Liam didn't respond. He felt numb. He couldn't understand why Elise would kill herself. Maybe they'd find a note.

On the elevator, the officer added, "I'm sorry for your loss" and, once they reached the lobby, "Have a seat on the bench over there. A detective will be along soon. They'll want to talk to you."

"Sure." Liam didn't see the point; the cops already knew everything he did. But he didn't see much reason to do anything else either.

He sat down on a metal bench that had been designed more for form than function. Directly in front of him, a flat screen TV mounted to the wall flipped between an ad for rooftop yoga and the status of the morning trains. Right now, all the lines had green dots beside them to indicate the trains would be running on time. Liam doubted that would last much past eight.

He called his receptionist's office line. Even if he didn't end up staying here all night, he'd be in no shape to go to work tomorrow. Her voicemail answered on the third ring and the message he left was brief. "Hey. I'm not feeling great. I'm going to be out Friday. Please reschedule any meetings." (While she would get the time with the message and might think he'd been out late drinking, the nice thing about being the boss was it didn't matter.) Then he called his business partner, David Hayes, and left a similar message.

After he watched the screen rotate a dozen or so times, Liam turned his attention to the bank of mailboxes beside the TV. 101. 102. 103. He read every apartment number up through the third floor and started again. Anything to keep from thinking about Elise's body.

The few tenants who came in or out were rerouted through the garage, so at least Liam didn't have to deal with them glancing suspiciously in his direction.

When the detective finally arrived, he stopped outside the building and spoke briefly with the cop by the door. He was wearing a charcoal suit and had a thick mane of gray hair brushed away from his face. The cop pointed to Liam. The detective entered the lobby and said on his way to the elevator, "I'll be right back. Stay put, okay?"

Liam nodded and started reading the mailboxes again.

The detective sat down next to Liam. For several seconds, he said nothing. Then he leaned forward, placing his elbows on his knees, and sighed. "That's a real shame." The detective waited another beat, perhaps giving Liam a chance to respond, before adding, "One of the officers upstairs tells me her name was Elise Whitman."

It wasn't a question, but since Liam could tell the detective was trying to engage with him, he said, "Yeah. It is," then silently corrected himself. *Was*. It *was* Elise Whitman. Because that was what happened when you died. You were no longer anything. And you certainly never *would* be anything. Like Elise Parker.

Liam had never thought seriously about them getting married. They had only been dating for two months; it was too soon for those kinds of thoughts. But the fact that the possibility had been ripped away seemed unfair.

The detective nodded thoughtfully, perhaps even sympathetically, and tilted his head toward Liam. "Sebastian Wyatt," he said. "Call me Bash."

"Liam Parker."

"How did you two meet?" the detective asked.

They had met at Ava's. In fact, Elise had even been one of tonight's six players, but had bowed out early, claiming a headache. Liam, of course, couldn't tell Bash any of that. The games were illegal. Still, he had to say something. "A bar," he replied. "Downtown."

"Which one?"

More specificity. Think. "The Tap."

"Nice place. A little out of my budget, but . . ." Bash shrugged. "So, tell me what happened."

"Well, I knocked on her door and when she didn't answer, I tried the handle to see if it was unlocked." Liam shifted in his seat a little in an attempt to make the metal bench more comfortable.

"Was it?"

"Yes, it was, which surprised me."

"Why is that?"

"Elise kept her door locked all the time."

The detective looked past Liam at the computerized directory on the wall. "How did you get into the building?"

"There was a girl going out. She held the door for me."

"Do you know who she was?"

"I've never seen her before."

"After you got inside the apartment, what happened next?"

"I found Elise in the tub," Liam said, uselessly trying to recount the actions without visualizing them. "I tried to pull her out. When I couldn't, I called 911."

"That's how you got the blood on you?"

"Yeah."

Liam remembered Chloe greeting him when he opened the door to the apartment. Where was she? He thought he'd seen one of the paramedics lock her in the bedroom, but he couldn't be certain. He wondered what would happen to her. With no owner to take care of her, Chloe would probably get put in a shelter. If she didn't get adopted, the shelter would most likely put her to sleep. Liam couldn't let that happen. Elise wouldn't like it.

"The dog," he said, shifting his gaze away from the mailboxes to meet Bash's, "can I take her with me?"

The detective frowned. "I guess so." Then he asked Liam more questions. No, Liam didn't know of anybody who was angry with Elise. He didn't know if she kept a spare key with the neighbors. He was at home before he came here.

Bash ended the conversation by asking Liam if he knew how to get in touch with Elise's family.

"I'm sorry," Liam said, "I don't."

"That's fine. I'm sure we can figure out how to reach them." The detective gave Liam his card. "Call me if you remember anything important."

Liam slid the card into his jacket pocket. "Detective Wyatt, you don't think somebody . . . ?" He could barely get the words out. When the apartment had been designated a crime scene, he had figured it was standard operating procedure, even for suicides. Now he wasn't so sure, and he didn't want to leave wondering if his imagination was running away with him. "You don't think somebody killed her, do you?"

"We don't know," the officer replied, which Liam figured was cop-speak for yes.

Fuck, Liam thought while he waited for Bash to return with Chloe. *Fuck, fuck, fuck.* Suicide was bad, but murder would be so much worse.

Jacob Reed

JACOB WAS, IN ALL manner of ways, forgettable. Some of that was by birth. (He was five-ten and of average weight. His oval face was neither particularly handsome nor ugly. His nose was straight and without defect. His eyes were a murky blue bordering on brown.)

But most of it was by design. He kept his blond hair short, had no piercings or tattoos, even though he wanted them, and shopped at stores like The Gap, buying their most nondescript items.

Jacob liked being forgettable.

People who were forgettable were hard to find. Even if anybody did remember what he looked like, a description to the police would be so generic as to be useless.

The tuxedo vest and bowtie he wore when dealing cards at Ava's were too distinct to meet his standards. Before heading home, he changed into an olive sweater, a wool coat with no distinguishing characteristics, and a pair of blue jeans. He packed his work clothes into a backpack, then took a bus north and made his way down West Bourbon, hands in his pockets and dodging pedestrians.

This was a popular area with college students and young professionals. Both sides of the street were lined with greasy restaurants, cheap bars, and hip boutiques like Wag-A-Lot and Berg's Apothecary.

Jacob had started his career in crime as a pickpocket. It was something he still did occasionally, mostly as a way of staying sharp.

Over time, he'd worked his way up through a series of increasingly complex cons and from there into the world of cybercrime. These days, he did a little of both.

He watched how the men and women around him moved, whether they staggered along in a zigzag or walked steadily forward. He noticed what they were wearing, if their coats were open or closed, if their hands were in their pockets, if the women wore their purses across their chests or over their shoulders.

Jacob didn't plan on stealing from anyone tonight. He was working something big, something involving Liam, and didn't see any good reason to take the risk. Still, he couldn't help looking for opportunities. It had become second nature.

He stepped to the right to avoid a couple holding hands, to the left to avoid a pack of college kids. Then Jacob saw a man exit a bar at the corner of Belmont and West Bourbon. He was built like a boxer and "dressed for show," as Jacob's mom used to say. His tailored suit was probably Armani, his patent-leather shoes most likely Corthay.

Jacob recognized him immediately. This man had been one of the first marks he and his partner had targeted. They'd worked a scam on him called The Ring. He'd caught on to it, though, and instead of simply taking off like so many others would, he'd beaten Jacob until he was just this side of unconscious and punched Jacob's partner hard, leaning into the swing and connecting with her right eye before pushing her to the ground. That had pissed Jacob off, but there wasn't much he could do about it at the time.

The man turned in Jacob's direction. The distance between them began evaporating quickly. Jacob's fingers flexed the way they did sometimes when he was getting ready to slip his hand into a stranger's pocket. He thought of himself as a man in control. He reminded himself that this chance encounter changed nothing. This probably wasn't the first time he'd passed a mark on the street. The smart thing to do was leave him alone. Still, his fingers flexed.

Jacob imagined waving the wallet in his partner's face and saying, "Look what I got," certain she would take as much joy from the theft as he would. He imagined this man going home, finding his wallet gone, and having nobody to punch but himself.

Jacob looked to his right, pretending to be distracted. He had to do it, he decided. It would be justice—or, at least, justice of a sort. He stepped into the stranger's path and they collided. "Oh, Christ, man. I'm sorry," Jacob said, putting one hand on the man's chest in a way that looked like he was trying to stabilize himself while at the same time reaching around to the man's back pocket.

The man pushed him away. "Idiot. Watch where you're going."

"Sorry," Jacob said again. He had his head down to make sure the man couldn't get a good look at him. His hands were now in the pockets of his wool coat.

Grumbling, the man went on his way. Jacob watched him as he charged into the distance, putting five feet between them, then ten. He felt a rush of adrenaline as he fingered the wallet. He wondered what he'd find inside. Cash, hopefully. Credit cards, for sure. Probably a license and an insurance card. But sometimes there were other things too. Once he'd found a punch-out card for Al's Beef that got him a free sandwich and another time he found a twenty-dollar gift card for Starbucks. He'd also found bus passes, dry cleaning tickets, and family photos.

Jacob thought of those photos as little treasures, glimpses into a life that could have been his if he'd gone a different way. He'd keep them for a while, carrying them around in the pocket of his jeans until they were worn out and cracked, pulling them out every so often to wonder what might have been and, perhaps one day, what might be.

The man was twenty feet away when he stopped, felt for his wallet, and spun around. "You little shit!" His square face was screwed up tight and his hands were curled into fists. He pointed at Jacob. "You think you can steal from me?"

Everyone within earshot turned to look. Upon seeing the man, some checked the traffic and scurried across the street.

Jacob broke into a sprint and the man came after him, moving just as fast. Jacob was slight and agile. He gracefully dodged pedestrians like a running back headed for the end zone. The mark, who might be able to stare down a bear if he had to, simply shouldered people out of his way.

Jacob turned onto Belmont. There was less foot traffic here. He could go faster. He passed a church and thought about trying the doors, but if they were locked, the narrow lead he had would be lost. He passed an alley and thought about running down that too, but what if it led to a dead end?

Beyond the Lincoln Belmont library, the street became residential, with old brick houses and small fenced yards. There was no one in front of him now but a homeless man pushing a shopping cart.

Jacob was getting tired. He could feel the mark gaining on him. Eventually he crossed underneath the Belmont station. Not sure where to go but unable to run much farther, he heard a train rattling to a stop on the tracks overhead.

That was his ticket out of this mess. His only chance. He broke to his left and ran across the street. A series of faces, cartoonish in proportion and color, had been painted onto the cement pillars supporting the tracks. He fished his metro card out of his pocket and fed it into the turnstile's reader.

If Jacob could have jumped over the turnstile, he would have. But Chicago turnstiles worked like revolving doors, with over eight vertical feet of rotating bars. The city had made sure that if you wanted to get through, you were going to pay.

The reader rejected his card. He could feel the painted faces staring down at him, telling him he wouldn't escape, not this time. He shook away the doubt and inserted the card again.

His pursuer's footsteps were getting louder, his winded voice shouting obscenities, telling Jacob to stay where he was, threating to kill him.

As tempting as it was to look back, Jacob kept his eyes on the reader. A wasted second might be all it would take to lose his lead.

This time the reader processed the metro card without issue. Jacob snatched it up and pushed into the turnstile. A hand grabbed his jacket and tugged, but his momentum kept him moving forward. As the turnstile rotated and the metal bars closed in behind him, the hand released.

"You son of a bitch!" the man shouted.

Jacob bolted up the stairs to the platform, taking them two at a time. The red, purple, and brown lines all came through this stop. He didn't care which train was up there. He just wanted to make sure he was on it when it pulled away.

The train's doors were still open when he reached the top of the stairs. Jacob slipped through them right before they closed. The car wasn't crowded—no surprise, considering the hour—and he took a seat by the window.

He watched the stairs until they were out of sight. That was close. Was he getting sloppy? He replayed the theft in his mind. Hand to the chest, hand to the back pocket. An apology. No, he wasn't. That was as good a lift as he had ever done. But this man had figured it out.

He pulled the mark's wallet out of his jacket. Inside, he found a stack of cash and counted it. Two hundred and thirty-two dollars. He slipped the money into his coat. Then he pulled out the only photo and pocketed it too. It was of the man and a much younger woman. She was draped over him in a loving way that, like so many wallet photos, reminded him of the relationship he wished to have.

Jacob was about to close the wallet, ready to dump it in the trashcan at the next station, when he felt something on an inside pocket that caught his attention. He looked, slid out a key. It was for a safety deposit box, that much he could say for sure. His curiosity was piqued. People kept valuable things in safety deposit boxes. What bank did this key go to? Jacob could find that out as long as he had a name. He checked the man's license. Christopher Bell. It sounded vaguely familiar. Perhaps it was just that the name was so ordinary.

Well, he decided, even if he was going to forgo further pickpocketing for a while (and, after what had happened tonight, he meant it), there was no reason not to see what was in this man's safety deposit box. Wouldn't that, too, be justice?

Liam Parker

THE NEXT COUPLE OF days were a blur of comfort food and crap TV. Liam slept when he could, which wasn't much, and cried when he needed to, which was often. He only left the condo for brief trips outside to walk Chloe and a stop at Petco for dog food. On the first of those walks, the concierge told Liam she was a nice-looking dog on the way out and said the kids are going to like her on the way back in.

Liam figured the concierge was probably right and, with a weak smile, managed to say, "Thanks."

By Sunday morning, he was starting to feel a little better. He was still a long way from being okay, but he was finally ready for some company. He called David Hayes to see if they could meet for lunch.

David said he could and suggested a restaurant called The Crown.

Liam wasn't surprised. It was David's favorite place for a burger and a beer.

Liam had met his business partner through his ex, and she had met David through his girlfriend, Alicia. The two women were regular volunteers at St. Ann's Church on Tuesday nights. They'd bring in snacks, set up chairs, and help direct visitors to the various addiction meetings—AA, ACA, Al-Anon, and so on. They were a comforting presence to new and returning attendees, alike.

Since their divorce, Catherine rarely showed Liam her good side.

But he knew she still had one because she still volunteered.

The Crown's floor was covered in long sheets of gray porcelain tile. The tables were made of cherrywood and polished to a shine. Exposed filament lightbulbs hung from the ceiling at uneven heights.

David was sitting near a window in the back. He was a tall man who looked tall even when seated. He was wearing gray slacks and a blue button-down. His suede jacket was draped over the back of the chair. With him looking down at his phone, Liam could see the bald spot forming on the top of his head and his large nose seemed especially pronounced.

"Can you believe these assholes?" David said, without taking his eyes off the screen.

"Who?"

"The *Tribune* says next year the mayor's going to put more meter maids on the street. He thinks it will bring in another four million in revenue. As if the city doesn't tax us to hell and back already. I take it you're feeling better?" He was referring to the message Liam had left the night of the murder. He still didn't know what had happened.

David tucked his phone into his pocket and finally looked across the table at Liam. His face contorted into an expression of surprise. Liam didn't look like himself. He hadn't shaved since Thursday, his hair was a mess, and he was wearing a pair of jeans and an old sweatshirt, which were well outside his usual attire.

"You're not sick, are you? What's going on?"

"It's Elise."

"You guys broke up?"

"She's dead."

David leaned in, his lanky frame casting a shadow across the table. "Really?"

Liam nodded.

"What happened?"

Before Liam could answer, a waitress came over. "Are you gentlemen ready to order?"

Liam asked for a glass of water. He wasn't in the mood to eat and alcohol didn't seem like a good idea right now. David ordered the same burger and beer he always got from The Crown, a medium-rare slab of meat with onions and bacon and a Budweiser on draft.

When the waitress was gone, Liam glanced over his shoulder to make sure no one was within earshot and told him the story.

"That's awful," David said, and, even though it sounded trite, it seemed to Liam perhaps the most honest thing he could say. It *was* awful. It would always be awful. Even when it hurt less.

The waitress arrived with their drinks. From the look on her face, he thought she might have been eavesdropping, so after she'd left their table for the second time, he made sure to speak softer. "There's one more thing. After Detective Wyatt was done questioning me, I asked if he thought Elise had been murdered. I just kinda got the feeling he was leaning that way. He said he didn't know. That sounded a lot to me like a yes."

David considered this while he sipped from his beer. "If she was, I'm sure they'll get to the bottom of it."

"I hope so. I just can't figure out why anyone would've done it. I've been running the scene through my head over and over. The place hadn't been ransacked, so it wasn't like it was some run-of-the-mill robbery, you know?"

"I get it. Sometimes something like this—it's hard to understand."

"Do you think there was something going on? Something I didn't know about? Detective Wyatt asked if anybody was mad at her. Do you think somebody could've been mad enough to kill her?"

David sighed. "I don't know."

Liam slumped further into his seat. He was merely asking David the same questions he'd asked himself. He needed to stop thinking about the murder, at least for a while, so he willed the conversation toward work-related matters, and didn't even mind when David, following his lead, once again pitched his plans for their firm. He wanted to turn ConnectPlus into a full-fledged advertising agency. TV and radio spots, billboards and print ads. "We don't have to limit ourselves to digital advertising," David explained. "We could become a one-stop shop for all of our clients."

It was what he always said when pitching the idea. In response, Liam said what he was always said: "I don't think that's something I can deal with right now."

But this time, it was more true than ever.

Order your copy today!

Go Here to Order:

https://geni.us/rk_redwoodcon

GET AN EXCLUSIVE COPY OF *THE LAYOVER*

Connor Callahan is back in this exclusive novella that takes place three years after his parents were abducted and prior to his first case in Atlanta. When he sees a man discreetly tag a stranger's suitcase with a black magic marker, he sets out to discover what is going on. It's a decision that will thrust Connor into a conflict far more dangerous than he could have imagined, and when it's over he will know one thing for sure: You're not always safer on the ground.

When you join my readers club, you will immediately get a free and exclusive copy of *The Layover*, not available elsewhere.

I usually e-mail once or twice a month with things I think you'll find interesting, such as behind-the-scenes stories, new releases, and fan discounts. Of course, you can unsubscribe at any time.

Join the readers club by signing up at

read.reagankeeter.com

ALSO BY REAGAN KEETER

THE CONNOR CALLAHAN SERIES

Gone

A Good Plan

Last Trip to London

STANDALONES

The Redwood Con

Misery Rock

99 Souls (as Gabriel Burns)

ABOUT THE AUTHOR

Reagan Keeter is the author of multiple Amazon bestsellers and a National Indie Excellence Awards finalist. He has worked as a writer and editor at Georgia newspapers. From Georgia State University, he earned his undergraduate degree in Journalism and from Southern Polytechnic State University his master's in Technical and Professional Communication. He lives with his wife and their two dogs in Atlanta, Georgia.

You can connect with him via:
His website: reagankeeter.com
Facebook: https://www.facebook.com/AuthorReaganKeeter/
Twitter: @ReaganKeeter
Email: reagan@reagankeeter.com

Printed in Great Britain
by Amazon